GW00535732

ABOUT THE AUTHOR

Andrew Lowe was brought to you by the North of England, the colour orange and the flavour coconut. He has written for *The Guardian* and *Sunday Times*, and contributed to numerous books and magazines on films, music, TV, videogames, sex and shin splints.

He lives in London, where he writes, makes music, coaches youth football and shepherds his two young sons down the path of righteousness.

This is his first novel.

@andylowe99
andrewlowewriter.com

the ghost

ANDREW LOWE

Copyright © 2015 Andrew Lowe

The moral right of the author has been asserted.

Apart from any fair dealing for the purposes of research or private study,
or criticism or review, as permitted under the Copyright, Designs and Patents
Act 1988, this publication may only be reproduced, stored or transmitted, in
any form or by any means, with the prior permission in writing of the
publishers, or in the case of reprographic reproduction in accordance with
the terms of licences issued by the Copyright Licensing Agency. Enquiries
concerning reproduction outside those terms should be sent to the publishers.

Matador
9 Priory Business Park,
Wistow Road, Kibworth Beauchamp,
Leicestershire. LE8 0RX
Tel: (+44) 116 279 2299
Fax: (+44) 116 279 2277
Email: books@troubador.co.uk
Web: www.troubador.co.uk/matador

ISBN 978-1784623-005

This is a work of fiction.
Any resemblance it bears to reality is entirely coincidental.

British Library Cataloguing in Publication Data.
A catalogue record for this book is available from the British Library.

Printed by TJ International Ltd, Padstow, Cornwall, UK
Typeset by Troubador Publishing Ltd, Leicester, UK

Matador is an imprint of Troubador Publishing Ltd

for tom and josh

And Lot's wife was told not to look back, where all those people and their homes had been. But she did look back, and I love her for that, because it was so human. So she was turned to a pillar of salt. So it goes.

Kurt Vonnegut, *Slaughterhouse Five*

PART ONE

SOMETHING WAS COMING UP the stairs.

It always did.

As usual, he was hiding in the corner closet, huddled between the musty pillars of comic annuals *(Topper, Whoopee!, Whizzer and Chips)*. He was crouched and braced, armoured only by sweat-crumpled *Superman* pyjamas.

Thunk.

Whatever was coming up the stairs didn't seem too concerned about stealth. The first few times he had added mystery – he had given the Something guile and motive. But over time, the nightmare had refined and resculpted itself, chipping away every fragment of agency. Now, it was bold and cold as gleaming marble – inexorable, inevitable.

Thunk.

This was the part where he waited – the part where, although he had no sight of the Something, he knew what it was and what it would do. He knew that it would soon enter the bedroom. He knew there would be no cinematic pause outside the door, no theatrical rattle of the handle. The Something would just come right on in, without air or grace or face (as yet).

In the early days, he had woken before the reveal. He had read about 'lucid' dreaming – how it was possible to collude with sleep, to blend the surreal with the real and redirect the flow of fantasy. Lately, though, his night terrors could not be tamed; they swarmed and scuttled in the insomnia-parched gloom, eager to smother and deliver him into this looping suspension.

Thunk.

The room was breached. He knew he would have time for one final flex of will. Maybe, at last, he would slip the tentacles, surge to the surface and gulp down the stale spores of the marital bedroom.

The closet door jerked open. Light flared in around the shape of the Something.

This was the part where he woke up.

Lights Down

DORIAN COOK HAD PASSED through the BFF Screening Rooms many times. The process was like medical triage – rhythmic and ritualised, with status as quantifiable as core temperature or pulse-rate. Most attendees were admitted casually, while emergency cases – broadsheet editors, TV pundits – demanded fast-track efficiency.

Cook typically presented in full film-critic uniform – boot-cut jeans, asexual shoes, unlaundered short-sleeved shirt. A shoulder-bag propped against his gathering paunch carried mineral water, freesheet, notebook, biro, and a recently published hardback – mostly for ballast. He would be greeted by a public-relations official employed by the studio which had produced the film being screened. The official's seniority would depend on the film's profile. (A limited-release indie might only merit a senior intern, while a major blockbuster would smoke out the Head of Publicity – a weaponised breed with an air-kiss of death and a sharkish nose for journalist blood vintage.)

Cook was mid-tier and so didn't warrant the full VIP schmooze-and-polish. But his connections earned him a personal pour of the warm white wine and an extra five minutes of shop-talk around the sandwich platter. He was

Associate Editor (Film) of *Widescreen*, a national monthly that specialised in cinema but also covered selective TV. Market share was steady, but circulation was down – had it ever been up?

"*Dorian!* How are you?"

Here, with guest-list clipboard, twirling a studio-logo ballpoint, was Christina Collins, a deskbound fixer temporarily elevated by maternity leave. She wore the hostess role with affected pride, like a toddler tottering in her mother's Blahniks. Cook received her small, bony hand with barely disguised indifference – it was like being invited to examine a sprig of damp lettuce. He returned an exploratory squeeze-and-shake, suppressing an urge to just swat the thing aside. Then, the cheek-to-cheek pantomime with lips pouting at nothing – a duty-bound double when neither had wanted a single.

"Hello, Christina!" he beamed, slipping into character. "Good, thanks. Very busy. You?"

The question was palpably rhetorical – on message with the general exchange. Collins answered it, anyway.

"Tell me about it! Pretty crazy. Not easy being a man – well, woman – down. We've had Pacino in for *Scarface 2*. That's been... interesting."

Cook laughed – at the absurdity of the film's existence, but Collins read it as empathy. Earlier that year, at a Miami junket, Collins had chaperoned Cook around an inert section of the *Scarface 2* set. The schedule – including a twenty-minute one-on-one interview with the lead – had been revised out of existence by Robin Leonard, Pacino's cartoonishly gay publicist. Cook had planned to doorstep Leonard at the final-day drinks party and charm him into offering top-up access closer to release. But Collins kept Cook muzzled with cocktails, squashing him into a corner with another journalist and over-sharing her thoughts on how she 'hated' kids but had *so* much respect for women who chose to have them.

"My mother was told she couldn't have children," she squawked over the DJ's *Scarface*-riffing playlist of retrofitted '80s synth-pop, "but we're a stubborn family. She proved everyone wrong and had me!"

"Pity..." muttered the other journalist, as Collins answered a cellphone call. Cook snorted in solidarity.

Later, when all chance of approaching Leonard had passed, Cook was clenching through a story about a 'brilliant' travel writer Collins had met during her gap year, when he tilted back his head and released a gaping, slow-motion yawn. Collins, drunk, raised both eyebrows.

"Oh! Sorry. Am I *boring* you?"

"Yes," said Cook, locking eye contact until Collins turned and elbowed her way to the bathroom.

Cook knew that Collins would have long since dismissed the moment as a pout – a swipe of petulance too feeble to unsettle her meticulous diorama. Even so, as he accepted her offer of a pre-sliced Pret A Manger baguette, he had the feeling he was being fattened up for market – or slaughter.

To Cook's irritation, the spread was already sparse and well rummaged. He was hungry, and had taken care to arrive with time to spare, knowing that a traditional last-minute dash carried the risk of hospitality turning into hospitalisation. Journalists, like pigeons, would never decline free food, and all those mobile breakfasts and deskbound lunches required a relaxed attitude to hygiene. He imagined a flurry of sneeze-streaked knuckles and earwax-tacky fingertips, prodding through the huddle of triangles, exhuming the fillings.

Collins' assistant handed Cook a copy of the film's production notes.

Running time – 137 minutes.

He sighed. As an episode of a TV sitcom was perfectly formed at around thirty minutes, a feature film, he felt, should last no longer than ninety. This made it possible to mentally split the action into two sections of roughly forty-five minutes each. After the first forty-five, if he wasn't engaged, then he could console himself with the knowledge that there was less than an hour to go. A two-hour film was tougher, but could be moulded to a similar principle – after the first sixty minutes, Cook would at least have an idea of how gruelling the second sixty would be, and he could brace for a manageable single-hour run-in, perhaps bolstered by one or two carefully timed text messages (screen brightness reduced to minimum).

But anything with a running time of over two hours was potentially unbearable. An hour could pass with little to no connection. What then? The same amount of time could be spent trying to stay sharp and locked in to a weightless narrative, as it floated up and away.

Collins saw Cook flinch at the running time. "I know," she smirked, "but honestly, it doesn't feel that long. I didn't even notice!"

Cook was certain that Collins hadn't seen the film – and that she would know that he knew, but not care.

"Can I get you a drink?" she asked, already moving beyond the mock-personal pleasantries in favour of playing the emotionally removed attendant.

"Nah, I'll leave it. Bit hungover."

Lately, Cook found that drinking at screenings lulled him into the limbo of half-sleep – too tired to stay awake, but too attuned to the embarrassment of falling asleep to fall asleep. He scooped a few rubbery crisps onto the paper plate next to his baguette, took out his water bottle and found a seat with a decent eyeline on the hallway TV.

More journalists arrived, checking in with Collins and slotting into the usual cliques. Cook imagined videogame-like labels hovering over their heads – 'Fighty Freelancers', 'Broadsheet Stalwarts', 'Crumple-Suited Hacks', 'Staffers', 'Liggers', 'Stringers', 'Shouty Editor-At-Large And His Interesting Hat', 'Origin Unknown But A Fixture At Every Screening'.

Cook was known and liked and he knew and liked many in attendance, but he made no effort to socialise. Glaring up at Sky Sports' typically hysterical build-up to a Champion's League dead-rubber group game, he moped at the thought of them all – himself included – as cogs in the studio promotional machine. The age of the 'respected' critic was over. Now that anyone with a wifi signal could declare themselves an 'expert', it was no longer enough to have put in the hours, to have seen more *quality* films than anyone else. No-one had time for depth any more – it was all about breadth. In a grand act of self-delusion, the *Widescreen* website offered the facility for browsers to add 'Reader Reviews' – as opposed, presumably, to the 'real' reviews of the staff.

Not that Cook couldn't hold his own. He enjoyed a fair fight on the merits of Bergman's undisputed masterpiece (naturally, *Persona*) and he could construct a sturdy position on Haneke's ongoing thesis of audience collusion, or why Meadows was more early Scorsese than late Cassavetes. He just found it exhausting that he had to stand alongside these people who thought that a vague memory of a couple of Kurosawa films qualified them for debate. The cultural shift had led Cook to insist even more stridently on how the view of an aficionado – such as himself – was indisputable in the face of just another opinion from a punter whose formative film was probably *Reservoir Dogs* – or, worse, *Jurassic Park*. He had developed a set of irritating but effective defences – most notably, the aggressive, empirical dismissal of any insight that contradicted his own. After a recent office argument with a junior *Widescreen* writer, he had sent her an email explaining how he didn't appreciate having his opinion 'disrespected' in earshot of the rest of the office. The subtext was clear – while they were both entitled to their views, his was the one that carried most weight.

Cook came from a world where a few people had a lot of insight into a small number of things. Now, he found himself among a lot of people with a limited insight into a lot of things. Everyone was a Jack-of-all-genres, while Cook was the crumpled king of but a few – an arcane craftsman working from an obsolete blueprint.

So, here they all were – sprawling at the blunt end, privileged by an early, ad-free viewing of the film and charged with delivering a verdict that would be picked over by Collins' office for favourable phrases to be daubed across promotional posters in high-footfall streets and stations.

This would hopefully compel shoppers and commuters to spend money on seeing the film, and a small amount of that money would, technically, contribute to their salaries. Cook recalled an old episode of *Wogan*, where a young Stephen Fry had described critics as 'parasitical'. He had always thought this a typical tortured artist's view, but now he felt its sting more keenly. He was tired of passing passive-aggressive judgement on that which had already happened. He ached to make something happen himself.

Cook finished his food and took a seat on the front row. He was lucky to get it – most of the prime territory had been pre-marked by the usual clutter of jackets and backpacks. Just before Collins closed the doors, Neil Hooper, a writer from rival magazine *Movie*, hustled over and hurled himself into the seat next to Cook. He pulled a notebook and pen from the pockets of the coat shaped around the seat-back.

"How's it going, Mr Cook?"

"Good! Looking forward to this. Bit long, though."

"Fuck! Really? Wish I'd sneaked my beer in now. Strange to see Christina out in the real world. Loving her earrings. On loan from Lady fucking Gaga!"

Cook squeezed out a laugh – stifled as he noticed that Hooper's pen was the type fitted with a mini-torch that would cast a self-important glow whenever he made a review note.

The screen curtains parted and Collins dimmed the lights. Cook kept his eyes closed and drifted down through the double-darkness into amniotic oblivion.

2
Antagonist

"Come on, Dor. Get yerself out of bed!"

The voice was furry with Rothman's phlegm. A good half-hour after his double-belled alarm-clock had been silenced by a flapping palm, this was the reassuring slosh and rattle that marshalled Cook every school morning.

"Come on, now. Up to middle-school today!"

Cook's grandmother, Esther, scraped open his frayed bedroom curtains and admitted the grey autumn light. Early sixties and already stooped, Esther listed from room to room in billowing, crinkle-folded A-line skirt and prehistoric slippers. All the weight she'd hefted through three wartime pregnancies had slumped and settled, leaving her bottom-heavy. She had compensated by staying top-nimble, keeping her synapses sparking with violent knitting and *The People's Friend*.

Cook staggered over to a chest of drawers, shedding his pyjamas. Esther wrestled him into a hug and butted a kiss onto his cheek. He was always shocked by her brutality of gesture – despite her age, it was oddly coltish, as though she had developed the dynamics of physical affection via hearsay. Esther hadn't yet installed her false teeth and Cook recoiled at the gummy yield of her jaw with its sheen of bristle.

He hopped into his socks and pants, tugged on saggy polyester trousers and layered a thinning vest under something scratchy and woollen. The school had no dress-code, but his wardrobe – browns and beiges and dark oranges – seemed to obey one anyway. There was no bathrobe – no midway point between pyjamas and full clothing. This was a morning survival ritual, whatever the weather. The house carried an unholy chill that flowed deep through its foundations, swelling up around the brickwork and swirling out of the pores of the walls – a vaporous spectre of cold that first stirred in late August and had the place comprehensively haunted by December. Installed heating amounted to a couple of tame electric-bar 'fires' and, outside of spring and summer, Cook was forced to dress as soon as he pushed back the bedsheets, before creaking down the narrow staircase, out of the bolted back-door and into the concreted yard for trembling communion with the outside toilet.

This morning, the yard's dividing wall was a scribble of glinting slime. Slug-trails criss-crossed the smooth top layer, flickering in the sunlight as Cook scampered past. The wall's gravel roots had been savaged by mining subsidence, and it slanted at an alarming 30-degree angle. His home, wedged into the middle of a terraced concertina on the edge of an industrial oil-works, was technically a slum – a slow-motion write-off, doomed to condemnation or collapse.

The loosely hung door scraped across the stone floor as Cook barged into the toilet. He emptied his bladder quickly, staring straight down into the bowl. This was no place for silent contemplation. In the daytime, it was a biological waste-bin – a functional space designed for briskly executed functions. By night, for a seven-year-old boy, it was a smelly and lightless pit of despair – a Petri dish for the imagination, infected with multi-limbed gutters and slitters and suffocators. The white plastic potty under his bed had recently been removed by Esther, who claimed that Cook was now a 'big boy' and therefore too old for it. But he had rescued the curved, cold mould from under the sink and still used it occasionally, sneaking it outside for emptying when he was sure his grandmother was busy.

Back inside, Cook stood on a crate and washed his hands over the kitchen sink, while Esther made him toast and milky tea. Their mongrel collie Rusty watched, as Cook tip-toed up to reach the top cupboard, sliding· out a Weetabix packet crudely daubed in Letraset *Doctor Who* characters.

"Can I have warm milk, nana?"

"Haven't got time, son. You're supposed to be out in five minutes."

Cook ate the butter-soggy toast (always 'best butter' for mornings) and drank half of his tea in a single guzzle, belching hard. Esther chuckled and Cook laughed along – a squeaky staccato. The two shared a relaxed attitude to body noises, sometimes to the point of mutual admiration. A few days earlier, they had been watching a TV wildlife programme, when Cook was alarmed by a hollow tearing sound, slowly rising in volume. At first, he had thought the noise was coming from one of the animals on-screen, but then he looked over to Esther's chair, to see her leaning to

one side, breaking wind with such gusto that it triggered a
barking frenzy from Rusty.

Cook ran back to the sink and pinched a blob of
toothpaste onto the ragged bristles of his favourite,
irreplaceable red brush. Esther swiped at his bowl-cut with
a comb as he scrubbed.

"Can I take one of my annuals?"

"Be quick!"

He scrambled up the stairs on all fours, crashed back into
his bedroom and opened the door of the closet in the corner
– a built-in wardrobe that Esther used as storage for toys, board
games and books. Cook stuffed a *Beezer* Summer Special (12p)
into his shoulder-bag, dashed back down through the front
room (or 'parlour' as Esther called it) and out of the main
door which spilled him directly onto the pavement.

The school walk was hardly life-affirming. Esther was not a
walker – she was barely a stander – and so Cook had to make
his own way. Today, he planned to pass by the house of Lisa
Goldstraw, a slightly older girl he had played with in the local
park. Lisa lived in a palatial semi in one of the moneyed back-
roads that branched off from Cook's direct route to school.
He was, of course, still beyond the grip of anything
resembling sexual longing, but his stomach somersaulted in
Lisa's presence and so, like a flower facing the sun, he tilted
towards her. With bright, yielding face and caramel-brown
eyes, she embodied emergent friendship, primal connection,
a proxy sister (Cook was a single child) and he pined for her
life and world. While his domestic realm was shrivelled and
austere, Lisa was blessed with a curious abundance of room,
food, heat and love. What could she possibly *do* with it all?

Lisa's mother saw Cook fumble his way through the garden gate and greeted him at the door.

"Hiya, Dor. She's already gone, darling."

Baby Rebecca squealed happily at the sight of Cook. She wriggled in her mother's arms and reached down to him. Cook smiled and lifted his hand. Rebecca coiled her tiny fingers around his thumb, flexing and unflexing.

"I'll tell her you called, though. Maybe try a bit earlier tomorrow. Be careful now. Watch the road!"

Cook speed-walked back down Lisa's street and re-merged into the flow of school foot traffic. He rode the current of dufflecoats and parkas, weaving through the rickety prams and skittering scooters. He passed the immense iron gates of the oil-works, where the factory walls, smeared with pitch, formed an S-bend as the pavement swooped and gathered into a steep incline that levelled off at the zebra crossing below Bethesda First & Middle. Cook's friend Michael Howell panted past on his Tomahawk. Cook had asked – begged – Esther for his own bicycle this coming Christmas. "We'll see…" she said, as always.

The children were greeted at the school gate by Deputy Head Mrs Mellor, a podgy matriarch in neutral cardie and lumpy tights. Her all-seeing eyes swam behind red-framed bottle-bottoms.

"Dorian! Mr Butcher. First room on the left."

Cook nodded and turned into the double-doors. Bethesda was built on two levels – nursery ('first') school below and primary ('middle') up top, separated by a covered stone staircase. Each school had its own playground, but both tiers came together to eat in a lower-level hall, where the tables were grouped by age and the air tingled with the tang of cheap mince. As the children merged with their trays in the serving queue, Cook always felt a twinge of threat from the older boys – they seemed impossibly quick and loud and large, bloated with impending violence.

He hung his coat on one of the pegs opposite Mr Butcher's room, summoned a surge of mock confidence and walked in. Back at nursery, the placings were informal, with flat plastic table-tops and comfortingly stacked chairs. Here, the traditional wooden desks (pen-grooves, inkwells, hinged worktops) were arranged in a formal grid pattern. Little-school primaries and plasticine had been replaced with big-school browns and chalk. There was an unwelcoming smell of burnished timber. Butcher – short, skinny, untidy black beard, leather-elbowed brown jacket – seemed less than elated with his new intake. As Cook entered, he was at his blackboard, double-underlining the word 'REGISTRATION'.

"And you are?"

He consulted a clipboard and cupped his ear, not bothering to look up.

"Dorian Cook."

Butcher hoisted his eyes from the clipboard and glowered into space. "Dorian Cook, *what?*"

"Dorian Cook, sir."

"Better! Sit yourself down and put your things in the desk. Wherever you sit, you'll stay there for the year."

All the window seats had been taken. Cook selected a desk towards the back, near the door. Most of the other children had bunched into mini peer groups and were chatting happily, apart from one girl at the back who was isolated by at least two desks in every direction. Michael Howell entered and raised his eyebrows at Cook. Butcher ticked him off the list and, to Cook's relief, Howell came over to claim the desk in front.

The room quickly filled. Cook knew about half the other children by sight and could count six or seven as friends. A boy he hadn't seen before was delivered directly to the classroom door by his worried-looking mother. He had bright, white hair and pale, near transluscent skin. As his mother coaxed him into the room, the boy's eyes glazed with tears and he clung to the door frame. The sideshow quieted the class, who looked on with predatory pity. Eventually, the boy slumped into one of the only few seats available, directly in front of Butcher's desk. He folded his arms into a tight huddle on the worktop and buried his face. Butcher approached the boy and carefully confirmed his name – John Ray. He gave Ray's hair a perfunctory ruffle.

"Come on, son. It isn't that bad."

Ray shuffled upright and pulled a blue-and-white handkerchief out of his back pocket. He mopped his eyes, blew his nose and re-pocketed the hankie – seamlessly, as if the three motions were well practiced. Butcher broke away to take the formal register and Ray glanced nervously over his shoulder, catching Cook's eye. His face was flour-white, the eyebrows a downy camouflage. If the flesh around his eye sockets hadn't been reddened by rubbing, he would have had no discernible contrast to his features. Ray's irises were clear as cut-glass, his lips hypothermic. He wore his hair collar-length, with a wispy, swept-over fringe. Some might have found his purity strangely beautiful, but here, among the lumpen textures of state-funded learning (remoulded textbooks, splintered chair-legs, colour-clashed students and Brylcreemed teachers), his ethereal edge was otherworldly and unsettling.

Butcher, needlessly, took the register. Cook was second, after a girl named Battison.

"Dorian Cook?"

There were sniggers. Cook had first awoken to the oddness of his forename at nursery class, with its Daves and Garys and Steves. His mother had once told him it was something to do with an 'actor' she'd met after a teenage theatre trip. He wondered if the actor was his father.

At playtime, Cook fell into a game of football with a group of older boys. They were indulgent – slowly passing him the ball, holding off and giving him time to compose and pass back – until one, frustrated at his poor timing, kicked the ball, full strength, straight at his face. Cook fell to the floor, grazing his palms. The kicker retrieved the ball and led a round of howling laughter, but the tallest in the group marched over and slapped the ball out of his hands.

"Sorry, Den. It was an accident."

'Den' helped Cook to his feet. "You alright?"

Cook said nothing. He leapt up and hurried away, nose throbbing from the impact. In the toilet-block at the playground's far corner, he splashed water on his face, gulping back the urge to cry. Outside, Mrs Mellor sounded an extended note on a tin whistle. This was new to Cook, but the message was clear – end of playtime. He left the toilets, dragging a sleeve across his nose. The tall boy was waiting outside.

"You okay, then?"

"Yeah!" said Cook, embarrassed.

"I'm Dennis. Will you help me put the football stuff away?" It sounded like a command rather than a request.

"Okay."

Cook was sceptical, but thought this might at least give him time to recover for the next round of lessons.

Dennis Mountford was two years older than Cook – a lifetime in their accelerated time-zone. He was remarkably clean and neat but somehow eluded the sense – common to all the other children – that he had been dressed by someone else. Mountford's clothes all looked new, his hair was styled rather than hastily tamed, his shoes unscuffed. He walked with jagged, measured steps, as though he could disengage his legs and break into a glide at any moment. The other boys regarded Mountford with suspicious respect. He had never followed up on any physical threat, but no-one had yet summoned the confidence to test him. He was officer material – the soul of a teacher in a pupil's body.

Mountford unlocked a shed by the girls' toilets and Cook helped him drag four concrete-base goalposts into a line against the wall.

"Dorian, yeah?" said Mountford, lobbing the football into a hanging pouch. "My mum knows your nan."

Cook nodded but didn't look up. He lingered a little in the cool darkness, nosing through a crate of swimming gear.

"You have to head the ball with your forehead, mate," chuckled Mountford, "not your nose."

"I wasn't trying to head it! He kicked it at me!"

Mountford smiled and ushered Cook back outside. He slid a chunky padlock through the door's bolt.

"Listen. If anyone tries to mess you about, come and tell me. Right?"

Cook studied him, uncertain about the idea of a protector – it felt like taking on a debt he knew he couldn't repay.

And then, a louder, deeper voice.

"Will you two get inside? The whistle went five minutes ago!"

This was the headmaster, Mr Austin – monolithic and walrus-faced – on the top step outside the school's back entrance. He tapped at the face of his watch.

"Coming, sir!" said Mountford.

Austin shifted to one side. Mountford scaled the steps and squeezed through the deliberately ungenerous space. Cook followed.

Cook was first out of the classroom door as the hometime bell rang. He took down his coat, ran across to the class opposite (Mrs Mellor's) and waited as the door opened and the children lined up to be released, alphabetically, according to surname. Lisa Goldstraw was the fifth to leave. She smiled as she saw Cook.

"Hiya, Dorian! Are you going home?"

"Uh, yeah…" said Cook.

To avoid the end-of-day crush around the pegs, Mrs Mellor insisted that her class retrieve their coats at afternoon break, and so Lisa was already wearing her dark blue quilted overcoat with detachable hood. Cook was annoyed at this – he had recognised the coat earlier and planned to bring it to the door himself.

"Y'alright?" said Lisa, as they passed through the huddle of parents at the main gate.

"Yeah. Got hit by a ball at playtime."

Lisa giggled. "That's daft."

"Couldn't get out of the way!"

She looked at him, doubtfully. "Shoulda been quicker, then!"

"I *am* quick!"

Lisa laughed and flicked up her hood.

At the crossing, the lollipop lady chatted to Lisa about a borrowed cooking dish she wanted her to pass on to her mother. Cook maintained a respectful distance throughout the exchange, hovering close enough to confirm himself as Lisa's companion.

They headed down past the oil-works and turned off onto the road that led to Lisa's street.

"Coming with me?" she said, as if only just noticing.

Cook was about to answer when she suddenly lurched forward, shouting, "Leave him alone!"

Half-way down a sloping side alley, almost out of sight of the main road, a group of four boys were standing in a semicircle. They faced a smaller figure who was squatting down with his back against a high wall, as two of the bigger boys aimed kicks at his legs and body.

"What's he ever done to you?" shouted Lisa.

One of the boys looked up briefly and then got back to business. Their target was foetal, hands covering his face. As Cook caught up with Lisa at the entrance to the alley, he saw a whip of white hair and realised it was John Ray.

"They're all so horrible to him!" shouted Lisa, dashing past the alley. Cook was not so phoney-brave as to plan an intervention, but he was shocked to hear Ray droning out piteous little wails of pain and protest, each punctuated by a pause as he inhaled enough breath to deliver the next. One of his assailants imitated the noise as he kicked, while the others sneered and sniggered. After each impact, Ray fell briefly silent and then resumed wailing, until the next blow interrupted him again.

And then, Cook felt himself stop and turn and run, carried by a surge of misplaced outrage. He pelted around the corner into the alley and saw that Ray had now coiled into a tight ball at the boys' feet.

"We could roll him down the hill like that!"

Cook was still running. In a few seconds, he would be within striking distance of the boys, although there was no question of making any kind of contact. So, what exactly was the plan? If he was supposed to be a bull – head down, horns cocked, hoof grinding – then his enemies entirely failed to cower before his uncastrated menace. They laughed – loud and cruel – as he slowed and shouted.

"Stop hitting him!"

The group turned away from Ray and faced Cook. A heavy-looking lad with greasy hair stepped forward.

"Why?"

Not, 'who says?' or, 'make us!' or, 'what are you gonna do about it?' Just, 'why?'

Cook had no answer. He stood there, in the glare of his audience, paralysed by intrigue and indecision – more watchful kitten than wild beast.

"Dorian!" Lisa was calling from the road junction at the alley entrance. "Come on! I'll get my dad."

The greasy-haired boy sniggered. "Is that your girlfriend, Doreen?"

Cook smouldered with impotent fury. He watched as two of the boys held Ray's arms while another trained the bright light of a pocket torch into his eyes.

"Keep his head still!"

Having assessed Cook and determined a nominal threat, the bigger boy turned back and rejoined the game. He gripped Ray's head firmly and forced his eyes open with his thumbs.

"Watch! He hates this!"

Ray was half-moaning, half-growling. He had gone limp – an exhausted quarry, downed by predators, resigned to the inevitable. The boy with the torch passed the beam across his eyes. Ray reacted as if his fingers had been pushed into an electrical socket. He bayed and bucked with agony, trying to shuffle himself up to a standing position. But his tormentors held him back, until he flopped forward and was allowed a few seconds of relief, before being prepared for another pass of the torch. The second time, as the light was tracked more slowly over his open eyes, Ray retched up a bellow of anger and thrashed his legs at the boys' feet, forcing them to step back.

One of the boys yelped in mock-surprise. "Look out! The ghost is getting angry!"

Ray's blue-and-white handkerchief had been used to tie his long hair up into a vertical stack at the top of his head – a joke ponytail. Cook turned and sprinted back down to the junction. A few hundred yards down the road, he could see Lisa, outside her house. She was waving and pointing, directing a large, slow-moving man as he emerged from the garden gate.

Cook backed onto the pavement, pivoted and ran to the main road, towards home, hands over his ears, muffling the sounds of John Ray's anguish until he was far enough away to pretend they had never existed.

3
Press Week

COOK EVICTED HIMSELF FROM the oceanic triple bed he had shared with the same woman for fifteen years. Gina had been awake and busy for so long, she had effectively lived through a parallel morning – showering, dressing, rousing Alfie and preparing his lunch-box, bringing Cook his morning tea, crunching through her usual bowl of muesli. (Cook, unfunnily, called it 'rabbit food' and mocked her asceticism. In turn, she sneered at his 'cardboard' Weetabix.)

Sex had been off the morning menu for two years and counting. (Gina still counted, Cook didn't.) At some point, post-Alfie, all the grappling and wheezing had started to seem faintly silly, certainly pointless – gymnastics without judges. Cook, always body-shy, was glad to be free of it all. He still flinched at the memory of their joint unveiling – Gina was slender, feline and pedigree, while Cook could only stand there, brandishing a slight, serviceable penis which jutted from a body that had accelerated ten years into the future in all directions. He was now 45 – in years and geometry. He leaned his age. Despite moderating all vice – alcohol, tobacco, chocolate, crisps, even *bread,* for Christ's sake – the bathroom mirror broadcast a clumsy clay rendering of creases, folds and unfortunate fuzz clusters. His scalp hair still carried a passing illusion of density, assisted by above-average height and judicious avoidance of overhead glare, but male-pattern baldness had clearly entered its final, irreversible, phase. With friends, Cook had a line for it – "I try to think of it as gaining head, not losing hair." But it sounded hollow, and he had no desire to acquaint the world with the curvature of his skull. He had spent his working life sitting in darkened rooms and dreaded exposure of any kind.

Cook showered, brushed his teeth and, almost fully swaddled in toga-like bath-towel, padded back through to the bedroom. The long-untouched Jockey briefs in his underwear drawer reminded him of Brigitte, a French unit publicist he had enjoyed a *thing* with a few years ago. (It was too erratic and uncommitted to call it an affair.) Back when baby Alfie was waking two or three times a night, Cook had staggered, sleep-starved and vodka-soaked, into Brigitte's world after a book launch party at a hotel bar. They had bonded over Bresson – Cook's favourite director – and swapped a few spurious industry anecdotes. The sex was lurid and cathartic, but it was the follow-up shutdown he mostly craved. At home, he was expected to put in a daily dawn shift, supporting Gina's uncomplaining breast-feeds with a glue-eyed bottle session. Escaping to Brigitte's for the odd weekend soon became more about rest than lust.

Downstairs, Cook tag-teamed with Gina across the breakfast bar.

"Alfie's had cereal. Could you make him some toast?"

He grunted acknowledgement, pecked her on the lips, and embraced his son, noting that Gina had already harried him into school uniform, a good half an hour before he would have bothered. As Cook made coffee and slotted bread into the toaster, Gina loaded her work-bag, flattened Alfie's hair, applied lipstick, signed a trip-slip. He cringed at this casual demonstration of the female multi-task cliche, and wondered how much longer his monthly boost to the joint account could keep him relevant here, dining out on the past provision of a healthy sperm.

Alfie was old enough to go to school by himself, but Cook walked with him, anyway – if only to stir himself to action. This morning, his son bombarded him with the baffling intricacies of an online 'monster-trading' game, and pestered for a monthly subscription. Cook offered token resistance, but eventually submitted. It was a glimpse of the future – already gone were the blissful, unstructured hours of Lego assembly, the heatwave water-pistol skirmishes, the improvised oneupmanship over reciting *The Tiger Who Came To Tea* from memory. All those Polaroid memories – all that was precious and immeasurable – was melting and melding into bipolar finance management. Would he pay for this or that videogame, this or that mobile phone, this or that school or bike or car or wedding? He and Gina would soon become little more than chief treasurers of their son's advance into adulthood.

This, of course, was life – a progressive disease. Furtive, undodgeable, terminal. With each passing year, Cook found less time to wallow in his favourite place – the moment, the now. He was wilting under the pressure of maintaining forward momentum, of always needing to press ahead when all he really wanted was to hang back and savour the flavours. But this thirst for the present fought with the unfinished business – the trailed-off sentence – of his past. That day, that decision – always clear, always present, scowling at his shoulder. If he could only turn around quickly enough, could he catch it and bag it – and change it?

At the *Widescreen* office, the mood was snappy exasperation. It was the monthly magazine's time of the month. The final print deadline had loomed into view, shadowing the adult staff in temporary adolescence. This was the time when the sub-editors unsheathed their scythes. Filling the pages was, effectively, the job of the section editors, but if their work wasn't all processed and produced on time, then it was the subs who would be called on to explain the lateness – and potential late-printing fees – to the publisher.

As Associate Editor, Cook nuzzled in the limbo between accountability and superfluity. Experience had furnished him with a layered geology of skills, but he was rarely required to dig deeper than the topsoil. He could write, commission and sub-edit copy, prepare and revise an issue plan, and offer informed instinct on commercial issues. He could, at a push, manage – ideally, over juniors who still saw him as imperceptibly distant and wise. In the absence of seniors, Cook led with status, rarely by example. Since he was broadly responsible for ensuring the section editors were briefed on forthcoming issues and, as his publisher insisted, 'big-picture editorial initiatives', press week held little fear for him. (Again, the elusiveness of the moment – his work kept him safely in the abstract future with no time to ponder the present, let alone reflect on the past.)

The lift to Cook's office floor stood at the end of a long, narrow corridor. It was possible to step inside, slip around to the right and be invisible to anyone emerging into the corridor at the far end. Here, Cook could indulge his misanthropic side. He loved to enter the lift and, on hearing someone emerge into the corridor, shift out of sight and hammer his floor button. The lift mechanism would pause, long enough to give hope to whoever was approaching. But then, the doors would silently and sweetly close, prompting footsteps to scurry for the call button – usually without success. Cook often began his ascent accompanied by a muffled 'shit!' or 'fuck!'. If the person did manage to lunge and force the doors to re-open, Cook's external headphones gave him an unspoken excuse. Today, to his irritation, he was delivered to his level without incident.

At his desk, he sifted through the usual deluge of email – boilerplate press releases, forwarded screening invites, templated internship requests, Nigerian friends, Estonian lovers, unsolicited newsletters, optimistic mailing lists. An update from a recently rebranded social networking site caught his attention.

Greetings from your new friends at PastLives.com! We've just undergone (Cook winced at that) *a website redesign and plugged in lots of exciting new features, including live chat, a cool 'Friendfinder' location tool and oodles* (another wince) *of new customisation options!*

It looks like you're still registered but haven't visited in a while. Don't be a stranger! Come and give us another try. We don't bite! (Well, the office dog does if you take his food away!)
– The PastLives Team

Cook opened the link. His browser autofilled the user/password details and he continued through to his profile page. At the top-right of the screen, a large number '2' on a red-circle background winked white and black. He clicked it and discovered two messages at the top of his inbox – one from the administrator welcoming him to the new version of the site, the other from 'Den'. He hovered his mouse arrow over the subject line ('*Long time!*') and clicked.

> *Hey Dor! Surprised to see you on here. ;-) Hope things are going well for you. I'm fully domesticated these days with a wife and (slightly less demanding) son (6). Be good to catch up. On top of all the usual stuff, I've got something I could really use your advice on mate. Can't really talk to anyone else about it – apart from Dave. My phone number is in the profile bit up there. Give me a call and we can have a beer soon. Really need to talk. It's been too long mate!*
> *Den*

Cook signed out of the site and returned to his email, weeding out the rest of the junk. He set up an out-of-office reply to cover holiday he was taking in a few days and moved on to his most recent message, marked '*Urgent: BBC News Channel!*' It was sent by Henry Gray, the *Widescreen* Editor-In-Chief. Gray was supposed to oversee the magazine's overall output. In theory, he was the head chef at the pass – the final line of defence for content quality control, editorial reputation and studio relations. In reality, he hopped in and out of the office seemingly at will, being careful to wave a hand over the glamorous decisions – cover presentation, feature headlines, photo-shoots – but lying low for any political fallout or strenuous deadlines. The email was a direct appeal from Gray to Cook, asking him to appear, on behalf of 'the brand', on a BBC News item about the forthcoming Academy Awards. Cook had just finished reading, when Gray called from the other side of the open-plan office.

"Dorian, did you get my mail about the BBC thing?"

"Yes. Just looking now."

"I imagine you're not crazy about this, but you know the Oscars and no-one else is available."

"I'm just shocked you didn't ask me first, instead of as a last resort!" bantered Cook.

Buried inside his levity, Cook's use of the word 'ask' was keenly honed passive-aggression, implying that the situation was negotiable. (Technically, this was true – Gray's credibility as line-manager was hardly robust.) His reply was postponed by the arrival of the magazine's publisher Laura Porter – frantic, mid-thirties, and, for a professional talker and hawker (she preferred 'marketeer') cursed with a blaring halitosis. As ever, she swished in with twinkly but strained fervour, like a supply teacher eager to connect with a problem class.

"Hi, guys!"

There was a surly chorus of acknowledgement. Cook barely bothered to raise his head. Most publishers, insisted the standard editorial wisdom, were overpaid accountants who knew the price of everything and the value of nothing. Porter simply knew nothing. As one-eyed ruler in the kingdom of the blind, she would have driven her subjects to revolt and revert to an unsighted leader. She was a jabbering ticker-tape of management cliche – 'actioning' this, 'escalating' that, 'facilitating' the other. She either absorbed ideas from the magazine staff and fed them upwards to the senior directors, or adopted business-level decisions from above and dribbled them back down to the magazine team, each time passing off the work as her own making. Porter was fastidious over everyone else's process and time management, but comically relaxed about her own. The days when she would mysteriously fall out of all contact were particularly ominous, and usually led to some grand new scheme or drive – as ever, clearly funnelled from upper management.

"Daisy?" Porter addressed the Online Editor. "Can I borrow you for a second?"

It was a frequent epithet which always made Cook shudder with irritation. As Porter and Daisy moved into a meeting room, Gray shouted over.

"So, are you clear to do that telly, Dorian? Details are all at the end of the email."

This now sounded more like delegation. Cook was clearly being advised – rather than invited – to accept. Gray pulled back slightly.

"Please? It'll be an easy gig. They just want an expert voice on the Oscar chances of the Whiteley movie. I think you'd be the best person to do it."

"The *only* person."

Gray absorbed the sulk without comment.

Cook had taken a media training course a couple of years ago, where he had learned how to steer a conversation towards prepared comment instead of letting an interviewer lead a discussion. "You should sit down with your own agenda," explained the instructor, "and stick to it. Talk about what *you* want to talk about, not what they want you to talk about." Cook was good at radio, but TV made him selfconscious and stammery. Apart from hating the unforgiving lights and the unerring stare of the cameras, he had a tendency to gum up on detail – once, embarrassingly, having to refer to a note in his pocket when asked about an actor's age. Cook's skills were solitary, not social. He was a decent writer, but a stumbling speaker.

"And there's really no-one else?"

Gray regarded him, pressuring with silence.

"OK. But what if I'm off sick?"

"Then I'll know you're faking," said Gray.

4

Mr Smith

A damp hand flattened across Cook's forehead as a glass thermometer slotted under his tongue.

"You *are* a bit warm."

His skull – taut and tenderised, his throat a knotted clench. Volcanic nausea simmered in his core.

The bedroom – a haze of fever-heat.

Esther peered over her reading glasses and narrowed her eyes. "No-one'll believe this, you know. It's Monday!"

Writhing under a wisp of a bedsheet, he craved the comfort of warmth, but was too flushed to tolerate the itchy blanket laid out by his sceptical grandmother.

Esther retrieved the thermometer and gaped at the gauge. "Bloody 'ell! You're not pretending, then."

Cook was too wretched for protest. He watched, heavy-lidded, as Esther threw on her coat and announced she was going to 'fetch the doctor'. She thundered down the stairs, tutting and muttering. The house flinched as she slammed the front door.

Dorian Cook had turned eight years old a few days earlier. Apart from those first few days at the Royal

Infirmary, he had slept in this room every night of his life, like his young mother before him. But this was the first time he had ever been alone here. His inception had been a double-problem – he arrived both inconveniently premature and too bulky for standard delivery (8lbs, 11oz). In the bed now moulded to Cook and his malady, the twenty-year-old Lily was shaken awake by scything contractions and driven to hospital in her brother's Hillman Imp, where her abdomen was unzipped by a terse consultant obstetrician. Cook was extracted from the dark and presented to the light – before his time, just as he was getting comfy, just as he was starting to fit. And then there were two, here in this room, side by side in a single bed – one freshly baked, the other newly blooded as an adult, also before her time, forced to get busy being old just as she was getting the hang of being young.

Cook lay on his back, X-shaped, hot and bothered by the unnatural silence. He felt simultaneously dry and clammy, sensitive and numb. His shoulders were studded with tiny pink eruptions, and his open pyjama-top exposed a join-the-dots swarm across his chest. He wondered if there was something slithering around inside him, rushing from point to point, attempting to prod and poke its way out, leaving a nipple-like scar with each impact. The thought made him want to scratch and smooth out the impurities with his fingertips. In these moments, Cook pined for his mother. Esther's love was fierce and protective, but he longed for the milky yield of maternity – a rare pleasure now Lily had moved out and visited randomly. The matter of his father's identity and whereabouts remained cryptic, beyond discussion.

Cook jerked out of half-sleep. On the other side of the flimsy wall behind the headboard, their neighbour – referred to by Esther as 'Mr Smith' – fired off a lengthy fusillade of death-rattle coughing. The tempo was familiar and near-constant – at first perilous and apparently final, then slowly settling to a single aftershock wheeze every few seconds. To Cook, Mr Smith was little more than a flutter of white hair just visible over the top of the yard wall – gliding, fin-like, out from his door to the bin and back again. Cook always dreaded the moment when the hair would stop, and, as Mr Smith raised himself on tiptoe, grow a waxy-grey forehead, then a pair of half-seeing eyes. There were never words or gesture to soften this moment – no cheery, 'Hello, son!' or wrinkled smirk. Just a rheumy great slap of a stare – an elderly invasion of Cook's unformed little corner of the world.

Cook sharpened his ears to the wheezing, which was now rolling in and out every few minutes, undepleted – a tidal eternity. Mr Smith was little more than a carbon chrysalis – shrivelled housing for a torment which strained to burst free and surge away. For a young boy, adults were powerful, inscrutable, fully formed. Cook could not project backwards to imagine the creature over the wall as the closing act of a life that had once been all sex and swagger, propelled by the unswerving rhino-charge of youth. But he could still feel the bottomless isolation, hear the sorrow raging through the babble and splutter. Something pitiless inside Cook made him want to silence all of this – to shut it away somewhere airless and sound-proof.

"Hiya!"

Downstairs, Esther was back, and there was a deeper

voice, too. Cook's delirium was now disassociative. He travelled through a ten-minute chunk of time in an instant, and then suddenly here was Dr Sherratt and his icy stethoscope and squashy hands and dazzling baldness and cat-food breath. Sherratt took out a miniature torch, leaned in close and studied Cook's eyeballs.

Watch! He hates this!

Mr Smith erupted again, and Cook saw Sherratt's focus drift a little, assessing the cough with a flicker of pity.

"Calomine lotion will ease the discomfort," he told Esther, closing his bag. "It tends to peak pretty quickly and then ease off over a week or so. Keep him away from school and don't let anyone who hasn't already had it into the house – certainly not into this room."

Soon, there was no Sherratt and no Esther, and Cook lay uncovered by sheets, basted in gloop, disfigured by a sprinkling of spots and blemishes. He had been dosed with (in Sherratt's words) a 'suspension', and now the room squirmed like a snakepit – a freakshow of fluttering shadows and splintered echoes. The nausea reared up, splashing around the base of his throat. He lay unnaturally still, fearing the slightest movement might provoke his stomach – or bowels – into spasm.

And then he was in the sitting room, blanket over head and shoulders, quivering before the black-and-white TV. Next door, as the retching fits tore through his neighbour's lungs, Cook's sheen of fever-fuzz absorbed and amplified the barrage. He turned up the TV volume and stared at the *For Schools & Colleges* intro graphic – a circle of pearl-like pellets surrounding the words 'History Around You'. Syrupy muzak soundtracked a clockwise circuit as the pellets crudely self-deleted, one by one. Cook stared and slow-blinked, synchronising his eye closure with the mid-wipe point of the erasure process, as if the act of not acknowledging the pellets was the force compelling them to disappear. He fantasised about doing the same with the spots and dots that had annexed his own skin, willing them out of existence.

The air was like broth. He could taste the salt in the sweat on his lips. His dog was there and his grandmother was there and, at one point, he even thought his mother was there – blonde and bright and white, sparkling through the browns and beiges of Esther's textured wallpaper. And then it wasn't his mother, it was John Ray – the shining hair, the phantom skin.

Suddenly, it was late afternoon – dusk – and he was eating warmed-up Ambrosia creamed-rice pudding and watching *Dr Who*. A shingle beach glazed in low sunlight, a gang of humanoid monsters rising through the riptide and shambling ashore – reptilian features frozen in grimace, mutated bodies draped in slimy netting. Each carried some kind of beam-gun that could deliver one-zap instant death. Cook was instantly, unspeakably petrified – of their bulk, their inhumanity, their deformity, and of their reaper-like dominion over death. He imagined them (the 'Sea Devils') entering the house at night, executing his pet, then his grandmother, then hunting for him – climbing the stairs, finding him in his bedroom, maybe even in his bed.

Cook shovelled in a mouthful of pudding and glanced over at the door that separated the sitting room from the parlour. He jumped – a jolt of shock – at the sight of a human head, with carrot-orange hair, peering around the edge of the frame at ankle level. The head slid slowly upwards until Cook's mother's brother, Russell, revealed himself by stepping to the side and bounding into the room.

"What are you watching?"

"*Dr Who.*"

Russell laughed, too loud. "Dorian, you crackpot!"

This was his standard irritating term of address, overused fluidly as insult or endearment. He dropped to his knees and shuffled in close to Cook.

"Chickenpox!"

Under his blanket, Cook glanced up, nodded.

"Don't worry, Dor!" said Russell, settling down on the floor cross-legged, zoning in to a beach-head firefight between Sea Devils and soldiers. "You'll live."

5

Motion Capture

COOK SECURED THE MORNING off work with a cryptic text message and padded down to breakfast, bathrobed and bed-haired. Alfie had prepared him a slice of white-bread toast topped with a few smears of strawberry jam. He gnawed his way through, chasing each sickly swallow with a guzzle of instant coffee. There should have been a truant-like pleasure to be taken from unjustified time off work, but Cook felt unease at anything open-ended. He quickly slumped from the joy of unhurried freedom to anxiety at the quantum sprawl of paths and possibilities. It was no comfort to imagine colleagues frantically covering for his absence – he was barely missed.

"Frankensteins," announced Alfie, "are made of dead body parts."

Cook smiled. "But how do they get that way?"

Alfie searched his bowl of Coco Shreddies for an answer. "They get struck by lightning and come to life!"

Cook shifted from cheek to cheek, finding comfort on neither. In half an hour, he would be perched and tilted on a gurney at his GP's office, trousers down low, knees up high. The insistent pinching and pulsing around his anus was, he reasoned, the initial stirring of a rapacious rectal tumour – a slow-burning cellular eruption that would steadily detonate from the arsehole in, consuming and subsuming him. He had recently developed an obsession with disease after seeing the film *Biutiful*, in which the lead character irredeemably succumbs to prostate cancer. Gina had indulged him, insisting that health awareness was healthy, and it was the men who avoided doctors, usually out of misplaced bravado, who ended up dying from conditions that had progressed beyond the treatable stage. But Cook knew his anxiety was less and less about decay, and more and more about the universal dread that rose, with advancing age, of no longer being here, there or anywhere. Death was forever inbound. It could be delayed and diverted, but it *would* arrive, and there was nothing on Earth – nothing electrical in the sky – that could send it away.

The doctor's office had recently installed a touch-screen arrival system, with appointments confirmed by sex and date of birth. Cook dabbed in his details, wondering if this was the wisest method of processing patients – a shared surface for them to soil with contagious DNA. The waiting room was fully stocked with the sitting wounded. Cook slumped into the only spare seat, beside a modest children's play table, and braced for the familiar limbo of irritation and alarm – later arrivals being called first, random gap between appointment time and consultation, the infernal bickering between inner defeatist and pragmatist. He shifted a buttock to one side, shuffling the painful patch away from the wooden seat base, which creaked loudly. This provoked a beat of collective curiosity – a break in the chorus of

coughing and sneezing and despairing and diseasing. At the
very least, there would surely be ointment – a week or two
of reaching down and around and blending chemistry with
biology. When young, Cook pondered, we use drugs to
entertain; when old, to sustain.

A speaker drilled into the ceiling wafted out an
instrumental saxophone version of Simply Red's 'Holding
Back The Years'. Cook read this as an ironic comment on
the uncertain longevity of the audience. He imagined a
waggish orderly in an elderly care-home cueing it up as the
theme for medication time.

His phone jangled, announcing an email which offered
'herbal penis enlargement' – a treatment which would
apparently transform any man into 'the Pied Piper of Hot
Chicks'. Cook doubted this. He had never been much of a
leader, and he wasn't convinced that an arbitrary extension
to the length of his penis was going to change that – not at
his life stage, at least. The newsletter from the redesigned
PastLives.com squatted conspicuously in his inbox. He
thought of the message – the invitation to 'catch up' – and
realised that he could never reply.

"Dorian Cook. Doctor Escott. Room 4."

Escott's domain was a schizoid shrine to Christian piety and
science-fiction – desktop Dalek, rosary draped over computer
monitor, *Serenity* mouse-mat, photo of waterfall with
motivational slogan ('Beauty – an act of God!'). As Cook
entered, Escott – fiftyish, crinkled polo shirt, lavishly bellied –
leapt from his desk and closed in for a double-pump handshake
with an odd little bonus – a shoulder-pat from his free hand. It
felt calculated rather than caring, and Cook prickled.

"Dorian Cook?" he wondered. No eye contact.

"I am!" said Cook, weirdly.

Escott waddled backwards, muscle memory guiding him down into his chair.

"And how are you? What seems to be the trouble?"

Cook sat down – too hard – on another firm chair. He shuddered with pain.

"I, uh, have a sore spot. On my…"

Anus? Arsehole? Asshole?

"…bottom."

The word burst into the room and hovered there, unwanted. Escott regarded it silently. He nodded and began clattering away at the keyboard of his decade-old PC. "Okay. And how long have you had this? Is there any discharge? Any blood?"

Cook looked up at the poster on the wall above Escott's examination bench – an enormous, scowling lion's face on a stark, black background. 'The Lion of Judah…' announced an ugly-fonted caption across the brow of the mane. 'Jesus Christ!' shrieked a larger legend over the lion's jutting jaw.

"A week or so. Bit of blood, yeah."

Escott looked up and raised his eyebrows. "How much? Roughly. Is it bright red or quite dark?"

Cook saw himself from the perspective of the poster – a beast's-eye view of a clenched and clucking nebbish. He was a critic, criticiser, professional pontificator, opinion-former (not any more), supplier of promotional quotes (rarely) – a middling, middle-brow, middle-aged middle-man charged with composing too many words for too few readers. The Lion-Jesus glared down – at a creature clinging to the illusion that people cared about what came out of its mouth, when there was more concern over what was escaping from its rear-end.

"It's bright red."

Escott was standing and nodding more vigorously, groping his way into a pair of surgical gloves. "Fresh. Hmm..." He muttered, eyes closed, visualising his symptom-prognosis flowchart.

"Let's have a quick look, then. I don't think there's anything to worry about."

Cook was unfamiliar with this concept. He sat up on Escott's bench, unhooked his belt and compressed into a compromising position. He coveted his doctor's world of relative certainty, in contrast to his own realm of bluff and bluster – the eternal tyrannies of, 'In my view...' and, 'For me...' and, 'Everyone is entitled to their opinion...' and, 'I hear what you're saying, but...'. Cook's worries amounted to a lot more than 'nothing', and he was both their cause and effect, architect and architecture – the sole engineer of a caffeine-bolstered contraption of obsolete biomechanics.

Escott, for one, was done with him.

"Pop your trousers back up! Yes... You've got a couple of fairly small haemorrhoids – probably caused by straining. Do you move your bowels every day?"

"Erm, I think so. Usually."

Escott chuckled. "Well, it's not really the kind of thing one keeps a record of, I know. Although there seems to be a 'blog' for everything, these days."

Fully dressed and no longer cowed by the spectre of colon cancer, Cook discovered his sense of humour.

"A log blog?"

Escott laughed a little too heartily. "Yes! Exactly. I'm just writing you a prescription for a lactulose drink – that will help keep your stools softened. And you might want to pick up a tube of Anusol to ease the discomfort a little. No need for a suppository."

Cook hurried back through the waiting room, where The Beatles' 'Something' was now being sax-murdered.

"Dor!"

William Stone – an ex-neighbour – had taken Cook's place by the play table. They had first become acquainted back when Gina was pregnant and taking an afternoon nap. Stone had shooed away a gaggle of noisy estate kids, after Cook had failed to persuade them to 'make a bit less noise'. They had smelt his fear, and he felt emasculated and hopelessly middle-class in the face of their reptilian contempt. In contrast, Stone – a short but stocky police officer – succeeded in convincing the kids that there were better things to do than vandalise a mound of abandoned builder's tools. They had slouched away, lobbing a few profanities over their pointy shoulders. Cook was grateful, but had the impression that Stone was trading on reputation rather than status.

"Hey, Will. How are you?"

Cook swaggered over, unconvincingly. He sat down – with care – next to Stone, wisely resisting the urge to slap him on his burly back.

"I'm alright, mate, yeah! What's the story here, then? Having the snip or something?"

"Ha. No! I've, er..." Cook winced and switched his weight from right to left buttock.

"Oh, I see..." said Stone, whispering. "Arse boil?"

"Sort of."

Stone considered this as he fiddled with the gummed-up wheels of a wooden toy train. "Fucking hell! Bum-grapes?"

Cook nodded. Stone leaned in close. It was early morning, but Cook could smell alcohol on his breath. "You know why, don't ya? Because you talk so much shit!"

Stone bellowed with laughter. Cook politely guffawed, despite seeing no sense in the remark.

"Well," he offered, "that's my job."

Stone smiled at that.

"I'm having a cholesterol check, mate. Weight's all over the fucking place!"

A white-haired old woman sitting opposite tutted and sent over a sharp look. Cook was suddenly keen to get away and so employed his standard method of bringing a chance encounter to a premature close.

"Listen. We should have a catch-up sometime."

Lately, Cook seemed to be in a permanent state of 'catch-up'. He could feel his grip loosening on the matters of culture he would have obsessively monitored only a couple of years ago. He was still prone to faintly teenage fixations with certain music, adrenalised hectoring on pop-culture issues, and even the odd cautious engagement with sport and politics. But he was befuddled by science, bored with art and borderline anhedonic over nature. He drank more from habit than for effect and, despite his name, had little interest in anything but basic food. His sense of the sheer absurdity of sex was now so developed that he could barely do it without sniggering and, while he used to set aside time for lengthy sessions of masturbation, he had gradually adopted the swift and functional approach – more soporific than pornographic. For Cook, the sensual world was another country. They did things differently there.

"Yeah," said Stone, "let's have a pint. I'm on nights this week but I'll text you. Maybe next Thursday?"

Cook agreed. Like the other aspects of his life, he was long overdue an update on Stone's typically colourful emotional wranglings.

On the way out, he opened his calendar app and checked next week's schedule. On Thursday, he was due to attend a screening of *Struisvogel*, a post-war Austrian political thriller about a young woman's attempt to track down her father, an ex-concentration-camp guard, also wanted by Nazi hunters. Cook mulled the inevitably 120-minute-plus meditation on Holocaust guilt and father-daughter redemption. He deleted the screening entry and tapped out a replacement – 'Drinks with Will'.

6

Mum & Dad

Cook burrowed through the darkness – thrashing arms, swimming legs, elbows prodding at the clinging blanket folds. His fingers brushed against bone and hair. Esther's nightgown was too short and her ankles protruded as specimen for his investigations.

"Welcome to the underwater world of Jack Coo-Stow!"

Cook's voice was throttled by the heavy undersheet. In deep winter, Esther layered her bed like lasagne – an insulating strata of thick and thin, rough and smooth.

"This rare species is a 'Nana Leg'. It's hard to capture!"

He grappled with Esther's bony foot.

"Gerroff! C'mon, Dor! It's too bloody early."

'Bloody' was rare. It meant Esther was serious, that her indulgence of horseplay had slipped into irritation. Cook slept in his grandmother's bed for warmth, when the seasonal chill made his unheated bedroom inhospitable. The electric blanket was an impossible luxury. It seemed companionable and organic – a life-giving, heat-radiating network of arterial cables woven into a skin-like membrane. Cook would always wait for it to warm to its highest setting before sliding under the covers for grateful and exquisite smothering. Back in his own bed, swaddled in double pyjamas, flat on his back, entombed beneath a heavy haul of blankets and overcoats, he played a nightly game of distraction – inhale deeply, pinch lips into tiny aperture, exhale, watch breath drift and swirl, repeat until asleep. Esther had finally rescued him last February, when she had leaned in for a morning forehead-kiss and noticed a sprinkle of frost in his eyebrows.

Esther rose, stepped into her slippers and embarked on her early morning expedition to the outside toilet. With a jolt of excitement, Cook realised it was Saturday. He sprung out of bed, scurried across the landing into his room, opened the corner closet and dragged out a large, thin slab of plywood – rough on one side, smooth on the other. His Uncle Russell had 'borrowed' the wood from a college workshop and he had helped Cook cover the smooth side with a green felt Subbuteo football pitch. But as he laid it onto the floor, Cook saw that the wood had warped and the pitch markings were now stretched taut across an alarming hump, with its arc peaking at the half-way line. He abandoned the pitch, retrieved a tatty Enid Blyton hardback from the closet and ran back to his grandmother's room, huddling back in with the baking underlay. Esther kept a torch under her side of the bed for nocturnal toilet trips, and Cook often used it to read, curled tight and safe in a den of blankets at the centre of the bed. He carved out a narrow tunnel of fabric to use as an air-hole and scanned the torch beam over the back cover of *The Adventures Of Mr Pink-Whistle*.

Mr Pink-Whistle is not like ordinary people. He's half a brownie and half a person, and he can make himself invisible whenever he wants.

Cook found this idea intensely exciting and resolved to achieve something similar as soon as he was old enough. He had mentioned this to Esther and been met with a gruff rebuttal.

"That's only make believe, Dor. And why would you want to make yourself invisible, anyway?"

"Because when you're invisible," insisted Cook, "it means that no-one can see you and when no-one can see you, they can't hurt you, but you can hurt them if you really have to."

"Yeah, but they could *hear* you."

"Not if you're really quiet. You could wear socks."

The front door clanged shut. There were murmurs down in the parlour, then raised, excited voices in the sitting room, then the noise of someone running up the stairs. Cook spread himself flat under the covers. Maybe no-one would notice he was there if he was perfectly still.

"Dorian, darling?"

It was his mother's sing-song voice. She saw him so infrequently, she could never seem to calibrate her mode of address with his age and awareness. Her latest guess, it seemed, was that he was around two or three years younger. Cook heard her enter his own bedroom, pause, then cross the landing. He stayed quiet, knowing it would be interpreted as a game.

Lily slipped into the room. Cook's concealment was comically obvious, but she played along, loudly wondering where-oh-where he could have got to. She held back a little, drawing out his barely stifled sniggers. Then, she pounced, digging her fingers into where she thought the boy-shaped lump's ribs might be, scrabbling and tickling and forcing Cook to clamber out of her reach, up to the top of the bed. She gathered him up, squeezing, plunging her face into his neck. He spluttered on a mouthful of brightly bleached hair and shouted for her ("Mummy!"). His tone was uncertain – excited, irritated, a little scared?

"Ooh…" She nuzzled into his cheek. "I could eat him all up!"

Cook broke away and propped himself against Esther's mound of pillows where he could get a good look at her and brace for what might be coming next. Lily was long and slender and, despite the cold, wore a short mini-dress patterned with psychedelic swirls. Her waist-length hair whipped and swished as she clicked open a bulky suitcase.

"Where have you been, mummy?"

The question carried an awkward ambiguity. In this case, Lily had 'been' to Spain. Her normally dry, pale skin was glossed olive, and she was a tottering *Buckaroo* of cases, carrier-bags and oversized souvenirs, most of which were now scattered around the floor. And now she wasn't there, she was here, materialised and in motion but less familiar than in her usual state – the unpresent, the unarrived. Cook was confused by his yearning for Lily. Did he actually miss her, or was he just rebelling against his natural preference for aloneness? Could you really miss someone who was too rarely present to remind you of the things you were missing?

"It's called Lanzarote," said Lily, fumbling inside the suitcase, "in a country called Spain. It was very hot there, Dorian. I think you'd have liked it. Cold in here!"

"Why didn't I go with you?" Cook was now sitting upright, vertically propped on a saddle of pillows.

"You're a bit too young, darling. Plenty of time for you to travel the world when you're a bigger boy."

Cook was surprised to hear that his bigness was in doubt, but he had no real interest in travel. His world was tighly compacted – it extended only to the play-park at the top of his street and the oil-works that lay flat and wide and toxic at the bottom. And, uncomfortably close just a few doors down, there was the old butcher's shop, its front and back doors obscured by crude layerings of heavy planks. Cook always took care to rush past the lonely old house on his way to school, telling himself that he couldn't look at it because if he did, the world would explode. He knew that the world wouldn't really explode, but he could never quite bring himself to check.

"Here it is!"

Lily produced a plush toy from the suitcase. It had dog-like features but was caricatured and stretched tall, with yellowy-white fur. Cook took it suspiciously and squeaked out a thank you.

"It's a poodle, Dor! Like Snowy!"

Snowy was Esther's previous pet dog. Cook was too young to remember much about him – apart from a warm tongue lapping at his cheek and a sense that the facts about the dog's fate had been kept vague. Cook shook the toy from side to side, smiling a little at the freely suspended plastic pupils, rattling and rolling inside transparent eyeballs. The gift was another illustration of his mother's feeble grasp of her son's development.

"Why don't you live with us, mum?"

The question ambushed Lily. She took a steadying breath, pretending to fiddle with a suitcase lock.

"I wish I could, Dor. It's really hard. I live with a friend. Not that far away."

"Is it my dad?"

Lily sidestepped this with an agility that gave Cook his answer.

"You can come and visit! That'd be nice, wouldn't it? I bet you'd love the flat. My friend has lots of comics you can read."

Later, Cook lay next to Esther, mummified in bed-socks, mittens, double pyjamas and his late grandfather's balaclava. He gazed at the grey outline of the toy dog, propped up inside an open drawer of the dressing table. Its synthetic fur blazed absurdly white through the icy twilight, off-centre eyes sightlessly regarding the thin curtains. Esther snored loudly and frequently, in an unsettling baritone. Cook considered refuge in his own room (he was dressed for the occasion) but decided the noise wasn't bad enough to brave the stumble across the landing, remembering to resist glancing across and down into the oily blackness that seemed to gather around the base of the staircase.

He removed one of his mittens and peeked a couple of fingers outside the duvet. The cold seeped over them – frosting the tips, stiffening the knuckles. He snatched his hand back, replaced the mitten and returned to staring at the dog. Soon, despite the rasping and roaring, he sank into a dream-busy sleep.

Something was coming up the stairs.

Cook crouched in his closet, flattened into a corner,

battling the urge to spring up and out and maybe dive through the window and take his chances with the pavement twenty feet below.

He heard the Something turn the corner at the bottom of the stairs and – slowly, always without urgency – begin its thunking ascent.

Dream-logic allowed him to simultaneously hide in the closet and watch from his window as a group of Sea Devils ambled through the shallow lake of caustic sludge that surrounded the oil-works. They slimed across the road, converging on his front door, barging into the house in ones and twos.

Thunk.

He heard the Something crash through the cheap bedroom door and thunk its way over to his hiding place.

7

The Price of Admission

"IT WAS ALL SO fucking *po-faced!*"

This was Jake Saloman, broadsheet critic, chairman of *Critics' Wire*, a film writers' collective which distributed screening news and hosted an annual, under-reported awards ceremony.

"But it's a serious subject matter!" barked Neville Smith, part-time reviewer, full-time gadabout. "You can't just throw in a load of irony. Sometimes you have to take things seriously."

Next, the overlapping squawk and squabble distinctive of a group of gawky film critics masculated by watery wine.

"I thought there was a lightness of touch."

"He just makes the same film over and over again."

"Why do you always have to have something to say?"

"Well, it's like 'My First Kubrick'."

Cook would normally wade in to this subjective jetsam with arms flailing, drink sloshing. But, here in the British Film Foundation bar – a menagerie of baying indignance – he was immobilised by ennui. The contact from Dennis Mountford had taken root in a gloomy corner of his mind, and it was not something that could be shrugged back into the past or forgotten from the present. Mountford was a lifetime gone and yet right there in the room with him – across the reclaimed-wood table, perched on the burnt-orange ottoman. In this vision, his friend was still a young boy, and Cook shuddered as he realised they hadn't shared the same space in the real world for over thirty-five years. He gazed into his barely depleted pint glass and forced a scared little smile.

"Look at *Citizen Kane...*" (Saloman again). "It hasn't aged well. The sign of a true masterpiece is timelessness."

Consternation, sneers of laughter.

"And the *Mona Lisa?*" challenged Malcolm Parker, weekend broadsheet film editor. "That's hardly 'aged well', but it doesn't make it less of a masterpiece."

"We're talking about two entirely different art forms," snapped Charlie Brent, listings-mag film-section editor. "You can't say that this painting is 'better' than that film."

Cook, a little drunk, drew in a steadying breath.

"Is *Citizen Kane* a five-star movie?" he demanded.

General agreement.

"And is the *Mona Lisa* a five-star painting?"

"Of course!" brayed Smith, through a splutter of house Rosé.

"How about what everyone had for breakfast this morning? Five-star bowl of Shreddies, was it? Five-star fucking brioche and coffee?"

"We're talking about *art*, Dorian," said Parker carefully, "not just general experiences. I know there's some debate over..."

"I'm talking about sensual – *sensory* – pleasures," Cook interrupted, slurring the S's. "Has anyone here ever had a five-star bowl of soup or a five-star blow-job? It's all about the moment! You can't judge anything – art, experience, arcn't they the same thing? – with hindsight. It's all about how you feel and react in the moment, when you're right there, on the ride! You can't stick a 'rating' on everything and then compare the components of life and culture, based on those ratings!"

"It's just a convenient yardstick," smiled Saloman. "We don't have the time or space to have lengthy conversations about…"

Cook yelped a strange little exclamation and held up his hand, palm facing out. It was a gesture of supreme arrogance, designed to cut the response short.

"But don't you think it's depressing – how we have to view films on this sliding, five-point scale, how we're paid to neatly package the unpackageable? It's not a fucking 'convenient yardstick'! It's a dance with the marketing devil. We provide the poster-friendly quotes and star ratings, and the studios use them to sell the films. Why do we – why does *anyone* – even bother writing long-form reviews any more? Do you know who reads our reviews? We do! Other film reviewers! It's not fucking 'writing', it's grandstanding. No… It's masturbating! We're basically just sitting around, wanking off in front of each other."

He sprang up from his seat, swaying.

"And you can quote me! On the fucking poster!"

After that, Cook spent a little too long sitting in the fragranced, air-conditioned toilet cubicle, staring down at the frayed underwear stretched around his ankles. He dug out his phone and opened the email inbox. One new message.

Enlargement supplement! Did you know that we have a formula that can elongate your manhood with no side effects?

Cook did indeed know this. He seemed to be made aware of it roughly every hour, as his ironically enlarged Junk Mail folder could testify.

He signed in to *PastLives.com*, opened the message from 'Den' and deleted it.

8
How We Used To Live

The children chosen to take part in Bethesda First & Middle's centenary celebrations were divided into two groups. The younger ones – Cook included – were allocated Victorian-era playground games, while the older bunch all contributed to a collage of thickly daubed watercolours depicting school life in 1874. Cook ground three marbles together in his pocket as he was guided to his spot on the upper-school playground. The day was being filmed for a historical TV show which uncovered evidence of past culture in present-day architecture. Cook's school had been selected because its original buildings were a social historian's wonderland of air-raid shelters and shoe-scrapers. The presenter – a bearded academic in a beige polo-neck – drifted around, chatting to the children. He stooped before Cook, referring to him as 'young chap' and resting a hand on his shoulder. As he spoke, his mouth barely seemed to open – saliva-glazed lips writhed like earthworms in the centre of the tangled scrubland that had overrun his chin and cheeks.

Cook spent the half-hour filming time engaged in an over-theatrical 'game' of marbles with an older boy, David

Brereton. They were instructed to repeatedly – but casually – roll smaller marbles towards a larger target ball, while everyone else skipped and hopscotched and leap-frogged inside strictly defined zones. Cook and Brereton giggled and bantered, rolling the marbles with too much pace and aggression, aiming them at a nearby group of skipping girls. Cook was pleasantly shocked by Brereton's disregard for instructions, how practiced he seemed at appearing to comply, but always adding his own subversive little improvisations. When one of the girls slipped on a marble, Brereton was quick to convincingly feign disinterest, focusing instantly back on the ground below, and abandoning Cook to a warning from Mrs Mellor.

On the way home from school that afternoon, Brereton caught up with Cook half-way over the zebra crossing.

"D'you wanna go to the marl-hole on Saturday?"

Esther had warned Cook to avoid the area near the deep pit of clay around the back of the brickworks, a short walk up from their house. Unguarded at weekends, the 'marl-hole' was a treacherous gouge of restless sludge, trickling screes and abandoned extraction tools. Cook definitely did not 'want' to go there on Saturday, but he felt oddly secure with Brereton – although he was clearly the type to attract trouble, he was equally skilled at deflecting consequences.

"Yeah, okay!"

"Come call for me – 28 Lowther Street."

Brereton veered off and Cook diverted to the corner sweet shop, where he bought a few Fruit Salad chews before rejoining his usual route home. A few minutes from his house, Cook noticed a group of boys, directly in his path, shoving and wrestling near the main gates of the oil-works.

His instinct was to turn back and find an alternative route, but he buried the sweets deep in his pocket and carried on walking. As he got closer, Cook recognised John Ray, at the centre of a restricting huddle, being yanked and buffeted around by three captors. Each time Ray made a dash for escape, he was hauled back into the centre. Cook switched pavements to avoid the scene, and was about to scurry past when he saw a blue-and-white handkerchief in the middle of the road.

"Come on!" shouted one of the boys. "You can go!"

Cook stopped and watched. The group had parted to form an apparent exit channel. Ray bolted for the gap, but was quickly blocked and forced back into the centre. He howled with frustration, and again, Cook thought of something animal – almost alien. Like Mr Smith's persistent hacking and heaving, he longed to silence the sound, to slice it out of existence.

Cook walked over and picked up the handkerchief. The boys were a little older, but he was high on confidence after his role in the filming, and the new connection with Brereton made him feel more protected – at least more monitored – than usual. He forced his way through interlocking hands and offered the handkerchief back to its owner. Ray's pallid skin was blotched red with anger. His jumper had split open at the armpit and something earthly had been ground into his feathery hair.

"Thank you," he said, taking the handkerchief and stuffing it into his pocket. Cook's boldness had stalled the boys, but as he turned and wriggled out of their circle, he felt a kick to the back of his leg which toppled him down onto the pavement. The boys' laughter was more gleeful than malicious. Cook's misfortune had broken the tension and, faces saved, the group scattered and scampered away.

"Are you alright?"

The question could have been directed either way, but it came from Cook to John Ray.

"Yes."

Ray sniffed. He took out the handkerchief, wiped his nose, buried it back in his pocket. As they walked, Cook offered one of his sweets, but Ray shook his head. For him, kindness was to be feared – it was a feint, a prelude to cruelty.

The road levelled off near the iron bridge. Ray quickened his pace and broke away with a doubtful, "See you later!" Cook was surprised to hear that his speaking voice was clipped and precise – almost posh.

At home, Cook dropped off his school-bag and headed straight out to call on Lisa Goldstraw. Her mum made them both a glass of diluted orange juice and they sat drinking, side by side, on the two swings at the bottom of Lisa's vast, immaculate garden.

"Lisa?" enquired Cook.

"Yeah?"

"Will you go out with me?"

She considered this, tugging both stockings over her knees. "I can't. I really like you, but I'm already going out with someone."

"But I could be, like, your second boyfriend?"

Her silence told him this wasn't possible. He hopped off the swing and wandered into the kitchen, where Lisa's mum had propped baby Rebecca in a high-chair and was smearing primary-coloured puree into her reluctant mouth. Rebecca squealed with joy at the sight of Cook. She strained her tubby arms to full stretch, reaching for him. Mrs Goldstraw smiled and handed Cook the jar of baby food. He rattled the spoon around and scraped out a blob of something that smelt of sweetened carrots. Rebecca was stilled. Her shining eyes tracked the spoon's movement as Cook lifted it towards her mouth, which opened wide, received the food and immediately re-opened for more.

9

Catching Up

WILLIAM STONE DRAINED HIS glass and rose for a second round. He quickly returned from the bar with two fresh drinks, handed one to Cook and clinked cheers. Cook had barely broken the surface of his original pint, but awkwardly slurped at the foam from the new glass.

"Look at him!" laughed Stone. "Two on the fucking go! What a lightweight!"

Cook tilted his glass and took on more beer than was comfortable. The liquid was lukewarm and chemical. Bubbles spiralled up into his nose and he had to disguise a gag as a cough.

"How's the cholesterol?" A deflection.

Stone lifted an eyebrow, wrinkling his brow. Here, in a mangy corner of the *Seven Stars*, under the hundred-watt scrutiny of a mock-antique lantern, Cook saw that the whites of his friend's eyes were scored with deep red capillaries, branching and pooling into bloodshot halos around the socket edges.

"Quack put me on some pills, printed out a little info sheet. Usual – more exercise, no smoking or decent food. I had a scare last autumn. I dunno. Gotta die of something."

He finished off half of his pint in what looked like a

single gulp Cook reverted to his first glass and manfully cut the content by around a third. The effort made his vision blur.

"How's Gina?" Stone asked, eyeing his drink lustfully, as if pondering how soon he could dive back in for the second half without appearing dependant. Stone had always given Cook the impression that he was a drinker by personality and capacity, when in fact he used alcohol as more of a tool than a toy – to dull the ache of a desolate marriage that was slouching towards divorce.

"She's good, yeah," spluttered Cook, mid-drink. "I mentioned I'd seen you and she said to say hello."

Stone smiled, looked up from his glass and held Cook's gaze a little, sensing – and expecting – more.

"But... Ah, you know. We're holding it together. Her folks would fucking disown her if she gave up, but I'm not sure how much longer that can go on for."

"Funny," said Stone, sloshing his beer around, "I always had you pair down as happily-ever-after types."

Cook snorted. "You can never really judge someone else's relationship from the outside."

This prompted a synchronised swig, noticed by both. Stone laughed, loud enough to turn a couple of heads.

"How's Lydia doing at school?"

Stone's daughter was fourteen going on eighteen, with a swelling sexuality that Cook regarded with both alarm and allure.

"I barely see her these days. She communicates more with her bloody gadgets than she does with her voice. I suppose Alfie is too young for all that?"

Cook winced. "He's well aware of it – more than I am,

anyway. I hate the idea of 'social media' – this culture of virtual vanity."

"It's an American thing," Stone confirmed. "They love bragging about their friends, talking about how successful everyone is. Brits used to find that a bit embarrassing but we've definitely got over it now."

Refreshment levels steadily increased and the conversation flowed into darker channels. Cook raised the topic of Stone's troubles at work – he had recently been assaulted during the policing of a street protest and, unwisely, had retaliated, socking his (female) assailant on the chin with his sizeable fist, and laying her out cold. His promotion prospects had been frozen and he would soon face a disciplinary hearing.

"Listen, Dor…"

Cook braced. Stone's tone and posture was now familiar – maudlin, head hung low and heavy, weighted with booze. He was breathing like a bulldog.

"Can you do me 2K? 3K at the end of the month."

It was a long-running arrangement. He would hand over £2000 in cash and, at the end of the month, always on time, Stone would deposit £3000 back into his account. Cook suspected a gambling debt, but couldn't make sense of the economics. He emptied his glass and, unkindly, left the question unanswered for a few seconds.

"Of course, mate."

Later, hot-faced and ravenous, Cook bought a steak pasty and settled into the corner of a quiet carriage on the last Tube train home.

He took out his phone and opened an email which

notified him of a new message on *PastLives.com*. He laid the paper pasty bag down on the seat beside him, logged in and opened his profile inbox.

> *Dor! I hope I don't sound too pushy – and I hope you're getting my messages. It'd be great if you could just give me a quick call mate! It's really important. Think I might have got in touch with Dave but he hasn't got back to me either!! Please mate. Just two minutes then I promise to leave you alone. Hope you're really well!! Den*

The train jerked away from the station. Cook deleted the message, pocketed his phone and slumped forward, elbows on knees, head resting on clasped hands. The journey was around twenty minutes and he stayed in this position all the way, uneaten pasty by his side.

10

Foreshadows

"City or United?"

Uncle Russell raised Cook onto his shoulders, crouching slightly. As he gradually unbent his knees, Cook felt the peaks in the ceiling's artex complexion brush against his hair.

"United!"

Russell drew himself almost upright, lifting Cook's head closer to the plaster spikes. Both were laughing.

"*City* or United?"

"City! *City!*"

Russell squatted down and Cook scrambled off his shoulders, brushing off-white flakes out of his hair. His uncle closed in for a follow-up armpit-tickle, but Cook saw it coming and was quickly up and running for the bottom of the stairs.

"Nana! Tell him!"

A knock at the front door, rather than Cook's plea, brought Esther thudding down the stairs.

"Leave him alone, Russell! What do you want for your tea?"

Russell gathered himself. Then, still laughing: "Egg and chips!"

"Can I have that too, nana?"

Cook followed Esther and hovered as she struggled with
the sticky front door.

"No. You're going out."

The door opened on the third tug, revealing Lily, frozen
in a rehearsed smile.

"Hello, Dorian, darling!"

As ever, Cook recoiled from the hug, keeping one foot
in the house and the other on the front step, torn between
his egg and chips and his mother.

Cook and Lily walked slowly and silently through the
Saturday dusk, up past the oil-works and down a deserted
side-road lined with houses whose windows were either
boarded or cautiously ajar, leaking statutory odours of over-
boiled vegetables. Cook tolerated the holding of his hand but
didn't squeeze back. As they traced the high perimeter fence
of honeycomb-patterned wire that bordered the Bethesda
School infants' playground, he saw that Lily had lost her
smile, but regained it briefly whenever she caught him
glancing up at her. After a careful crossing of the busy road
that climbed up to the football stadium (City), Lily released
Cook's hand and pulled a single door-key from the fur-lined
pocket of her coat. For a second, Cook thought she was about
to let herself into the *King's Head* – a buckled old pub on the
corner, long since marked for demolition but somehow still
upright. Instead, she cut into a narrow side-passage and Cook
followed as she lifted the latch on the poorly hung gate at the
end of a smelly back yard. The key admitted them into a
narrow kitchen where they crab-stepped past toppled
columns of saucepans and dinner plates which seeped over
the rim of a china sink barnacled with mould and matter.

The living room was certainly lived in. Cook cleared away a heap of damp clothes and settled into a squashy armchair which, despite its smooth PVC upholstery, had managed to retain an impressive crust of dust. A large-to-overlarge man in T-shirt and pyjama bottoms emerged from a storage room under the staircase, bumping his head on the door frame. Lily leapt to his aid, rubbing at the bump, her pink nail varnish contrasting with his inky-black hair. She turned to her boy as she soothed her man.

"Dor, this is Tom. Remember – I told you about him a few weeks ago."

"Hiya!" said Cook, mock-cheerfully.

"Y'alright, Dorian?" enquired Tom. He pulled away from Lily's fussing and dumped a mound of comic-books on the floor next to Cook's chair.

"Ee'yar… Have a look at them, then. *Spider-Man*, *Hulk*. Think there's a few *Superman* ones in there, too."

"What d'ya say, Dor?" said Lily.

"Thank you!" sing-songed Cook, ruffling through the pile. He took out an issue of *The Amazing Spider-Man*. On the cover, the Green Goblin was in mid-fight with the costumed hero, while the pair's alter-egos taunted each other in flashback. Tom gave Cook a small bottle of orangeade and a packet of cheese-and-onion crisps. Cook guzzled and munched and rustled, hardly noticing that Tom and Lily had disappeared upstairs. When it grew too gloomy to read, he just sat there in the dark, tracing spider-web patterns in the armchair dust, re-imagining the comic stories, projecting them onto the blackness where they played out as animations – vivid and looming and leering.

On the way back to Esther's, Cook happily threaded his fingers through Lily's.

"I like my dad!" he declared.

Lily snatched in a breath. "That's really good, Dor."

11

The Uninvited

THERE WERE FEW REQUESTS more humbling than being summoned for a second sitting in make-up because of a producer's concern over 'shine'. Cook was in position, installed on a minimalist sofa, side-on to camera, when a perky young runner interrupted their chat about the new wave of British realism and, with tender diplomacy, shepherded him back to the light-bulb mirror. He was re-powdered and re-deposited at the sofa area, where a second guest – Dan Machin from *Movie* magazine – had taken his spot, forcing him to sit further along and concede a subtle relegation of status.

"I think I actually prefer it to go out live," Machin was telling Jonathan Trotman, the *Talking Pictures* presenter. "You can lose confidence in what you're saying if you have to repeat it too many times."

"Oh! Is this live?" said Cook, sounding a little more concerned than he'd intended.

"Yeah," smiled Machin.

Trotman, a wily power-ligger who had once been Cook's section deputy, stepped in. "It'll be pretty straightforward, Dorian. Just five minutes of general chat with hopefully a bit of debate."

"Don't worry," added Machin – to Trotman, "we'll try not to agree on too much".

Cook swallowed reflexively. He was confident he knew the topic, but always felt cornered under the gaze of live television. Recording offered a fuzzy buffer of abstraction – he could do the job, walk away and get busy denying the sharp realities of the broadcast, shunting it into the fog of the future. But in a live setting, he was shoved into centre-stage to perform for a chorus of rolling eyeballs and curling lips. He felt like a fraud.

"Can I use the bathroom?" Cook asked Trotman.

"You'll have to be quick. We're on in five minutes."

The runner guided Cook to a shabby rest-room around the back of the sound-stage and he slipped into a cubicle, locking the door. Without sitting down, he pulled out his phone, tapped through to the email inbox and skimmed a self-sent message of Wikipedia notes on the director of the film under discussion. He was about to pocket the phone and hurry back to the studio when the ping of his New Mail alert triggered a flutter of anxiety.

Two messages had arrived simultaneously. Cook's trembling index finger opened the first by accident.

From: Sample enlarge <symptotephil@wyx.com>
Subject: So hard you could break an egg!
Message: Forget the old memories where your pals laughed at you in the locker room, grow larger today.

He dismissed it with a sideways jab of the screen and opened the second new message – a notification from *PastLives.com*. He logged in and accessed the inbox.

Dor! I've managed to get a message to Dave and I think he's up for a meet. We've got to talk mate. I'm freaking out. I think it's…

There was an urgent knock at the cubicle door which made Cook jump and close the message.

"Dorian? Are you okay? We need you back in the studio! Live in two mins!"

"Yeah, coming now!" Cook shouted, failing to conceal a wobble at the base of his throat. He flushed the toilet and walked out – practically into the runner's arms. She scampered off ahead and he struggled to keep pace, disrupted and queasy.

"How does this compare to Whiteley's previous film, *Low Blow*?"

The studio heat was on. Cook and Machin sat stiffly, side by side, while Trotman – animated, informed – gently interrogated.

"I don't think anything could have prepared us for the progression," offered Cook. "It's the difference between, say, *Reservoir Dogs* and *Jackie Brown*. *Low Blow* is the work of a promising talent, but it's solipsistic – there's too much of Whiteley's own prejudice in there. *Shifting Sand* is a much more mature work. It's hard to believe that both films are from the same director."

"I'm not sure I agree with that," said Machin. "It's clear that Whiteley is an enormously exciting filmmaker, but he seems to have fallen into the trap of believing his own press a bit too much."

"Early reviews gone to his head?" offered Trotman.

Machin nodded. "Exactly."

Cook released a strange noise – somewhere between a sneer and a scoff. Machin glanced at him, but kept focus on his point.

"Any artist who wants his work to engage with a mass audience must engage with them himself to some degree, and Whiteley has committed the schoolboy error of thinking that he only needs to engage with his critics – with the acclaim – and can safely ignore the dissenting voices, because they're mostly coming from less esteemed circles – the people who still *pay* to see films."

Cook was subtlely shaking his head. Trotman spotted it, but stayed locked on to Machin.

"So, where does this story fall down for you?"

"I think he's sacrificed plausibility for stylistic indulgence. He obviously wants the film to be seen as some kind of *Midnight Express* update, but the cinematography is all exotic travelogue. He's infatuated by his filming location and has lost sight of how the character would actually behave in that predicament. *Midnight Express* has its problems, but it tells a similar story in a more accessible – and plausible – way."

Cook was now shaking his head so vigorously, the camera was picking up tiny jiggling movements around the edges of the Machin shot. Trotman turned, gearing up a segue from critic to critic, but Cook was quicker on the beat.

"I'm sorry, Dan. That's crazy talk. We have the most exciting British filmmaker since Lindsay Anderson, and he's made an absolute masterpiece – *for his second film*. How many other home-grown directors have produced something indelible for their second effort?"

Machin swivelled slightly to face Cook.

"Welles did it with his first."

"It's hardly like for like."

Machin caught Trotman's eye. There was reassurance in the gesture – confirming he wasn't about to let the dissent lapse into discord.

"I thought we were discussing the film's place within the director's slim body of work, rather than making comparisons with other more established directors."

"No, but if you're going to compare this film to racist drivel like *Midnight Express*, then we can pick and mix other irrelevant references from across cinema history."

The comment carried an impressive economy of insult – it managed to dismiss Machin's taste, implicitly accuse him of xenophobic leanings and discredit the whole tack of his contribution. Machin greeted it with a stunned laugh.

"So, Dorian. Uh…" Trotman faltered. The director hissed into his earpiece: "Focus on the film!"

"…what do you think makes *Shifting Sand* so, as you say, indelible?"

"He's taken an incredibly difficult subject and presented it from so many different angles – political, social, sexual. And all framed inside this gorgeous photography – like something from Roger Deakins. What's most amazing is how he doesn't shy…"

"Hitchcock!" Machin interrupted.

"Hitchcock?"

"Yeah. His second Hollywood feature – *Foreign Correspondent*. Incredibly mature."

"It's a glorified B-movie!"

Cook could feel his lips gumming together. The pitiless

lighting had him surrounded, flaring down from multiple angles, searing through his thinning hair, baking his brain, boiling his blood.

"Well, that's the conventional wisdom," said Machin, smugly. "Watch it again, though. It's actually improved with age. For a film that's over seventy years…"

"Hitchcock wasn't British, anyway!"

This was an ominous incision from Cook – calm and measured, but clearly intended to wound. He carried on.

"And if filmmaking is all about plausibility, Dan, then you're dismissing several genres right there. Or maybe you can only stand to watch documentaries?"

"Did you just say that Hitchcock wasn't British?" Machin's smile was bright and broad.

"Well… I meant he's not *perceived* as British."

"He was born in Leytonstone, Dorian!"

Now, Cook was diverted by Machin's nicotine-yellow front teeth, his coarse little goatee (grown to distract from a double-chin), his overwashed check shirt. And, yes, he was actually wearing *cords!*

"Anyway," said Cook, spluttering, "this business of engaging with the mass audience. You can't produce art that second-guesses the sensibilities of those who might consume it. That's just marketing. Whiteley is shaping up to be one of this country's most essential artists, and if he's going to reach his full potential, he needs to *ignore* the masses and be a complete fascist when it comes to his artistic integrity. That's what he's done with this film, that's what makes it such a success and, I think, that's what every filmmaker who has ever made something truly great has also been aware of."

"Dorian, I don't think I can take a lecture on film from someone who doesn't know the nationality of one of our all-time greatest directors."

This was unnecessary, but effective. Cook was hushed. His eyeline detached from Machin's smirk and became unmoored, drifting off to the right – up, up and away, straight into the camera lens, returning its laser-guided glare. The dolly-mounted Sony NXCAM was happy to accept the staredown challenge. It stood firm, unflinching, taking photograph after photograph, exposure after exposure, blasting its subject out of the past and into the nearly-present – ageing, bloating, defiling. Cook absorbed the silence like a stolen peace, willing it to extend into eternity. And then, somewhere out there in the ribbons and refractions of light, he could have sworn he saw a ghost – something no longer imprisoned in soundless void, something dead and gone and yet somehow alive and here again. The idea stirred him from stupor, and he was mortified to discover himself unswallowed by unopened ground.

"Is it me?" he said weakly. "Or is it hot in here?"

They were the first words to be spoken in the studio for at least ten long, gaping seconds. Trotman guffawed, gratefully seizing on the remark as self-deprecating. Machin, head tilted, studying Cook with awe, spoke slowly and carefully in triumphant sympathy.

"I'm pretty sure it's you, Dorian."

12

Low Gates, High Stakes

May, 1974

Uncle Russell shunted the two boys to his usual spot on the City home terrace and pulled two flasks from his work satchel – milky instant coffee for himself, 'orange' for Cook and Mountford. Unusually, the surrounding cluster of fans could comfortably be described as a crowd, and the air was a churning brew of stale sweat, cigarette smoke and meat-pie belches. According to Cook – and, a little more reluctantly, Mountford – the two were now 'best mates'. As milk monitor for the term at Bethesda School, Cook always tried to hold back an extra bottle for his visit to Mountford's classroom and occasionally managed to slip it onto his friend's desk unnoticed. Mountford had not formally requested this privilege, but he accepted the gesture and, despite their age difference, the two boys were never far from each other's playground clique.

The match was listless – early bursts of chanting were soon replaced by a murmur of cautious apathy. Mountford took to gripping the horizontal section of the terrace bar with both hands, tipping himself forward, legs straight, scuffing his feet on spectators behind.

"Mind out, son!" barked a scrawny man in a cloth cap. Cook and Mountford giggled conspirationally, and Cook copied the trick, swinging even further forward and drawing similar irritation from nearby fans. As attention shifted from a fruitless set-piece, his uncle came round to the commotion.

"Dorian! Are you watching the match or do you want to go home?"

Cook resumed the pretence of watching the match. Mountford did likewise, prodding and goading his friend into cackles and heckles, squawks of mock-protest, and theatrically defensive 'dead-arm' punches. As the three filed out at full-time, Cook complained about the 'bore draw'.

"It was 4-0 – to them," snapped Russell. Neither Cook nor Mountford had been aware of a single goal.

After dropping off Mountford at home, Cook and Russell took an unfamiliar route back to Esther's, along the cycle path around the edge of the play-park. In the unwaning teatime sunshine, the gravel was warm and crunchy under Cook's cheap plimsolls. Russell quickened his step and slipped into the corner shop, emerging – just as a delighted Cook caught up – with a lollipop.

"School alright, Dor?" said Russell as they turned into Esther's street.

"Yeah," shrugged Cook, lapping at the lolly. "There's a boy who gets bullied a lot and I don't like it."

"Oh, right. That's not good. As long as it's not you."

"No, it's not. But he gets bullied all the time."

"Has he told the teachers?"

"I think so, but they don't do anything."

"It's up to his mum and dad. Don't get involved!"

"But should I tell the teachers, as well?"

"Stay out of it, Dor. You might end up as the one being bullied if you're not careful."

"I think they must really hurt him and I wish he'd stand up for himself."

"Does he not do that?"

"He tries, but they just keep hurting him. I've told Den and sometimes he helps out 'cos he's older but they just do it again when he's not there."

The two reached Esther's door. Russell lifted the hinged metal knocker and let it fall, twice. The clangs were loud but unnecessary, since Esther was already in the parlour and had the door open in seconds.

"Just leave it, mate."

"Leave what?" demanded Esther.

"Nothing," said Cook, too quickly.

"Must be something, Dor," said Esther. "Y'can't leave nothing."

13
Going Social

INCREASINGLY, COOK'S HOME OFFICE reflected the junk and jumble of his thoughts – a mini-museum of the unresolved, the unattended, the unexplained. Gina called it his 'man cave', while Alfie preferred 'daddy's den'. Cook, pompously, insisted on 'study'. (The only time it saw actual study was when he surrendered it to Gina and Alfie for homework help, after conspicuously resetting the computer's browser history.) Gina's sessions regularly concluded with her resolving to 'freshen the place up', but the room had long since settled into a benign obsolescence – wheezing PC, beige Anaglypta, rarely punctured corkboard, 2003 edition of the *Writers & Artists' Yearbook,* clumps of unwatched (sometimes unwrapped) DVDs, and an enormous and ugly crystal ashtray that Cook – now a non-smoker – retained for its writerly allure. It was the Sunday morning after a late evening dinner party, hosted – by Gina and, nominally, Cook – in honour of a friend's fiftieth. Cook had drank heavily, eaten lightly and, buffered by alcoholic bravado and the comfort of acquaintances, reassured himself that his performance on *Talking Pictures* would at least lead to fewer TV gigs. All the guests were comfortably removed from Cook's work circle and were unlikely to have been watching. (Will Stone – the last to leave – had mentioned the show, naturally referring to it as *Talking Bollocks*. But, given its late transmission time, Cook was sure that Stone had only caught it by accident, beercan in hand, kebab balanced on knees.) But now, he hung his hungover head and slotted the door's internal latch into place – always quietly, as there was shame in the self-indulgence of wilful withdrawal.

A short stagger, a nudge of the mouse and, with the standard groan of middle-aged angst masquerading as joint pain, down hard onto the lumpy chair.

Cook glared at a scattering of uninvestigated bills, flinched a little at a sagging shelf over-burdened with the unopened (sterile film theory books), the unexplored (stalled script treatments) and the unloved (a DVD series on iconic directors which featured his depressingly young self wearing the same shirt in different locations). After a brief wander round a couple of news websites, he logged in to *Mogul*, a movie-studio simulator he had found oddly compulsive during a flight from Los Angeles to London a few weeks earlier. Cook usually preferred the abstract strategy of chess or backgammon, but the game's varied challenges – setting release schedules, taming greedy producers, green-lighting, budget-balancing – had locked his attention and torn a chunk out of the flight-time.

An hour or so later, as he adjusted the virtual admission price for an underpopulated public tour of his virtual studio, Cook was bothered by the sense that he was avoiding something. On cue, his email alert sounded and he cautiously accessed the inbox. To his relief, it was an informal commission from the Features Editor of the broadsheet currently sitting (unopened) on a side table by the computer desk.

> *Hi, Dor. We're working on a special issue themed around the current state of play in social media – all the new channels and how they compare to the early start-ups, etc.*
>
> *Thought you might be interested in a personal piece from the perspective of a media type who opts out. Nothing too furious – just a bit of balance. Maybe sign up to the sites, take a look at what they offer and structure it as a critique? Nice and personal. 800 words.*
>
> *Let me know if you'd be up for it and I'll send over something more formal.*
>
> *Hope all's well, chap.*
>
> *Best,*
>
> *Tim.*

Christ, thought Cook. Working on a Sunday – for something so banal. He was a militant opponent to all forms of online social 'sharing', and his first thoughts of easy money were quickly replaced by a vision of the amount of work involved – trawling the sites, registering phantom profiles, dredging the lakes of self-regarding shit for occasional shimmers of substance. It was a job that would require him to engage with a culture he both despised and feared. He retained a pathological grip on his privacy, despite having little in his life that would be of interest to snoopers or strangers. His career path had meandered to its current position via a series of seemingly arbitrary waypoints local newspapers (wedding photo captions as an intern, unsustainable clashes with section chiefs as a dispensable contractor), church magazines (a brief dalliance with Catholic conversion in his mid twenties), writing and subbing (and, to the amusement of colleagues, subbing his own writing) at a pipsqueak movie monthly called, naturally, *Popcorn*. Then, a rush of freelance pontificating for in-house arthouse mags, and sideline script-work at an over-ambitious film-quiz radio show, before wriggling his way up through the ranks on-staff at *Widescreen*.

In the early years of their marriage, after Gina had cautiously educated him on the pleasures of mid-priced wine, Cook had considered moving into food criticism, attracted to the job's absurd, alias-based culture of secrecy. But he was ironically surnamed, with a palate eroded by years of low-grade meat. He mocked the pretension of oysters, openly retched at offal, and generally avoided any food which required skill or practice to consume. The thirtysomething Cook had once stormed out of a Chinese restaurant after his dining companions had gently mocked his clumsy chopstick technique. ("You need to get a grip, Dorian!")

Now, he was being drawn deeper away from centre-stage, blending and fading into the background. He had regressed from the boiler-room bustle of the news desk to the templated mediocrity of copy-fitting, fact-checking and adjectival preening. His ego offered spasms of resistance, but he knew it was all means to an ultimate end – of shadow and silence and, crucially, anonymity.

He tapped out a response, accepting the commission with an uncharacteristically affable request to discuss details 'over coffee'. Almost immediately after sending the message, his email alert sounded again – a notification from *PastLives.com*, as if in rebuke to his buoyancy. He navigated from email subject line to website to message.

> *Hello, Dor. I saw you on TV! Totally by accident, mate. You don't look that different! At least I know you're definitely still alive! Hope you're actually reading my messages (it says you are on the Read/Unread list thing). Drop me a line mate. Please. Don't worry – I'm not after money! Den.*

The mention of money at least gave Cook a sense of what he was now dealing with – a friend in need. He typed a formal but sympathetic reply, saying that he would love to help but didn't actually have much money himself. At worst, Cook hoped he could avoid a meeting and just transfer a token payment that would feel reasonable but final. His curiosity about Brereton – and Mountford's predicament – could probably be satisfied with a couple more messages. He would then delete his account and move on.

He scrolled the reply window and noticed that Mountford's original message was automatically quoted underneath – with an extra line Cook had missed, a few returns below the main chunk of text.

> *PS. It's about the ghost.*

14

Corporal Punishment

June, 1974

"Two times two is four! Three times two is six!"

This was 'maths' – a modulated drone-through of the first twelve integers and the results of multiplying them all by each other. Cook sat with chin on desk, arms flat and sprawled, laminated number-grid propped upright.

"Sit up straight, Dorian!"

The children knew that Mr Butcher had plenty of potential bite behind his bark, and so, as Cook jerked himself upright, most of the others instantly mirrored – a conditioned pulse that, for Butcher, vindicated his hive-mind regime. The class resumed its synchronised chant.

Cook felt something brush against his shoe. He glanced down and saw a small, multicoloured rubber ball that David Brereton had kicked along the floor. Brereton was smirking and nodding towards the front of the class, where John Ray sat, within ear-cuff distance of Butcher. Ray was in a reverie of recital, gossamer hair bobbing and wafting as his bloodless lips launched the words up into the air above Butcher's desk.

"Six times two is twelve! Seven times two is fourteen! Eight times two is sixteen!"

This enthusiasm wasn't just for Teacher's benefit. Ray had a head for figures to go with the body for bullies. Numbers, for him, had rules and form and structure, while people were volatile and amorphous. For his classmates, the times-table repetition was numbing and medicinal – an educational analgesic. To Ray, the effect was ecstatic, psychotropic.

"Ten times two is twenty! Eleven times two is twenty-two!"

Cook scuffed at the rubber ball with his shoe, sending it rolling towards Ray's desk. It bounced off a chair-leg, skittered up and landed in Ray's empty inkwell, where it settled with pleasing snugness. Butcher looked up from his text-book. A movement had flashed across the edge of his vision – had something been thrown? The ball's pink and blue swirls alerted him to Ray's usually unadorned desk-top.

"John Ray! What is *that?*"

At the sound of his name, Ray startled with such violence that his desk tilted, dislodging the ball. It dropped to the floor and ricocheted around – to the childrens' delight, and Butcher's fury.

"Pick it up!" he bellowed. "Pick it up and bring it out to the front!"

Ray sprang from his seat and broke into a strange, cowering stoop, scurrying from desk to desk, flailing and lunging. The ball finally settled in a corner under a radiator. Ray retrieved it and approached Butcher. After a beat of calculated tension, Butcher nodded and Ray raised a trembling hand, revealing the ball in his open palm. Butcher immediately swiped it away and, gaze fixed on Ray, dropped it into his desk-side bin.

Ray began to lower his arm, but Butcher reached over with his right hand and slowly closed his spindly fingers around the boy's wrist. The gesture was sinister and well practiced – a massage with a message. He reached into a desk drawer with his free hand.

"Mr Ray," said Butcher, retrieving a thick wooden ruler, "you seem a bit confused."

"No, sir!" Ray spluttered, not understanding the point but anxious to soften Butcher's intent.

"Playtime is not for another twenty minutes, son."

Butcher placed the wooden ruler onto his desktop. The whole class – clenched and mute – winced at the weighty thunk. Ray started to cry.

"I know, sir. I'm sorry, sir!"

Still holding Ray firmly by the wrist, Butcher pivoted him around to face the class and peeled open his fingers one by one. And so, this frail specimen – snared by circumstance, barely eight years in the wild – was presented to his classmates with arm outstretched, palm up but empty-handed, offering nothing. Butcher took up the ruler. He grasped Ray's arm just below the elbow and stroked the wood across the boy's fingers, extending and flattening them to prepare for the first strike.

"Sir…" sobbed Ray. "Please. I don't want to!"

Butcher turned to face his audience and offered a mirror-cracking smile to the front row.

"Perhaps you would rather sit next to Angela?"

Angela Battison was a short, silent girl who had been quarantined at the far-left back corner, behind an exclusion zone of two adjacent empty desks. She suffered from a recurring infection which formed pustular abscesses on her arms, legs and face. The condition could be eased, but it was fickle and restless and slathered her skin with a permanent glaze of decay. At their peak, the scarrings were large and painful and exuded a necrotic odour.

John Ray looked over at Angela, who was pretend-busy doodling. She had expected Butcher's offer and didn't want to catch anyone's eye. Ray took out the blue-and-white handkerchief and dabbed at his nose and eyes. His silence was enough of an answer for Butcher.

"Sit down at the back! Next time, there will not be a choice."

Ray trudged to the desk beside Angela, stepping inside her fetid ecosystem. He dragged out the chair and sat down, coughing a stifled retch into his handkerchief. The children all watched his shuffle of shame in impotent silence – except Cook.

"Sir, don't be so tight on him!"

Butcher's head jerked up. He skewered Cook with a stare of startled amusement. Then, slowly, enquiringly…

"Bring yourself to the front, Dorian."

Cook instantly stood and strode over to Butcher's desk with a vigour that seemed suicidal to his classmates. Butcher looked back down into his textbook and let Cook stand before him in silence for a few awkward seconds.

"Mr Cook," said Butcher, finally lifting his head and locking eyes. "You have a problem – it's called a mouth."

Cook's response was rapier improv – a thrust for the gallery of brutalist bowl-cuts and chequered knitwear.

"*You've* got a problem!" he sneered. "It's called a face!"

The mockery was witless, but Butcher absorbed it with strained respect. He lifted his pitcher's mitt of a hand and whipped it, palm open, into Cook's head, striking him so squarely the noise could have been mistaken for the slamming of a desk-lid. Cook yelped in shock and tilted over, touching his fingertips to the dusty floor.

"Mr Austin's office. Now!"

Eyes streaming, ears buzzing from the blow, Cook pivoted away and stumbled out of the door. He climbed the steep rack of uncarpeted wooden stairs to the headmaster's office and rapped twice on the door.

"Come!"

Inside this pompous, oaken lair, with its broad window nosing down on the classrooms, Cook was given no counsel or airtime. Austin favoured discipline over detail, and he slid a thin wooden cane from an umbrella rack and brought it down hard, three times, on Cook's palm, before returning to his marking, and waiting until the boy could no longer suppress his sobs before telling him to go.

15

Slight Return

COOK REMOVED ALFIE'S SHOES and socks, restrained him gently by the shoulder for a brief food and drink request ("No, thank you!") and launched him into the play-centre's sprawling fort of tunnels and ladders. When he was sure that his son was safely monkeying across the rope-netting with children equivalent to his age and build, Cook turned and surveyed the droopy parents huddled around an island of plastic-topped tables near the food counter. Here, a buffet of broadsheet supplements was occasionally inspected, but mostly there was tablet-swiping and phone-poking and, Cook noted with distaste, very little conversation or physical book-reading. His gaze was drawn to a tall, hunched man in an ugly maroon polo shirt, trudging back from the serving window, triangular sandwich-pack in one hand, plastic cup in the other. Mountford was still unmistakably Mountford – there was just more of him. Overweight, overgrown, over-burdened – a scaled-up model of the character in Cook's past life. He seemed compressed and off-centre, both familiar and unfamiliar – a cartoonish interloper in the real world. He moved across the sticky floor like an astronaut, as if each slow, steady step carried both novelty and peril.

Cook had repeatedly played out this scene in his mind – the hang-back, the shudder of clarity, the awakening, the hurried retreat through the bright blue exit barrier to sink back into the dusk. But he was surprised to find himself simply and confidently walking over, stopping a few feet away from Mountford as he was settling into his seat, back turned.

"Hello, Den."

Mountford jumped a little but turned his head to face Cook with oddly muted interest.

"Mr Cook!" said Mountford, and then checked his ironic pomposity. "So glad you could come, Dor."

Mountford heaved himself upright and smothered Cook in a brief and brittle man-hug. Cook gasped beneath his friend's bulk and inhaled the polo-shirt's collar – a clash of expensive cologne and cheap fabric-conditioner. As they broke their embrace and Mountford turned to sit, he almost elbowed his coffee-cup off the table, and Cook was shocked to see him deftly jab out a hand to correct its tumble. That first impression of sluggish vulnerability had been misleading – perhaps wilfully so.

They sat, stiffly, in the interview position, face to face across the Formica.

"D'you want anything?" wondered Mountford, nodding towards the food counter.

Cook forced a smile and shook his head. "Is your boy in there?"

"Jake, yes. He's six. He's amazing. I never thought I'd be any good at it, Dor – being a dad. Doing alright, though. He's the one by the swing."

Cook scanned the play-area and saw a short, borderline

plump boy waiting patiently for his turn on a rope-tyre. He was waving at his dad, smiling happily. Mountford waved back – a slow, window-wiping motion which looked more like a signal for help than a gesture of connection.

"Alfie's in there somewhere, too. He's nearly nine."

Mountford nodded and took a slurp of coffee. "Both left it a bit late, then."

Cook shrugged. "My wife wore me down. I never really wanted kids. Pram in the hall, and all that."

Mountford smiled. "I suppose writing about bloody films is a sort of art."

Cook laughed, a little defensively. "What are you up to, these days?"

"I do signs," said Mountford. "Awnings, shop-fronts, occasional big stuff like stadiums or public buildings. It's okay. Got my own business. I did graphic design, so…"

A short silence descended, ponderous rather than uncomfortable. Mountford displaced it by unwrapping his sandwich. Cook checked on Jake, who was now sitting inside the tyre, being shoved and swung in looping circles by a group of other boys, including Alfie. All were laughing and shouting to each other.

"So," said Cook, "what made you get back in touch?"

Mountford was lifting the sandwich to his mouth, but the question diverted him, and he slotted it back into the plastic.

"Lots of weird messages, Dor. Worrying."

"Why do you think it's got anything to do with us?"

"I've had stuff through the post, as well."

Mountford pulled a backpack from under the table, dug out a small envelope with his name and address typed onto the front, and skimmed it across the table. Cook took out the contents – a torn away magazine cutting. The edge of the page was missing and Cook couldn't place the design, but judging by the paper quality, slack typography, grammatical errors and inconsistent tenses, he guessed it had been taken from something cheap and specialist. A patch of awkwardly compressed copy had been highlighted, with one section encircled in red biro.

Apports are materialised objects produced by mediums during Spiritualistic seances. These objects can range from flowers, jewellery and even live animals. The production of the apports was and is still one of the most prominent and effective aspects of the seances. Their behaviour vary from flying through the air, to hitting the sitters in their faces, to landing on the table or in people's laps. A favourite is to scatter perfume over the audience. However, during scientific testing in seances numerous frauds have been discovered even when ordinary precautions were taken. Often the fraudulent medium concealed the apports in the room or on his/her person. While the seances may have been conducted by unscrupulous procedures, often it was discovered that no fraudulent intent was intended.

Cook finished reading and looked up at Mountford, who had turned away from the table, cowering in the presence of the envelope and paper.

"Have you seen the other side?" said Mountford, still with his back turned.

For a moment, Cook misinterpreted the question as some kind of paranormal or philosophical challenge.

"The other side? Of what?"

Mountford turned back to face Cook. "The paper!"

Cook flipped over the cutting. A section of tightly packed classifieds had been defaced with a message written in red biro.

DO YOU BELIEVE?

The letters were neatly arranged and uniformly spaced. The question-mark was a strange mirror-image 'S' above a deeply prodded point. Cook examined the words, admiring the presentation.

"Looks like some kind of viral-marketing campaign for a horror film or something. It's too well designed."

"The online messages are directly to me, Dor. You can't find people on that website without searching."

Cook re-folded the paper and slid it back across the table. Mountford stared down, keeping his hands out of sight. Now, the silence was localised vacuum – it cloaked over them, amplifying their unrest. They were alone together, marooned in a crossfire of drumming bare-feet and jagged Tannoy. Back at Bethesda, Cook and Mountford had been part of the primary palette – yellow-cardiganned, bowl-haircutted, bell-bottomed birds of paradise, strutting and fluttering against a backwash of tweed and torpor. Then, they thrived; now, they subsisted, in the negative alternative, where all was colour while they were grey. The two men had both, to different degrees, accepted impending obscurity, and now here was this – rekindled significance.

"I don't know. Go to the police, Den. I'm not sure how I can help."

Mountford scooped the paper and envelope into his backpack. "I've already spoken to them. They can't do anything until there's a specific threat – and even then…"

"What are the website messages like?"

"Just strange. Rambling."

Cook fiddled with his wedding ring, rotating it around the finger. He glanced over at Alfie and Jake – they were now both barrelling up the chute of a slide, arching their legs as other children squeezed through.

"Den, it's thirty-odd years ago."

"No, it's not! It's now. Look – can't we just swap numbers?"

Without waiting for agreement, he took out a pen and, like a bashful bet, nudged it into the centre of the table. Cook wrote his number on the back of the food receipt, and Mountford snatched it up, packed away the uneaten sandwich and carefully climbed to his feet. He was slow and creaky again – back in character.

"It's been really good to see you again, Dor."

"You, too."

Neither men sounded convinced or convincing. They shared a brief, transactive handshake and Mountford plodded off to collect his son. Cook watched them wriggle out through the narrow exit barrier, ready with a wave – but his friend didn't look back. He bought a coffee and browsed the film sections. Around half an hour after Mountford had left, Cook received a text-message.

Thanks for today. Maybe CU again soon. Den.

Cook scowled at the text-speak and fussy sign-off. He typed a reply.

> *Yes. Lovely to see you. Jake is great! Maybe get together for Christmas drinks…*

The ellipsis, rather than question-mark, confirmed closure – to the text conversation, to the meeting, to the reason for the meeting and, for Cook, to the relationship. He considered adding Mountford's number to his address book, but instead he deleted the message and slotted the phone back into his pocket, where it immediately sounded an email alert. He took it back out and opened his inbox.

> *YOUR SECRET WEAPON! Penis enlargement in a patch. "My personal ability to control ejaculation is truly incredible. SizeGenetics (tm) helped my erect length increase from 6.5 to 7.8, with erect girth from 5 to 5.5."*

Cook smiled, deleted the mail and, feeling cleansed, returned to his reading.

16

Play for Today

July, 1974

On Saturdays, Esther worked a part-time cleaning job at a local insurance company and Cook was usually home alone until early afternoon. This morning, at 8am, the day was already floodlit – pre-baked in mid-summer shimmer. He tumbled out of bed, ran to the landing, sat on the top stair and shuffled, step by step, down to the bottom. Rusty was curled in a tight bundle on the hearth-rug and raised his ears as Cook hurdled him, paused, and tried to do a standing jump from the back edge of Esther's armchair to the kitchen step. He made it in three attempts (his record was two). In the kitchen, Cook dropped two Shredded Wheat into a bowl and slathered them in sterilised milk. Bowl in hand, wearing nothing but Y-fronts, he opened the back door and stepped outside.

The yard was long and thin, with a choppy topography of fractured paving. Subsidence had failed in its effort to topple the dividing wall and was now redirecting its energies towards the foundations. Barefoot, Cook tiptoe-surfed the undulating stonework and hitched himself up onto the rubber lid of the dustbin propped against the gate. Here, in one of the planet's least salubrious sun-traps, Cook raised his face to the mild morning beams, eyes closed, gnawing through the cereal. As the sun's position shifted, casting him in the chilly shadow of the outside-toilet roof, he abandoned his bowl and crouched down to investigate the surrounding mound of heavy house-bricks which Uncle Russell used to hold the bin in place. He heaved up the largest rock and flipped it over, scattering a crowd of woodlice. Most of the creatures made it into the safety of the paving cracks, but one had been tipped onto its back and was scurrying and thrashing its legs in an attempt to correct itself. Cook captured it with a gentle pinch, slowly lifted himself upright, and studied the brickwork of the leaning wall. He found a recently re-spun spider-web, hung horizontally like a hammock, spanning the interior of a crevice. He reached in and precisely – almost tenderly – positioned the woodlouse in the sagging centre of the structure, where it immediately intensified its wriggling. The movement only ensnared it more deeply, and it gradually mummified itself inside a ball of gummy webbing which restricted its struggle to sporadic spasms.

Cook turned his head to the side – he knew his breathing could cause unnatural vibration. And then – *there!* – in the web's darkest corner, four sharp and spindly protrusions appeared instantly, as if by materialisation. Within seconds, a burly spider emerged, gripping the woodlouse and biting it into submission. Next door, Mr Smith launched into a deathly-dry coughing fit, but Cook could not be distracted. He gaped as the spider detached its prey – his offering – from the surface of the web and dragged it deep into its lightless lair.

Mr Smith coughed and coughed and coughed, and Cook heard him stumble into the kitchen, run a tap and, after a pause, burst into a more lubricated splutter which quickly degraded back to its arid origin. He grabbed the cereal bowl and skimmed across the jagged ground, back into the house, through the kitchen and into the living room. Rusty twitched at the commotion, but stayed low and bundled, greeting him with a limp tail-flap. Cook lunged at the TV and cranked the volume on an episode of the cartoon serial *Arabian Knights*. Still, Mr Smith coughed and coughed, but now his distress was at least dampened by cheap incidental music and regular waves of canned laughter.

"Size of a buffalo!"

Cook was breathing heavily. He thought of the spider, deep in the dilapidated wall – undisturbed, enjoying his breakfast in the dark, injecting liquidising venom, feasting on the nutritious mush.

Later that morning, Cook dragged his kick-scooter through the parlour and out of the front door onto the hot pavement. As he fiddled with the door-lock, the scooter slowly keeled over, as if wilting in the staring sun. He snatched it up and clattered off to Lisa Goldstraw's house. Esther had still not yielded to his regular bicycle request, and he felt conspicuous and overgrown on the rusty red device – particularly in the solar spotlight.

He trundled past the abandoned butcher's shop (still not looking) with both legs on the scooter platform, side-on. He turned the corner and scraped his way up the steeper, scrub-lined lower avenue which peeled off to the right, up to Lowther Street – Brereton's road – and beyond, to the forbidden jumble of industrial waste known as the marl-hole. He veered left, up past the newsagent at the corner of Denbigh Street, hiding his scooter shame by clattering up the cobbled entries that separated the brown and grey terraces. He soon emerged at the edge of the play-park and into Lisa Goldstraw's neighbourhood, with its deep driveways and stone-clad semis, and children who didn't know him well enough to risk any catcalls. Cook's heart quickened at the thought of Lisa, and his lungs greedily inhaled the oxygen of anonymity.

To Cook's consistent astonishment and envy, Lisa's house had a back-garden veranda bursting with toys and books and board-games. Baby Rebecca had transformed into Toddler Rebecca, and she teetered and stumbled from one primary-coloured object to the next, yelling with delight. Lisa showed Cook her latest acquisition – a plastic 'barber-shop' chair with a crank-handle which oozed Play-Doh through the perforated skulls of grinning models, like a benign meat mincer. Rebecca held a pair of blunt orange scissors in both hands, cropping the coloured strands while Lisa styled them neat with a broad-tooth comb. As ever, though, Rebecca was more interested in Cook himself – cuddling him, gaining his attention for babbling announcements, stroking the claggy comb through his hair.

The midday heat, which had been brooding all morning, was now fuming – up in the low 80s. Lisa's mother had thrown open all the veranda windows, inviting a weedy breeze which drifted around to little effect. As she lifted Rebecca away for a nap, Cook noticed a small, slitted scar underneath the toddler's chin, scored across the width of its tip.

"Come on, Trouble! Let's get you down for an hour."

They listened as Mrs Goldstraw settled Rebecca in an

upstairs room before returning with two glasses of blackcurrant squash, a single ice-cube bobbing in each.

"Little Becky fell out of her pram last week. Didn't she, mum?"

"She did, darling, yes. It was a really nasty cut. She's okay, though."

"And she now calls Dorian 'Dor-Dor'."

Mrs Goldstraw chuckled and stole a sip from her daughter's glass.

Cook scootered home through the afternoon haze. At the forking point to Lowther Street, he was surprised to see David Brereton, Michael Howell – and John Ray, all on Tomahawk bicycles, pedalling uphill towards the park. They shouted and waved but didn't stop. Cook span round his scooter and followed them, along the perimeter cycle path and, eventually, into an upscale estate where the houses hid behind tall double-gates and pruned hedges. He tracked the cyclists to the back of a mid-sized house with a dark blue facade. By the time he emerged from a corridor of topiary, tracing the edge of a lawn as green and pristine as snooker baize, all three bikes had been laid flat on a panel of decking outside open French windows. Cook hopped off his scooter and wandered inside – to a broad and tidy dining room adjoining a kitchen that was laboratory-clean and lavishly equipped. Brereton and Howell stood before the wardrobe-sized fridge, guzzling fizzy pop and cooling their faces in front of the open freezer door. Ray was crouched down, face hidden inside a cupboard, searching for something.

"Hey, Dor!" said Brereton. "Where did you get your scooter from?"

"Yeah!" spluttered Howell, through a mouthful of Tizer. "Really want one of them!"

"Shut up…" muttered Cook, too focused on his surroundings to compose a comeback. Having previously visited both Brereton and Howell's houses, he assumed – correctly – that this was where John Ray began his journey to school each morning. The opulence enthralled him. Everything – layout, surface materials, colour choices – blazed with the gloss of good taste empowered by ample income. Esther's walls were bare, her shelves loaded with Toby jugs, cadaverous imps and awkwardly posed porcelain figures. Here, the pattern was reversed, with shelves free of ornamentation and walls displaying what could confidently be called art – abstracts, landscapes, photography. And it *smelled* good – light and sweet and fresh. Cook was used to interiors fouled by the essence of reconstituted lard and harsh detergent.

"It must be upstairs!"

John backed out of the cupboard. His face looked oddly reddened, as if he'd been dabbing it with blusher. He dashed out of the kitchen and clambered loudly up the stairs.

"He's got a thing," said Howell. "He has to put cream on when he's out in the sun."

"Yeah," smirked Brereton, draining his bottle. "Or he dies – like Drac-lee-a."

"It's Drac-*yew*-la," insisted Cook. "And anyway, vampires aren't real."

"Yeah, they are," said Brereton, "and you can only kill them by setting fire to their hearts."

"I need a pee!" bleated Cook, jigging from leg to leg.

"So do I," said Howell, "but John says we're not allowed, because his dad will go mad."

"Do it down the grid!" smiled Brereton.

Around the corner from the open kitchen door, a metal drainage grid swallowed the house's waste water. To use it, Cook would have to step out into the garden and risk being seen by neighbours. There was no plausible threat of consequence, but the exposure would be unbearable.

"Is there a bottle or something?" Cook searched through a couple of cupboards underneath the sink, but they were crowded with dishcloths and cleaning fluids.

"Finished with this!" announced Brereton, handing over his almost-empty bottle of apple juice. Cook removed the cap and unzipped his trousers. He turned his back to Howell and Brereton, poked out his penis and slotted it into the top of the bottle.

"Errrr! He's not even emptied it!" shouted Howell. Brereton shushed him.

Cook held the bottle steady and, after a short pause, warm urine trickled out and blended with the cold juice, raising a little steam. Brereton nudged Cook in the back, but he kept steady, spilling nothing. After a few seconds, the bottle was almost full. Cook zipped up and tipped half of the liquid down the sink.

"Give us that!"

He took Howell's half-full juice carton and diluted his potion until the bottle was two-thirds full of something yellowy-greeny and convincingly chilled. Howell snatched back his almost-empty carton and Cook replaced the cap on his bottle. Howell and Brereton looked at him, confused, until Cook's half-smile inspired a shudder of sniggers from Howell, and soon all three were giggling in sordid solidarity.

John Ray re-appeared with shining skin. "I have to use a

really high factor!" he explained, in that precocious cadence, every vowel rich and ripe. "My skin doesn't have enough melanin. It used to be worse than this but I can go out now."

"Do you want a drink, John?"

Cook offered the bottle. Ray regarded it suspiciously – the liquid's colour seemed strange and the brand label had been almost completely scratched off. But if this was a trick, it didn't match the mood.

"It's really nice," offered Howell.

"Yeah," encouraged Cook, "it's a new lime drink. It's called Jungle Juice."

Ray studied Cook's gaze for a few seconds, then took the bottle, opened it and, without sniffing the content, drank deeply. The sun-blushed skin on his forehead furrowed into a frown and he pursed his waxy lips. Cook and Howell caught each other's gaze, and their poker faces flickered. Brereton was openly laughing.

"It's warm!"

Ray wiped his mouth and, for a second, his tainted cheeks were chalk-white again. He looked from Howell to Brereton, who both instantly shifted their eyelines down into the kitchen floor, suppressing their sniggers. He turned to Cook – who didn't look away – and the two boys stood there, still and silent in the burning air. As Ray's eyes reddened, Cook's gaze calcified into a stare, then a glare, and then – with the faintest twitch of one eyebrow – transformed into a challenge.

The front door clanged shut.

"Hello?"

Ray tipped the 'Jungle Juice' into the sink and dropped the bottle into a bin.

"Johnny?"

Ray's half-brother, Darren, hustled his way through the door from the sitting room, struggling with a large cardboard box. He was a few years older than John, but carried none of his sibling's frailty or whiteness of complexion. He had dark, darting eyes and a commanding tone, reinforced by his pre-adolescent height and heft.

"Boiling fucking hot! Hope you've used your cream, Johnny! Help us get these outside."

John Ray took one edge of the box and side-stepped past the others out into the garden. Cook, Howell and Brereton watched as they hobbled past the kitchen window and set the box down, behind a tall bush, out of sight of the street. Brereton and Howell instantly followed them outside, but Cook was uneasy and joined them only when he heard a burst of helium barks and whimpers. In the garden shade, Cook peeked over the top of the cardboard box and saw a squirming huddle of around ten light-brown Labrador puppies.

"Aaawww," cooed Brereton, "can I hold one?"

The dogs trembled and squeaked. Cook squatted down and carefully reached his hand into the box, where it was immediately smothered in a delirium of nipping and licking.

"They're hungry!" said Howell.

"Course they fucking are!" snapped Darren. "They ain't been fed."

"Can we give 'em some dog-food?" Brereton directed his question to John – which seemed to anger Darren.

"Can't give 'em cat-food, you little twat!"

"DARREN!"

All five jumped in unison at the shout – a deep, dark voice from somewhere at the front of the house.

"Back 'ere!"

From his crouched position, Cook saw the head of Frank Ray – Darren and John's father – emerge from the sitting room and bob through the kitchen towards the back door. Frank – mid-thirties – had a flowing crop of colourless candyfloss hair which made him look at least twenty years older. He shambled out into the garden – short and fat and slow, but with an unchallengeable aura of adulthood. He unlocked a small side-cellar and began sifting through a pile of tools on a top shelf.

"How many of the bloody things did you sell?"

"Haven't sold any, dad. I couldn't…"

And then, Frank Ray – not so slow after all – was there among them, swiping his grubby fist in a wide arc of anger, connecting squarely with the side of Darren's head. Cook flinched at the bludgeoning *thunk*. Darren covered himself with both hands and ducked down low, wailing.

"I can't carry 'em, dad! And no-one wants 'em!"

Cook backed away, bumping into Brereton who had edged closer to the path which led to the street. But Frank now stood directly in front of the back door, blocking any passage out of the garden. Cook noted, with envy, that Howell had already managed to escape, but for himself and Brereton, the moment had passed. John, too, had disappeared – probably back into the house. The peer connection for Cook and Brereton was now severed, and there was no sense in staying, but there was clearly no question of them leaving.

Frank stood over his son, steaming in the afternoon heat. He retrieved a large iron bucket from the side-cellar and clattered it onto the floor between them. Darren moved his hands away from his face and glared, hatefully, up at his father.

"Fill that up! If you can't get rid of 'em, I'll have to!"

Darren scrambled to his feet. For a second, Cook thought he might lunge at Frank, or at least bolt for the path. But he picked up the bucket and shoved past his father into the kitchen. There was a shudder of plumbing as he opened the tap.

"Fetch us that block will ya, lads?"

Crouching down beside the box of puppies, Frank aimed the question at both Cook and Brereton, but didn't bother to turn his head to confirm.

"Which block?" asked Brereton.

Frank petted the puppies, offering the upturned palm of the hand he had used to strike Darren. The hungry and thirsty dogs leapt and writhed, tasting the sweat on the coarse skin. Again, Frank didn't turn to face the boys.

"The one by the hosepipe."

The 'block' was a large chunk of wood used as a base to hack away at knotty kindling. Cook and Brereton each gripped an end, and, with difficulty, dragged the wood across to Frank. Darren re-emerged with the bucket, rim-full of cold water. He hauled it over to the box and carefully set it down, spilling very little. Frank scooped up around five of the puppies and transferred them to the water. They squealed with outrage, thrashing and splashing. As Frank lifted the others out of the box, Darren nudged the paddling dogs back into the centre. Frank tipped the remaining puppies into the water, lifted the chopping block and set it down on top of the bucket. Some water had displaced, but the puppies still had no space for air, and the wood was solid and level enough to prevent any more water from escaping. Sealing the rim – and the dogs' fate – Frank sat down on the block, carefully centering his weight to prevent the bucket from tilting. He reached into his pocket and pulled out a squashed cardboard packet.

Frank Ray lit a cigarette and smoked it with steady relish, as the dogs drowned beneath him, and his eldest son sat, morose and silent, on the doorstep.

Brereton spluttered and sobbed as he trudged away, down the path, collecting his bike.

"C'mon, Dor!"

Cook remained rooted, his back flattened against the fence, spellbound by the scuttling clamour from the bucket. The puppies' watery protests took forever to dwindle, and Brereton had long gone before they were silenced completely.

Frank Ray flipped away his cigarette, and the flash of burning ash prodded Cook into action. He peeled himself from the fence and ran, ran, ran away from this – out of the garden, across the decking, onto his scooter.

17

The Big Picture

MINDS WERE MEETING — SMALL minds, feeble minds, high minds, dirty minds, a couple of borderline brilliant minds. One mind was notorious for being rigorously closed, another freely mocked for its exploitable openness. The *Widescreen* editorial conference room was pure and bright with sparkling white right-angle chairs and an appalling oval expanse of cornea-scorching lime green table-top. But every Monday morning at ten, dullness descended like a shower of dust. Minds were meeting, but only on behalf of their matter – woozy, weekend bodies shuffling into formation for another five days of PR jousting, flatplan-tweaking and freelancer-chasing. At table-head, and so default mind-concentrator, was a badly ironed light-blue shirt containing Editor-In-Chief Henry Gray, his baldness eggish and emasculating. With precarious authority – transmitted through the occasional thrust of a Starbucks spout-cup – Gray presided over Cook (notebook tilted to conceal doodling), Nigel Smith (smarmy freelance fixture – on staff to cover absence), Alison Truman (swashbuckling sub-editor with jazz-hands for copy-blanding and sharp elbows for gala screenings), Jennifer Croucher (harpy high-priestess editor who had evolved a muddling of rudeness and directness to the level of behaviour disorder), Mark Harford (remarkably unremarkable reviews editor), Warren Plant (likeable and talented late-thirtysomething art director who would have moved on a long time ago had he not burned all his industry bridges as a cocaine-snuffling early-thirtysomething), Daisy Hillman (writer, online editor, Wes Anderson bore), and Leah Barton (picture editor and asset manager who, to Cook's annoyance, had no interest in the magazine's subject matter, and who he unwisely referred to – in pub and office – as a 'JPEG Jockey').

Gray ran through the state of the issue, consulting with each team member. Words were too little or too late (never in abundance, never unchased), pictures lingered in approval limbo. The Reviews Intro page – due at last week's meeting – was uncomposed. (Harford was behind schedule after three days of spurious sick leave.) Croucher – red-eyed after a delayed flight back from Los Angeles – was spared the spotlight, while Plant, as ever, beamed it straight back into Gray's face, meeting exasperation on the state of the cover with a dismissive shrug at the editorial team's poor co-ordination on image-gathering.

Gray clunked an elbow onto the table and half-supported his drooping head by pinching and folding the forehead skin with nicotine-bleached fingertips. He spoke down into the table-top.

"Nigel, do we have everything for the TFF piece?"

To Cook's irritation, Smith had snaffled a dream gig covering the Taiwan Film Festival. Despite Cook's insistence of his superior knowledge of 'world cinema', Smith had landed the prize (2400 words, five days' waddling around in beige cargo shorts, sweating a sliver of waistline flab into the tropical air) by waiving accommodation costs.

"I'm writing it up tonight," smirked Smith. "Leah should have all the images from the PR office."

Heads turned to Barton. She was nodding.

"How was Taipei?" asked Plant.

"Bloody hot!" said Smith with mock-laddishness, mock-confidence, mock-shock. "Some very strange telly! Good job the hotel had English channels. I caught your performance on last week's *Talking Pictures,* Dorian."

"Yeah," said Cook quickly, hoping to deflect. "Not my finest hour."

"Very entertaining, though! Did they not tell you it was live?"

Gray lifted his eyes from the table – towards Smith and then Cook. The room temperature dropped a little. Cook, etching a dreamscape of fangs and fur and spirals into his notebook, didn't look up or stop doodling.

"I'm surprised you had time to watch it, Nigel. We all know about the unique nightlife pleasures in that part of the world."

And now the minds were drawn away from their meeting and fixed onto what had suddenly become the main event. Croucher drew in an exaggerated gasp of outrage. Smith held his smile, although the expression was slipping from quizzical to defensive.

"And what would they be, Dorian?"

Cook raised his head, set down his pen, inhaled deeply and stretched his arms out wide, as if imploring his audience. He limbered his head from left to right and spoke through tensed neck muscles.

"Well, apparently there are boys who look like girls."

The door jerked open and Laura Porter bustled in, trailing a borderline obese man in a saggy suit, laptop slotted under one arm.

"Hi, guys! Sorry to interrupt but I just wanted to introduce you all to Mark Holt. He's our new User Experience genius!"

For Porter, everyone with a degree of competence was a 'genius'. Plant was a design genius, Croucher an editing genius. No doubt her gardener was a grass genius.

"Hello, folks!" said Holt, sitting and opening the laptop. Porter settled in next to him – too close. She brought her upright hands together as if in prayer and rapidly clapped them together in girlish rapture.

"This is so exciting!"

The guys and the folks struggled to empathise.

"What is it?" demanded Barton, determined to be the least impressed.

"Okay. What's my role?" said Holt, with caution. "I suppose I'm here to bridge a gap – between editorial and advertising. Why do you need me? Because your subscription base is declining and we have to find new ways to attract a new generation of readers. Now if I'm Johnny or Jenny Movie-Fan, then I'm getting all my movie news pretty much on demand, as and when I want it. And where am I getting it from?"

He let the question hang.

"*Movie* magazine, I'd say," sneered Plant. "Looking at the sales figures."

Porter frowned at him.

"*Online!*" confirmed Holt. "Your audience behaviour is

changing. Your content is quality, but it's not enough to deliver at monthly intervals any more. I'm proposing a whole new ecosystem for the brand – a more granular subscription model, and a metered web offering integrated with mobile."

He turned his laptop around to face the room. The screen displayed a new version of the magazine's logo, modified with an ugly, vertically stretched single 'W' which hovered to the left of 'idescreen' and 'eekly' – double-stacked.

"*Widescreen Weekly!*" squeaked Porter, clapping again.

The silence was violent. Plant released a barely suppressed snort, Cook registered the logo with quiet exasperation and returned to his latest doodle – a simplistic outline of a four-windowed house overlooked by a large sun with a mane of multiple straight-line rays. He sketched wide wooden boards across each of the windows and finished the scene by consuming the building in crude, curling flames.

As Holt continued, Smith leaned over and hissed into Cook's ear.

"It's Thailand, not Taiwan!"

"What?"

"*Katoey.* Ladyboys."

Cook's text-message alert bleeped loudly, drawing a look from Porter. He muted the phone, navigated to his inbox, and opened a message from Dennis Mountford.

Dor please call. Dave is up for a meeting. Had another weird letter. He's had phone calls! Can you do Friday night? Please call. Need to sort this out.

Cook shifted the phone down below the table, out of sight, and typed a reply.

8pm? Send an address. Not public.

October, 1974

'Playtime' at Bethesda Scool – a tangled uproar of doctors, nurses, cowboys, indians, cops, robbers, good guys, bad guys, killers and killed, kissers and kissed. Despite the mild autumn air, Cook had been aggressively padded, by Esther, in three tiers of unyielding polyester. Jammed sideways into a narrow passage behind the utility shed, he gulped down jagged, lung-scarring breaths. He was the chased, the yet-to-be-kissed – and a notorious 'naughty' girl called Beverley Leonard had made him her prey.

Beverley had repeatedly faced Mr Austin for such degeneracy as standing on a chair and lifting her skirt, usually to reveal underwear. She had recently escalated her victims from pupils to teachers, and was only allowed outside for one playtime a week. Cook's hiding place, in the cramped and under-visited upper school yard, was dark and sheltered and difficult to spot in passing, but it was well known as a refuge for smokers and skivers. He compressed himself deep into a cluster of nettles and weeds, listening to Beverley's flat-footed stomp as she searched around the front of the shed. She rattled at the padlocked door – for effect – and then pounced, peering round into the hidey-hole *("Dorian Cook!")*. But instead of dragging her target out into the daylight, Beverley wriggled in next to him. He could smell the Vosene in her dark curly hair.

"I'll kiss you if you show me your widgie."

In a panic, Cook turned to the opposite end of the passage, but it was blocked by an impenetrable tangle of weed coiled around a rusted bicycle frame.

"I know you're Lisa's boyfriend," reasoned Beverley, "but it's okay. I've kissed loads of boys with girlfriends."

Cook squirmed and tried to hustle past her, but she was bulky enough to hold him back.

"I'll tell your mum!" said Cook.

Beverley laughed. "She already knows!"

Cook cowered down lower still. A nettle barb prodded the back of his neck. He yelped and sprang upright, giving Beverley her opportunity. She leaned over, closed her eyes, and pressed her lips onto his. Cook tasted authentic sweat and synthetic fruit – her chewing-gum. He endured the 'kiss' and, as Beverley disengaged with an exaggerated puckering squeak, he reached up to frantically scrub a sleeve across his polluted mouth. Ordeal over, Cook motioned to squeeze past, but, instead of shuffling backwards to allow him a clear exit, Beverley wedged in closer and tighter.

"Let's see, then!"

Cook immediately covered his crotch area with both hands, clenching at the starchy corduroy. Beverley laughed again. "I won't do anything, don't worry! But you've got to show me! That's how it works!"

"I didn't say that!" bleated Cook. "You made me!"

"If you don't show me," said Beverley, "then I'll say you pulled down my pants."

This was no empty threat – the accessibility of Beverley's pants being widely recognised.

Miserably, Cook unzipped his trousers and slid them down to thigh height, revealing saggy red briefs with a white 'Y' lining. He tucked both thumbs into the elasticated hem and pulled down, exposing his shrivelled shame. Beverley studied the curl of skin and tissue.

"Oh! You've got a really little one! But I like your sticky-out belly-button!"

Cook felt his forehead and cheeks flush with anger and embarrassment. He quickly re-covered himself and shouldered into Beverley, who at last stepped outside of the gap and gave him room to pass. Their emergence went unnoticed, due to a commotion which was drawing pupils to the central playground. Cook stumbled towards the teacher voices, zipping up his trousers. Beverley sprinted ahead, skirt swishing.

The playground was overloaded – with all the pupils in both upper and lower schools. Mr Butcher jostled the children into parallel lines according to form, while Mrs Mellor scurried up and down the groups, counting heads. As Cook joined his classmates, he saw a thick, dark cloud drifting up the connecting staircase. David Brereton, two lines up, shouted across.

"Dor! Someone's set fire to the shelter. It's brilliant!"

"It is *not* 'brilliant', Mr Brereton!" roared Butcher. "It is very serious and you need to keep in your line while Mrs Mellor makes sure everyone is safe!"

The old air-raid shelter was used by the lower school

mostly as bicycle storage. It was a long, shallow concrete enclosure with a flat, stone-cladded roof and a padlocked wooden door at either end. The roof could be reached via a short leap from the middle of the staircase, but children were barred from playing either on the roof or inside the shelter. Stray footballs had to be retrieved by a teacher using stepladders, and the school caretaker, convinced that children were intentionally aiming objects up there, regularly lobbied for the roof to be surrounded by netting – or, ideally, barbed wire.

The form groups were herded out of the main gate and reassembled in the teachers' car-park. Butcher led the operation, funnelling the children, line by line, through the narrow entrance yard, muting any chatter with disproportionate threats. As Cook's class shuffled through the gate, a fire engine parked up and two firefighters in breathing masks unravelled a scorched hose, threading it in through the gate and down the staircase, which was now obscured by a rising swirl of black smoke. At the far end of the car-park, Cook could see Beverley Leonard at the head of her form group, crouched in a scrum with two other girls. As Cook lined up, Beverley turned and caught his eye. She whispered something to her companions and they sneaked a glance over before cackling and re-huddling.

"Dor!!! It was brilliant!"

Brereton had snuck in next to Cook, unseen by Butcher. He was hopping on the spot, trembling with pleasure, perhaps even pride.

"You should have seen it burning! We were in the dinner hall and we went up the stairs and all the fire was coming out of the shelter and you could feel the heat."

19

Meaningful Dialogue

"SPACE IS MORE DANGEROUS than killer whales!" insisted Alfie. "It's even more dangerous than volcanoes."

Cook flipped the over-fried bacon. "Volcanoes are pretty dangerous, Alfie."

"Only if they're activated!"

Gina, dressed down for a day off work, sat beside Alfie but screened herself out of the debate with strong morning coffee and a copy of *Vogue*. This was her refined survival skill – simultaneous absence and presence. Cook's method was swagger – a studied visibility. He sang and hummed and whistled, prepared comfort snacks, sneaked up the volume on his record player. In the absence of connection, Dorian and Gina Cook had settled for collaboration, resculpting their arrangement from loving relationship to working partnership. Mostly, this was punishing emotional graft – a choreography of bluffs and feints, joshes and jostles. Mutually assured self-destruction. Breakfast, though, was usually relaxed – foggy brains blunted to conflict, the urge to refuel serving as repellent against lingering melodrama. Lunch and dinner, to a lesser degree, carried the theme – natural communion around food forcing a welcome interval from the pantomime. Like a gloomy teenager, it was a marriage that now emerged only at mealtimes.

Cook scored a ragged incision down the centre of a bread roll and pressed two rashers of bacon into the slot. He snaked a squiggle of brown sauce over the top and handed it to Alfie.

"Use a plate, darling!"

This from Gina to Alfie, not from Gina to Cook. Another survival trick – using children as conduit for confrontation avoidance. Cook slid over a side-plate without comment.

"We should go to the Adventure Playground!" announced Gina.

"The one with the Pirate Ship?" said Alfie, through a mouthful of bacon.

School was closed for training and Gina had booked the day off to do 'outdoor things' with Alfie. She had volunteered this to Cook by text message several weeks ago but, as if to illustrate the toxicity of their recent communication, he had deleted the message without reading it, and had also taken the day as leave. Now, they faced the uncommon anxiety of double-parenting. Cook had planned to spend the morning holed up in his study with Alain Resnais' adaptation of Ayckbourn's *Private Fears In Public Places*. But he needed to bank sufficient goodwill to allow him to disappear in the evening – for his meeting with Brereton and Mountford.

"Yeah, that'd be good. I'll come, too!"

Gina paused, midway through a page-flip, and looked up at Cook. "Really? Oh! That would be nice."

"Yay!" bounced Alfie. "Mummy *and* Daddy Day!"

They both knew that 'nice' was a charitable forecast.

At the park playground, Cook and Gina deposited Alfie into the relative safety of the stress-tested rope-ladders and rubber-floored gangways. They were both quick on the draw with their phones – Cook prodding at work emails, Gina scrolling through various social media feeds. Cook spotted an unoccupied wooden bench and motioned for Gina to claim it, but she was too slow, and they were forced to hover as a nuclear family moved in and set upon a box of pizza slices.

"We can give him an hour or so," confirmed Cook to his phone-screen, through a daze of task-juggling (answering an email, checking his bank balance, dismissing an alert, flapping at a wasp). "I've got some work to do and then there's this reunion thing later."

Gina pocketed her phone. "Let's just wait until he gets tired or hungry. Probably not long. He didn't have much breakfast." (Economical passive-aggression – a dismissal of her husband's lazy 'hour or so' assessment with a side-swipe at his unloved, half-eaten bacon rolls.)

Bothered by insects, the pizza family scattered ("Let's eat on the grass like a proper picnic!"). An elderly couple loitering close to Cook and Gina were clearly considering a claim on the bench. But Gina swooped first, establishing territory with an aggressively draped overcoat. As Cook sat beside her, a distant muscle memory almost drifted her hand into his, but she disguised the impulse with a diffident pat on his knee.

"Tell me more about this 'reunion thing'."

Cook, still peering into his phone-screen, was immersed in a story at the top of his BBC news feed.

POLICE WIDEN SEARCH
FOR MISSING WOMAN
Detectives hunting for a 38-year-old woman who vanished
from her home are studying several reports of sightings.

Police, who believe Eleanor Finch could be with people she knows, made a direct appeal to the woman on Sunday afternoon, calling on her to return to her 'distraught' family.

Eleanor was last seen leaving her home at around 4pm last Monday. Police have been conducting house-to-house enquiries nearby, and have now expanded their search.

"Uh?"

"Your meeting later – with the old school-friends!"

Cook re-read the opening paragraphs of the story. He looked at the woman's name, then up at her age, then back down at the name again.

"Just a quick drink. We were all at school together."

"When did you last see them?"

"I saw one recently – Dennis. It was his idea to get together. I hadn't seen him since we were at school."

"God, that will be so weird."

"It's strange, yeah. He didn't seem like the same person at all. But then I've never met him as an adult."

"Well then he isn't the same person. Really."

"I suppose not."

They shared a few seconds of nothingness, to the sound of shouting and laughing children. Gina slid her hand back to Cook's knee. There was comfort – rather than affection – in the gesture.

"Dorian – I don't mind who you meet, you know."

Cook clicked his phone to stand-by – if only to wrench himself away from the news article – and tilted his head to catch Gina, eye to eye.

"What?"

"You don't need to give me stories about meeting old school friends."

"Stories?"

"MUMMY!"

The moment was ruptured by Alfie, red-faced and bawling, lurching into his mother's arms.

"Darling! What's wrong?"

After the comfort, the call for justice.

"Daddy! An older boy is being horrible. He's bullying the other children and he pushed me over!"

Alfie's features were warped and defaced – smeared with mud and sweat and torrential tears. Cook knew that the reality would be milder than the report, but there was something in his son's devastation – in the jagged sobbing and retching, in the despair and fury – that threw a switch. He sprang to his feet and squeezed Alfie by the hand, urging – almost yanking – him away from Gina, across the grass, past the pizza family and into the playground area. Alfie's 'Pirate Ship' was a vaguely galley-shaped framework of wooden oars and braces tethered by a network of ropes and netting. A central ladder led up from the sandpit base onto a broad 'deck'. This entrance was currently impassible, due to a stocky boy – a couple of years older than Alfie – blocking the path and demanding 'treasure' from other children.

"He's there, daddy! That one!"

"Okay, son. You stay here."

And now, on wings of outrage, Cook glided over to the boy, to the bully.

And there was the side entry and John Ray.

Watch! He hates this!

And there was the gates and John Ray.

Come on! You can go!

And there was Uncle Russell.

I'd stay out of it, Dor.

"What the fuck do you think you're doing?"

The boy – the bully, in a grubby green polo shirt – turned to Cook, standing a few feet away, within striking distance, tremoring with confrontation anxiety.

"What? I'm playing! Are you police?"

"No!" snapped Cook, a wobble in his voice. "I am not 'police' and you are not 'playing'. You are frightening younger children. You aren't playing with them. You are *bullying* them."

"What's the problem, mate?"

A tall, angular man with a shiny shaven head stepped forward from a crowd of adults at the edge of the play area. Cook briefly caught his eye before redirecting his glare back at the boy. "He's the problem! He's been bullying the other kids. He made my son cry." Cook was alert to the man's threat, but continued to build his case. "I've just seen him demanding money."

"*What?* Who's been demanding money?"

This was clearly a redundant question, but Cook assumed that the man hadn't fully understood. "*He* has!" said Cook, pointing to the boy.

And now, with curtain raised and audience enchanted with fear and fascination, Cook felt the urge to improvise, to season the drama.

"Is this your boy?"

"Yes, mate," said the man, immediately – confidently. "*This* is my boy. *My* son."

The man shuffled from stage right to centre, towards the main ladder, towards Cook and the boy, the bully. Cook pivoted – to receive him, braced for something ugly. If it was to come, he would be prepared – and that would be unexpected. But the man, head sparkling in the sunshine, walked past Cook and gripped his son, the bully, by his forearm.

"Liam! What have I *fucking* told you? Don't mess about with other kids!"

"I wasn't doing anything!"

The man squeezed his son the bully's other forearm and he pushed and pulled with both hands – forward and back – causing Liam's head to jerk against the motion. With this, Liam Sr. shook out the payback for Alfie, as Liam Jr. wailed and sprayed mucus and tears, the fluids atomised by violence.

"Steady on!"

This from an elderly man hoisting a young girl down from one of the climbing frame's high beams.

Liam Sr., now the bully, turned and snarled and released his son, the victim, who collapsed to the floor, clenched and shuddering, sobbing with shock and hurt.

"Don't tell me to steady on! I'll discipline my child the way I fucking want!"

"Is that what that was?" said Cook.

The bald man turned back to the balding man. "You what?"

Gina, crouched down beside Alfie.

The elderly man carrying the young girl.

Two rigid vertical furrows between Liam Sr.'s eyes.

Three horizontal grooves in Liam Sr.'s forehead.

Liam the victim unfurling, standing, shuffling towards Alfie, saying I'm sorry, I'm sorry.

"Pretty fucked-up kind of 'discipline'."

The elderly man setting the young girl down by an elderly woman, keeping his eyes on Cook and Liam Sr.

"Dorian..." (Gina).

"You think he's learned his lesson, do you? Now you've shaken him half to death?"

Gina comforting Liam as well as Alfie.

Liam Sr. mouth open.

Grooves, furrows.

"Fuck off! You're the one that made this a big thing!"

"Maybe if you stopped your kids extorting money off other kids, it wouldn't have happened in the first place."

This felt desperate and off-target, but Cook, the bully, was marshalling his *Critics' Wire* debating composure.

"What do you think you're teaching your kids – doing that to them in public? You're teaching them that it's okay to make something physical, as a knee-jerk. You're teaching them that the natural progression from anger is abuse."

Gina comforting Liam and Alfie.

Gina staring at the ground.

Grooves, furrows.

"I do not abuse my kids!"

Cook, smiling. "Oh, yeah. We can all see that!"

And now, Liam Sr., pointing at the air, prodding at the space a few inches from Cook's face.

"You've got a fucking big mouth!"

And there was Mr Butcher.

You have a problem – it's called a mouth.

Cook drew back his right shoulder and swiped his fist up and around and into the side of Liam Sr.'s smooth, shiny head. The connection was barely a glance, but Cook immediately recoiled and snapped out another punch. This one landed – more out of luck than precision – on the edge of an eye socket, with an unsatisfying, near-silent clunk. It jerked back Liam Sr.'s head, forcing him to stumble down onto one knee. Cook shuffled backwards, braced for retaliation, but Liam Sr. stayed down – there on the dank grass, on one knee, hand over his eye. It looked like a surreal proposal of marriage.

"You *cunt!*"

"Dorian!" (Gina).

Liam Sr. – still not fully upright – scrambled towards Cook, head down, his skull now a polished cannonball. Cook almost managed to sidestep the charge, but Liam Sr. half-connected with enough force to send the two men tumbling onto a honeycombed safety mat beneath a toddler climbing frame. In the initial wrestle for dominance, Cook was surprised to find himself the strongest. He dug his boot-heels into the rubber and shoved Liam Sr. to the side, wrestling his way into an absurdly sexual straddling position – Cook on top, Liam Sr. face down on the matting. Cook aimed a couple of uncharitable swipes to the back of Liam Sr.'s head, his fists clunking onto bony dome, squishing into leathered nape. Liam Sr. wriggled onto his back, flailing his arms up at Cook, slapping not punching. He rocked from side to side, trying to force his attacker off-balance, but there was too much bulk to shift.

And now, Cook appeared paralysed. He held his position, keeping Liam Sr. pinned, but only offering defensive flaps at incoming blows.

"Get off me!!"

Hands on Cook's back, prising him away.

A crying child.

"Daddy! Stop!"

"Leave him alone!"

"Dorian! Stop this!"

John Ray screaming, John Ray howling.

What's he ever done to you?

The ghost is getting angry.

Cook leaned back, just outside Liam Sr.'s punching range. He turned and saw that the hands belonged to Alfie – red-faced and crying Alfie. ("Daddy! Stop!")

Red-faced and crying Liam. ("Leave him alone!")

Gina, shielding Alfie. ("Dorian! Stop this!")

And now – rage filter lifted, natural rhythms and hues restored – Cook was calmed by concern for his son. But as he clambered away from Liam Sr., who was immediately embraced by an hysterical Liam Jr., he groped for Alfie but found him not there, shielded instead in his mother's arms.

20

Protagonist

On a cold, cold afternoon in the nineteen-seventies, Dorian Cook and David Brereton zipped up their fluffy-hooded parkas and hustled through the bottleneck at the school gates. As they passed by the teachers' car-park, they barged apart a huddle of older girls and broke into a top-speed run, squawks of outrage at their heels. Their improvised escape route delivered the boys to an estate of pampered semis which Cook recognised from the summer's day at John Ray's house. They slowed but, neither wanting to be the first to stop and show weakness, wrestled each other to a halt – Brereton yanking Cook's hood down over his face, Cook locking Brereton's head into the crook of his arm. Spent, they bent double, breath billowing.

"I've got a secret!" panted Brereton.

"Yeah?"

"I set fire to the shelter."

"Liar!"

Brereton raised his head. Cook saw anger ignite in his eyes. "I did! No-one saw me but I did!"

"Why did you do that?"

Brereton shrugged. "Felt like it."

"If you get caught, you'll get done!"

"Won't get caught."

They bought a fistful of Refresher chews from a corner shop and meandered back through the side-streets near Cook's house, with a vague plan to listen to records and play Subbuteo.

"I heard you were going out with Beverley Leonard," said Brereton.

"No. I might go out with Lisa."

"What? Have you asked her?"

"Yeah. She's nicer."

"What did she say?"

"She said yes, but only when she's stopped going out with Pecker."

'Pecker' was Martin Pekar, the son of Hungarian-born immigrants who lived in a bland little bungalow by the far end of the play-park. He was an odd mix of exotic and scruffy, and Cook had occasionally seen him emerging from a lunchtime remedial English class.

"He smells. Nearly as bad as Batty Battison."

At the bottom of Cook's street, the boarded-up butcher's shop squatted, sentinel-like, challenging them both to pass. Its large shop-front window space had been rendered opaque by an overlapping stack of oblong planks, while the first-floor windows had all been sealed with grimy brickwork – apart from the one overlooking the adjoining street, which had somehow been breached from the inside. A few poked-out chunks of house-brick lay below, at ground level, in a mound of rubble, walled off inside a yard area cluttered with abandoned builder's equipment – wheelbarrow with no wheel, rusted scaffold tubes, propped steel sheeting, a skeletal wooden chair-frame. An attempt had been made to bar access to the yard by padlocking the back gate and nailing up a 'Trespassers Will Be Prosecuted' sign, but the wall was topped with an inviting layer of curved stone, and the gate's bottom hinge had been kicked away, leaving a gap easily accessible to the wily and wiry.

"Dare ya to go in the house and get up to the window!" announced Brereton. "You've got to wave through the gap so I can see you've gone all the way up."

"Dares go first!" countered Cook.

Shouts came from the narrow entry alongside the butcher's shop yard, round the back of Cook's terrace.

"Leave him!"

Cook and Brereton sprinted past the padlocked gate and turned in to the entry. There were four boys – Michael Howell, two who Cook had never seen before, and Darren Ray – older, bigger, stronger. Darren was gripping the coat collar of the first unknown boy in one hand, while repeatedly punching him in the stomach with the other. The second boy watched, terrified, his exit nominally blocked by Howell's position. Brereton stopped dead at the bottom of the entry, but Cook just slowed slightly. As he approached the group, he saw that John Ray was squatted down a little further up, buried beneath an overlarge dark-green parka, bloodless face framed by the fur-lined hood. Cook's movement caught Darren's eye and he called over.

"Dorian! Get here! Hold him for me!"

Cook turned, but – true to form – Brereton had scented trouble early, and had disappeared.

The second boy seized the moment and bolted past Howell, down the entry towards Cook.

"Stop him!"

Cook shoulder-charged the boy, but he was bulky and thundered past, propelled by momentum and panic. The glancing contact bounced Cook to the ground, where he disguised his feeble intent by staying down, feigning pain and injury.

"Y'alright, Dor?"

Michael Howell was suddenly close, helping Cook to his feet. They both began to move away from the Rays and the beaten boy, hurrying to take the corner at the bottom end of the entry.

"Hey!! Get back!"

Howell and Cook immediately turned and walked brightly back towards the group, as if the attempt to escape was just some sort of directional confusion.

"Them two got me and John," whispered Howell. "There was another one but he ran off up the top. They threw his bag over there." He nodded towards the butcher's shop back yard.

As they reached Darren and John, the captive boy made an attempt to break free, but Darren was too strong and held him firm. "Right. Keep him still!"

Cook and Howell took an arm each, preventing the boy from wriggling. He had taut, curly hair and his head and face seethed in the icy afternoon – cheeks scalded by hot tears, nose a swollen blob of blood. They angled him to face Darren Ray, who punched him again in the stomach. He wailed, wilting forward as much as Cook and Howell would allow. Darren gripped the boy under the chin, squeezing his cheeks until his lips formed a ragged 'O'. Howell sniggered at the distorted features – a parody of a pout.

"Where's his bag?" Darren leaned in close to the puckered mouth.

The boy struggled to gather himself. He inhaled a few shuddering breaths, swallowed, tried to sniff away the sobs. But Darren drew back his right arm and (like father, like son) swung round his open palm, connecting hard and heavy with the side of the boy's face.

Thunk.

Cook took a faceful of blood, snot and tears. Darren Ray repeated his question – this time soft and sinister.

"Where… is his fucking bag?"

The impact's aftershock stirred a fury in the boy. He writhed free of Howell and Cook's grip, and burst forward, searching for the space and energy to break away. He fell, scurrying briefly on all fours, before hauling himself upright and running.

"I'm telling my dad on you!"

Cook dragged his sleeve across his face, smearing away the wetness. Darren made no attempt to pursue the boy. Instead, he walked over to his brother, crouched down beside him and tenderly peeled back the fur-trim hood, exposing that expressionless pallor – the cherry-red pupils, the wafting white hair.

"Where did they throw it, Johnny?"

"Over there."

John Ray spoke from a distance – calm and clear. He raised his arm a little, offering a barely perceptible – almost arrogant – gesture towards the wall of the old butcher's shop.

"Get in there and get his bag!" barked Darren.

Howell scurried off, jumping to order. Cook complied more slowly, backing away, turning only when he had exchanged a glance of recognition with John. At the gate, Howell squatted and leaned his full bodyweight into the hingeless corner, opening a gap which Cook shuffled through. The shoulder-bag rested, with curious precision, in the tray of the wheelless wheelbarrow, on top of a dusted-over bag of cement. Cook snatched it up, posted it through the gap to Howell and lingered for a closer look at this imposing, decomposing half-world, just a few doors down from where his grandmother fried her chips. The back windows were boarded solid, but the door-frame brickwork had been partially smashed away, the hole unconvincingly blocked from the inside by a flimsy wooden panel. He pushed at the covering and peeked through the gap – into almost total darkness, dappled only by soft daylight trickling in through the gaps between boards.

"Dor! Come on!"

Cook began wriggling back through the gate as Howell held it open. He stopped, distracted by a flicker of colour in the dusty-grey clutter – John Ray's blue-and-white handkerchief, draped over the peak of a triangular pile of scaffold tubes. Cook stuffed it into his pocket and squeezed out through the gate, where Darren and John – bag over shoulder – were waiting.

"What's it like in there?" demanded Darren.

"Dirty. Boarded up. Pretty dangerous."

Darren snorted. Cook and Howell stood upright and joined the brothers, completing an awkward little circle of solidarity. The light was dimming, and with no adrenaline insulation, Cook was reminded of the chill. Coat-hood still down, John Ray sniffed and rubbed at his nose.

"I found this, John," said Cook, producing the handkerchief from his pocket and handing it over.

"Thank you," said John Ray.

21
A Little Knowledge

WILLIAM STONE TAPPED DORIAN Cook's number into his phone and passed the few seconds between connection and reply with a sip from a glass of rich red wine. It was 7pm on Friday evening and the alcohol had been beckoning since mid-afternoon – a singular craving which gripped him gradually. (First, a faint essence, then an odour, then something moist and tangible – a tingle on the tongue.) At that point – usually around 5pm – Stone's actions became almost remote, cellular. Far deeper than a struggle between wills, it transformed into a groping *for* will – a battle to retain his autonomy.

"Hi, mate. How are you?" Cook sounded distracted and duty-bound.

"Bad time?"

"No, no. Just busy."

"What are you up to? You out?"

"On a bus. Bit noisy. I'm okay, yeah. What's up?"

Cook knew that a call from Will was never purely social. There was usually subtext – to be established via a serpentine pantomime of banter, until the inevitable, "Listen, Dor…". This time, though, the voice was strained and shaded. Stone cleared his throat and coughed up his business without delay.

"Community fucking order! That's what's up. Three months. Common assault, mate. Common assault!"

Cook felt nothing at this. His friend's troubles seemed shrivelled and disproportionate next to his own. The bus was approaching the stop suggested by Mountford – the stop near to Brereton's flat. He rose up, shimmied past the bony legs of his seat companion, and, phone-hand occupied, staggered forward to the exit-door, steadying himself with a lunge for every pole.

"Ah. Sorry to hear that, Will. Can't you appeal?"

"Doesn't work that way. Suspended as soon as there's an allegation – and this isn't the end of it. I've got an internal misconduct enquiry still going on. Plus, I've got to pay the bitch – who attacked me first! – compensation, and attend an 'alcohol treatment' course."

The bus juddered to a halt and Cook was almost delivered into the lap of an elderly man who smelt of something acrid and carbolic.

"Sorry. Excuse me!"

The man tutted obligingly, but didn't avert his window-stare. As the doors opened, the squash of people outside parted to form a sardonic guard of honour. Cook wriggled through and swerved into a side-street.

"Well. You can go back to work, right?"

"Yeah. But I can forget about any promotion."

Cook pulled a scrap of paper from his pocket – directions dictated by Mountford. "Will, I'm so sorry. That's harsh."

"Too fucking right it's harsh! Could have been even worse, as well. They wanted to put an electronic tag on me! The judge said he felt that my case didn't warrant it because

I wasn't an 'ongoing threat'. Since when have I been a fucking *threat*, Dor?"

"I suppose you can think of it as something you've learned," suggested Cook, scanning the house numbers.

"Mate, the only thing I've 'learned' is that seventeen years' service means nothing next to the word of a fucking little *thug* with..."

"Sorry, Will. I've got to go. I'm already late. Can I call you back later?"

"Yeah. I might be out, though. Got sorrows that need drowning!" He laughed – too long, too deperately. "Listen, Dor... Before you go, can you sub me for 2K? I'll make it 3K in three weeks. I've just got to get myself together."

Cook was standing at the door of a town-house flat-block, squinting at the handwritten name-cards above the intercom – 'R. Saltwell, M. Dutton, J. Mortlock...'

"Uh, of course. I saw the other money had gone into my account. I'll get that sorted."

"Thanks, mate," said Stone, relaxing. "I owe you one!"

"You owe me three, Will. Three thousand!"

Again, the overbaked laugh. Then, he was gone – no goodbye – and Cook reached up and pressed the button next to the card which said 'D. Brereton'.

"How many messages have you had?"

This from Dorian Cook to David Brereton – the boy so watchful and slippery, now a man eroded by friction. The three old friends (if that was what they were) convened in a council of shame, gathered around a dirty-white plastic kitchen table: Dennis Mountford – lumpen and malformed in an offensive maroon sweater, chain-chewing stick after stick after stick of gum, never discarding an old lump, just refreshing it with a new strip; Dorian Cook – unstylishly nearly-bald, palms cupped around a mug of tepid tea, still bruised by the playground confrontation, less and less convinced that he was only here out of curiosity; and a taller, tauter, scruffier David Brereton, who appeared to have provided most of the bodyweight now being carried by Mountford. Brereton had retained his hair and those backlit eyes still sparkled with mischief, but his skin was callow and gauzy, stretched cellophane-tight against a jutting skeleton, as if eager to shear off and slide away.

"Five or six…" Eerily, the timbre of Brereton's voice tallied precisely with the version in Cook's memory, barely shifted in pitch. "It's some weirdo who thinks he knows what happened. Winding us up."

Finally out of gum, Mountford was now dismantling the cardboard casing of the packet. He looked from Brereton to Cook, transferring the dismissal, inviting it to be exposed as false confidence. "I don't think so."

"What *is* it then, Den?" snapped Brereton. "Who exactly is going to bother with this shit after so long?"

Cook fixed his gaze on Mountford. "Maybe that's all it is – a reminder. Someone making sure it isn't forgotten. I can't see what they can do about it all now, though."

"Dorian…" Mountford was twisting panels of cardboard into gnarled little rods and then coiling them together. "I've had messages signed with a 'D'."

Brereton laughed – constricted, asthmatic. "It isn't *you*, is it, Dor?"

"You know who it fucking is!" Mountford seemed close

to collapse. Cook was shocked at the contrast between the younger, bolder child-man and the cowed animal now before him. Brereton rose to his feet and shuffled to the far side of the kitchen, lighting a cigarette to break up the journey. "Beer?"

Cook and Mountford shook their heads. Brereton slid a can of something out of a squat little fridge and settled back at the table. He slurped at the drink and drew elaborately on his cigarette, piping smoke out through his nostrils.

"Dave, I've got to ask…" said Cook, cautiously. "What have you been up to?"

Brereton flashed him a look, and for a moment, Cook caught something familiar – an ambiguity between anger and suspicion.

"I work in a hotel kitchen, Dor. Sous-chef. I'm not the boss but I sometimes get to be the boss. It's the best way – you don't get blamed when things go wrong, but you can claim a bit of glory when they go right."

He grinned and gulped back a lungful of smoke. With every toke, he tapped off non-existent ash into the air and rolled the filter side to side between thumb and forefinger. Cook wondered if Mountford could also sense the confected bravado in these tics and twitches.

"You're both married, aren't ya? I had a couple of goes at that."

Mountford scooped up the chewing-gum sculpture and plunged it into an overflowing pedal-bin. "Look. Never mind what we've been 'up to' in the past. What are we going to do *now?*"

"We should report it," insisted Cook. "No need for all the details on who we think it might be or why or whatever.

Just make it clear that we've been receiving threatening messages and we'd like to know what our options are."

Brereton shook his head. "What are they going to do about it? Shut down the fucking internet?"

"We need to make an official complaint!" insisted Mountford.

Brereton mashed his cigarette into an ashtray and posted it into the empty beer-can. "Thank fuck we've got a legal expert on the case!"

"Well, what do *you* suggest?" The corners of Mountford's eyes were glinting with tears. "Solve it with sarcasm? I've got *kids,* David! So does Dorian! These messages aren't some 'weirdo' trying to wind us up. Someone wants to hurt us!"

Brereton crushed the can, tossed it towards a small recycle bin, missed. He smiled, raised both hands – palms out – up in front of his face, and extended all the fingers, wiggling them around for mock-spooky effect.

"Someone. Or some-*thing!*"

22

Near Bathpool

Cook gouged a lump of unspreadable 'best' butter over a round of bleached white bread, layered on a row of crinkle-cut chips and splattered them with a few forkfuls of baked beans. He squished another slice of buttery bread on top, lifted his creation – with both hands – to a fully gaped mouth, and bit into the centre, displacing beans and bean-juice onto a dinner-plate balanced on his knee. In the kitchen, Esther laboured and muttered, preparing steak and kidney pie, more chips, and a dessert of improvised apple turnover made with excess pastry. That was for tea, later. The baked-bean sandwich was a standard after-school snack which Cook consumed on Esther's TV chair, Rusty curled at his feet. He munched happily, eyes fixed on *The Wombles*, worrying the dog's nose with a big toe which poked out through a hole in his sock. Two-thirds of the way through, he'd had his fill and, in penance for the bothering, laid the plate on the floor next to Rusty, who immediately inhaled the bread and chips before lapping the plate clean.

"*Lesley Whittle, the 17-year-old heiress kidnapped from*

her Shropshire home 52 days ago, has been found at the bottom of a drain shaft."

The Wombles gave way to *John Craven's Newsround* – usually a sign for Cook to dash up to his bedroom, to his comics and record-player and the impenetrable science-fiction novels handed down by Uncle Russell. But today, the normally jovial John, in tank-top and tie, spoke with a compelling note of alarm.

"Police made the discovery after a three-day search of Bathpool Park at Kidsgrove in Staffordshire, where Lesley's brother Ronald had tried to meet the kidnapper some seven weeks earlier. It is thought she had been strangled."

"Nana?"

"What's the matter, Dor? I'm doing something!"

"Police are convinced she was taken by the killer known as the 'Black Panther', because of his dark clothing."

"The telly says that they found a girl!"

Esther emerged from the kitchen, wiping her hands on a tea-towel. She gazed at the TV, tutting, gently shaking her head.

"Oh dear, dear, dear."

"What's a drain shaft?"

"The car found later abandoned in the town contained Miss Whittle's slippers and some office tape."

"It's a hole underground. They stop flooding when it rains. The water goes down there instead."

Cook reached forward and switched off the TV. "But why did he hide a girl in one? I bet it was really wet and cold."

"And dark!"

Esther had limited empathy for Cook's recent

introspections. She saw little point in shielding him from abstract cruelties, preferring to focus on his immediate physical needs – keeping him alive and warm and well fed. He often overheard her, chattering to herself, discussing her own woes – arthritis, constipation, insomnia – in lurid detail, as if openly auditing pain could relieve it.

"He was trying to make some money, Dor. He took her away and said he wanted a lot of money before he would give her back."

Cook thought of the drain shaft – smelly, deep and dark. "But why didn't he just make her stay at his house?"

Esther sighed. "I don't know, Dor. Because he's not a very nice person."

"Have they put him in prison now?"

"They haven't caught him yet. But I'm sure they will really soon."

Later, in his bed, throbbing stomach bloated with pie and beans and chips and apple turnover, Cook lay on his side, knees to his chest, and wondered if the girl had been given some food or if she had been forced to eat rats. (But how would she have caught them in the dark?) He thought she probably wouldn't have been able to scream and shout for help because her mouth would have been covered up by the man. But if that was true, how would she eat *anything?*

And then.

Something was coming up the stairs, but the closet felt safer and darker than ever. Even if the door was opened, it would be too dark for him to be seen.

Thunk, thunk, thunk.

As the bedroom door opened, Cook realised that the inside and outside dark wouldn't help him, because the Sea Devils would be happy with both.

The closet door opened – to no fresh light. Cook kept his eyes screwed shut.

And then Something climbed into the closet with him and closed the door from the inside, shutting them in together.

Morning was usually announced through the bedroom wall, by Mr Smith, prematurely stirred by an extended spasm of dry coughing. (Uncle Russell called this phenomenon 'Cough-a-doodle-do'.) But pangs from the overeating had needled Cook in his sleep all night, and he was awake and browsing the 1974 *Buster* annual before he realised there was something missing – no coughing, no sobbing, no babbling.

At breakfast, Esther poured far too much heated milk over Cook's Shreddies and laid a foil-wrapped parcel on the table. "Before you go to school, can you take a turnover round to Mr Smith's?"

On top of being her neighbour's sole witness to his existence, Esther routinely kept Mr Smith in fruit and cake and pastry products, delivered by Cook. There was a suggestion of repaid debt, but Esther saw it as more philanthropy than duty – redistributing a chunk of state pension away from her Bingo budget and into the care of an old acquaintance who had long since drifted from any kind of consistent self-provision. Mr Smith had been a mine worker – riding the rickety lift, hacking at the fractured seam with pick and shovel, dislodging the strata, gulping down the gas and the steam and the dust. Even as he retired, and rose above ground, the Earth retained its claim on his derelict lungs. He was soiled and soil-bound from his final punch-out at the colliery.

Cook unlatched Mr Smith's gate and tiptoed down the yard to the pale-green back door. He would have been happy to leave the parcel on the ledge, knock, and dash away, but Esther had asked Cook to 'check on him'.

"Mr Smith?"

Cook's voice sounded detached and remote. He knocked – too loudly – to cover the apprehension.

"Mr Smith?"

The silence wasn't unusual. Mr Smith was almost completely deaf and only came to his door when he happened to be in the rear sitting-room and could see Cook waiting – after peering creepily through the filthy net curtains.

Cook approached the sitting-room window. He balanced the pastry on top of the coal-scuttle, formed a light-blocking tunnel with both hands, and looked inside. The room appeared to be empty – although, oddly for early morning, Mr Smith's black-and-white portable – perched on a tall table at the bottom of the stairs – was switched on, broadcasting the test-card. All three bars of the electric fire shone light-orange.

"Hello?"

He would take the parcel into the house, put it on the table, call out, say that he was sorry but he had to leave to get to school on time.

Inside, the kitchen smelt starchy, as if it had long since been abandoned as an area for food preparation and was now just dead space – a memorial of pans and Pyrex. From the sitting-room TV, the test-card session musicians cranked out a circular dirge of droopy funk. Cook set the pastry down on the kitchen table and walked through the connecting door. On the TV screen, a hair-banded young girl was posed and frozen, playing noughts and crosses with a green-bodied clown puppet. On the floor, behind the sofa, Mr Smith was flat out and face-down. Cook tried to do several things at once – speak to Mr Smith, not look at the body, shout for Esther, turn and run. But he just stood there – by the hinged dining table, by the doilies, by the dark wooden chairs and the clunking grandfather clock.

Mr Smith's left arm was folded underneath his upper body, his right skewed up and out at an unnatural angle, hand resting flat against the peeling skirting-board. There was a terrible sense of tableau, as if the body had been propped in place. Cook crouched, and reeled at a faecal reek that only seemed present in the lower half of the room. He jerked back upright and, carefully, allowed his eyes to slide past the shoes (no socks), the formal but ill-fitting trousers, the dark green cardigan – up to the wrinkled, reptilian nape with its edging of cheaply trimmed white hair. The face was under there somewhere, and Cook imagined it eyeless and skeletal – brow bloodied, nose inverted. Fearful of glimpsing a contorted grimace, he shifted his eyeline sharply to the other side of the sofa, where a pair of NHS glasses – arms yanked from hinges, frame buckled, lenses cracked – lay upended against a leg of the TV table. Another shift of gaze and he alighted on the hallway beyond, with its transparent plastic faux-lino flattened loosely to the floor, home now to a set of ejected false teeth which had skated almost all the way to the front door, trailing a forked smear of saliva, upper and lower gums resting side by side.

"Dorian?"

Uncle Russell's shout came from outside, from the far end of Mr Smith's yard. Cook wanted to reply, but found that he couldn't open his mouth to try. His breathing had slowed, but now each inhale was sharp and stammering.

"Oh no!"

Now, Uncle Russell was in the room behind him, but Cook didn't turn. He stayed fixed on the false teeth, now appalled and terrorised at the thought of how the dead body's presence could be re-confirmed with just a minor eye movement.

Hands on Cook's shoulders – and he startled and turned and scurried out through the kitchen and the open gate, down the back-entry, to the front wall of the boarded-up butcher's shop. He squeezed through the gap and into the yard where he had retrieved John Ray's bag and handkerchief, squashing himself into the corner by the still untouched wheelbarrow, hiding from he didn't know what. He looked up at the boarded windows, then down at the door with its partially demolished brickwork – and now, no wooden panel attempting to repair (or disguise?) the damage on the inside. From here, he could simply stand up and, with a crouch, walk right inside. Instead, he took up a fist-sized chunk of chalky rock and ground it across the grey stone wall by his head, at first scraping out a few random straight lines, then scoring in a couple of circles which transformed into squiggles, then melded into a continuous, random, savage scribbling.

23

Tension/Release

COOK HAD ALWAYS NEGOTIATED his attendance at the Cannes Film Festival with a voracity that denied both the event's declining reputation for hedonism and his own diminishing media profile. However brightly it had blazed in the days of MTV-bankrolled degeneracy at the Palais Bulles, Cannes was now a pale ember, out-twinkled in the festival firmament by mid-September Venice (leaner awards, keener movies, younger talent, older churches). Where once the tone was sybaritic abandon – overnight cocaine airlifts from LA to Nice, porn-industry yachts moored offshore, unquenchable beach parties – now there was only distaste for sleaze and disdain for excess. But still they came – for the withering shrugs and the refurbished tourist menus, for the Rosé refills and the hateful caste system of pastel screening passes (white down to blue – from the high-priesthood of major media critics to the untouchable local-paper hacks and freesheet liggers). The uninitiated would detect self-esteem issues behind this docile clique insulated by elitism – conspirators without crime. But for Cook, it was tribal – a scramble for sterile turf in a demilitarised zone of round-table interviews and parochial embargos. For film critics, Cannes had become Coppola's Saigon – when they were away they wanted to be there; but when they were there, all they could think of was getting away.

With his yellow pass (fast-track admittance to all screenings) and self-proclaimed 'superior knowledge of world cinema', Cook was usually the King – or, at least, mid-ranking prince – of Cannes. But this year, he couldn't seem to find a foothold. The interviews were slippier and chippier, the PRs less fawning, the talent access joylessly micromanaged. Having talked Henry into assigning him for the full ten days, he was restless by day three, and now, on the Saturday of the first weekend, had partially hatched a domestic crisis as an excuse to return home – although the invention hardly demanded much effort.

Gina had dropped him at the airport, following an inch-by-inch burrow through motorway congestion. A jovial Radio Four panel game jarred with their brimming squabble over the playground incident. (*Grown men behaving like children... Appalling example for Alfie... Teaching him that violence is an option...*)

Alfie was blissed and oblivious in the back seat, shielded by headphones, tablet computer and *The Incredibles*, his barks of laughter out of sync with the gloom up-front.

"We should take a break, Dorian."

But then, a news report. And, for the first time in fifteen years, he had *shushed* her – a loud and insistent hissing which made her double-take in outrage.

"*The ex-husband of a missing mother-of-two has issued an appeal for her safe return. Gareth Finch revealed that he was aware his wife Eleanor had been suffering from depression for some time, but insisted her lack of contact was 'entirely out of character'.*"

"Why the sudden interest in the news?"

"Ellie. If you're watching... We all love you. Amy and Joe just want their mum back and whatever differences we've had, we can work something out. Please get in touch. Everyone is so worried."

"How awful."

"Detective Chief Inspector John Barrett, who is leading the enquiry, has admitted that his force are struggling for leads."

"Let's put some music on."

"We are extremely concerned for Eleanor's safety, given she was last seen on CCTV over a week ago. We are conducting enquiries near the family home and around Eleanor's place of work, but I can't comment on any information received. We know that some money was withdrawn from Eleanor's bank-card last weekend, and her passport is still at home, along with her car."

"Did you hear me?"

Cook felt car-sick. He closed his eyes and reclined. Oh, to transform! To become membranous – porous – and sink into the structure of the seat, to settle there, coiled around the moulding, grinding through the gridlock with supreme indifference. Eleanor Finch was another old acquaintance – unforgotten. Back at the beginning of Cook's career, when he was a staffer on a free reviews and listings magazine, he had written a feature on a film about an obsessive chat-show host attempting to track down his first love. Each of the magazine's writers was asked to contribute eighty words to a side-bar on their own 'lost loves'. Cook's submission managed to be both economical and indulgent.

Lisa Goldstraw. I used to walk her to school and was convinced I would marry her one day. She moved away. I told myself that I'd moved on – but never quite believed it.

At first, Eleanor had written to say how lovely she thought this was. Soon after, she wrote again, saying how lovely she thought *Cook* was (based on his monochrome byline picture – side-on, conspirational smile). Then the letters arrived at least once a week – coloured envelopes smothered in concentric heart-shapes and lurid declarations. Inside, the prose was purple, occasionally blue, always loaded with self-loathing and pleading for validation. Cook had wisely left the letters unanswered, but the silence only made Eleanor bolder. She started to etch potential meeting dates into the petals of the pre-printed flowers which lined the margins. Cook was twenty-four years of age, brooding behind owlish spectacles, hair side-swept and – he regularly winced at the memory – sprayed rigid. Eleanor was barely fifteen. Within a year, Cook had left the magazine, to his first newspaper job, and his admirer had fallen silent. Until recently.

Here now, dashing down the croisette, hurdling the dog-leads, heading for an early-morning screening of a Ukrainian film about a taxidermist torturer, Cook was shaken by the need to stir. He felt simultaneously besieged and marooned, a man without mooring – alive and alert to his assailants but absurdly unarmed and without base. This was not a good time – for the unsmiling doorman outside the Debussy theatre to refuse to even touch his pass, for a wordless redirection to a low-status queue of murmur and morning-breath, for the sight of *Movie* magazine's Neil

Hooper swaggering past security with a flash of orange pass.

"Fucking fascists!"

This was a surprise – to both his fellow professionals and to Cook himself. Usually, he managed to drive a filter between thought and mouth, but, in a disturbing new development, process time had apparently now dropped to zero.

Two doormen approached, leaving a third to consult with a two-way radio.

"Sir…"

"Oh! Now it's English! But when you're on your petty fucking power-trip, you hide behind French!"

"Sir, the two lines are based on level of accreditation. It is the only way to manage capacity."

"Fuck off! Half of the people in this queue don't even know what they're seeing, anyway! I'm here to *work!* I have to see this film for my *work!* You are trying to stop me from doing my *work!*"

A fourth official had materialised to the side, on the edge of Cook's vision. He slithered forward with a sinister confidence – older and tauter, dark blue suit in autonomous contrast to the uniforms of his colleagues.

"Could I see your accreditation, sir?"

"I have already shown you my 'accreditation', and apparently it isn't fucking creditable enough!"

Cook produced the lowly yellow laminate with smouldering self-portrait and wafted it sarcastically, a few inches in front of the official's nose. The card was taken, vaguely studied – and retained.

"Please attend the festival office within the hour, sir."

"Attend?"

Cook's voice could now be heard by anyone in the surrounding area – queue members, festival staff, kiosk attendants, passers-by with their umbilical bichons frise. All heads lifted, eager for drama.

"What is it, a fucking court hearing?"

The official had already walked away and was re-entering the theatre, Cook's pass in pocket. After a few seconds of outraged realisation, Cook burst back into life – teeth flashing, spittle splashing – with a barrage of French and English insults. He was now that most redundant of species – a civilian in Cannes. He had been cast out – to out-of-competition theatres showing out-of-date films. He would be turned away from scheduled interviews with stars who would insist (reasonably) that their interrogator should at least have seen the film under discussion. Parties and PR drinks were still within reach, but he would feel sidelined in any discussion of the festival programme and, in a day or two, his absence at the after-screening street huddles would be conspicuous. With a week to go, he'd only fulfilled a third of his *Widescreen* brief, and was commissioned for two major freelance projects. He could stir up an outrage, claim a grotesque overreaction to a genuine admission grievance. But the episode had been seen by too many – possibly even photographed or filmed. As research for his recent feature on social media, Cook had been forced to engage with the babble and squeak of Twitter. He had fumbled together a sparse profile page, attempted a few stilted acknowledgements of fellow critics and industry pals, and quickly settled into the dreary habit of intoning mini-reviews. ("A film of quiet power and grace with extraordinary central performances. Breathtaking and heartbreaking. Four stars.") But, as his piece demonstrated, he knew enough of the culture ('petty prurience', 'maximalised playground lore') to imagine a response to the confrontation.

Jon Trotman @JTrotman
Just seen major diva moment outside #fillmein screening. Journo had pass confiscated. Earpiece brigade are like waiters – don't mess! #cannes

Cook slouched back to his hotel, downed a room-service espresso and composed a resignation letter (five redrafts). Later that morning, in attendance at the festival office, he was assigned a mid-ranking but well-briefed press officer who explained that the 'altercation' was 'unacceptable' and that the festival security adopted a 'zero-tolerance approach to employee abuse'. Cook's accreditation would remain revoked and the case would be reviewed in late summer, with the possibility of a ban for future events.

In a dark corner of the festival coffee bar, Cook spent a miserable half-hour gnawing on a baguette and emailing the news of his pariah status to various editors and colleagues. It was a skilfully woven but overcooked tale of mistreatment, sprinkled with a few limp asides about legal advice and human-rights violation. He booked an evening flight home and logged in to his personal email.

There were five messages – a mail from Dennis Mountford, a profile alert from *PastLives.com*, and three spams with headers that made him splutter with laughter.

'Lesb1ans! get y0urself a tr1ple serv1ng of r0ast beef!'
'Like naughty teen doing accurate bl0wj0b?'
'Do you want women to spin around your b1g d1ck?'

Three taps of the 'delete' button scrolled the list down to Mountford's subject-line and message.

> Need a plan!
> Dor,
> I think we should get together again soon. Are you around next week? I had a direct message on PastLives! It said 'I enjoyed our mutual friend's performance on television. Hope to see you soon.' Dave is still not bothered but it's just too weird. Hope you're okay. Please get in touch mate. I've left you messages but they're going to voicemail. Is your phone alright? Are you abroad or something?
> Den

Cook logged in to *PastLives.com* via a link in the final email. The previously read notifications were greyed out, but a message at the top – from '@beth_s' –was marked in bold. He tapped the subject line ('No Subject') and the message expanded to reveal a blank content area. Cook gazed into the screen, baffled. A few seconds later, a narrow, dark-edged rectangle appeared at the top of the space and began to slowly extend, revealing an image that Cook recognised before it had even half-downloaded. It was a recent-looking street-level photograph of a sparsely populated car-park, next to the now undeveloped site where Bethesda First & Middle School used to be. At first, Cook thought it had been simply pasted from the Street View feature of Google Maps.

But he lifted the phone up close, to eye level, and saw that the sunlight, shining from behind the point of capture, had cast a tall, slender shadow across the pavement where the school gate would have been. The shadow's arms were raised to its face, elbows jutting, frozen as it framed and shot the picture.

Cook jumped to his feet and scurried over to the festival pigeon-holes, where official documents and promotional flyers were posted daily. Henry Gray was due to arrive that evening for his customary weekend of client-schmooze and party-crashing. Cook slid his resignation letter into Gray's section and began typing a text message to William Stone.

24

Out Of Mind

June, 1975

In the flat – Tom's flat – round the back of the *King's Head*, Cook sat cross-legged on the crusty PVC armchair, eating cereal, *Incredible Hulk* comic balanced across one knee. It was unnaturally early, but Tom was also up, standing topless over a tiny sink in the corner, daubing his chin and cheeks with shaving-foam. Cook finished a page and looked up. Tom's form startled him – bulge of midriff blubber hitched up by tracksuit-trouser drawstring, bare feet dusted with talcum powder in a vain attempt to obscure their persistent, sour, working-man musk. Lily had told Cook that Tom was a machine-worker at the pottery factory ('pot bank') where she also worked. He was tall, but top-heavy and distended, propped on stubby, shambling legs – a species apart from the spindly male teachers at Bethesda School. It was an hour before Lily's usual clock-in time, but today they had planned to all go in together, taking Cook along for 'a treat'. There was talk of driving a fork-lift, of hot meat pies and rejected plates ripe for smashing. Tom took a silver-handled razor to his cheeks. Cook winced at the shearing and scraping and tuned back in to his comic.

Then, Lily's footsteps on the stairs, a groggy good

morning and soon, tea and toast at the rickety table. Tom buttered a slice and dunked it into his mug. He slurped and nibbled at the soggy corner, grinning at Cook, drawing indulgent scowls from Lily, who lit a cigarette in riposte.

If this *was* his dad, then why did it all feel so new and strange and strained?

The women – including Lily – were arranged along columns of adjoining tables – side by side, elbow to elbow. Each had a rigid chair, an adjustable overhead lamp and a newspaper-lined workstation of stacked ceramics and paintbrush pots. There were many hands – dipping, dabbing, scrubbing, scoring – but it was far from light work. At the core of the factory, the kiln oven was loaded with clay-moulds and fired daily, forging hard-baked batches of household crockery to be cooled and scoured and inspected and wheeled in to the women, who would call on unskilled runners to refresh their table-stacks. This was the palatable top layer of hard labour – decorative, delicate, exclusively female. Behind the veil, beyond heavy double-doors and inch-thick strips of shredded plastic sheeting, the men toiled. Young men – placers – were sent in to the barely cooled ovens to retrieve the ware, emerging with bleeding noses and baking eyeballs. (Blurred vision was the daily standard, with premature blindness common before forty.) Not-so-young men – Tom included – operated the transfer machines, locking bowls and plates into treacherous grip-clips and imprinting them with template designs. Older men prepared the ingredients – confecting the liquid clay, stirring and pouring, flooding the moulds, smearing off the excess. The women received the men's dirty work and made it clean, their skill passed down from mother to daughter. They dipped and glazed and smoothed and glossed, dabbing cobalt-blue edging onto rotating plates, adorning bowls with freehand flora.

The factory, and hundreds more like it, had been built by the Victorians, with no regard for aesthetic or environmental health. Its titanic, bottle-shaped stone ovens loomed over ranks of modular terraces, shrouding the streets in smoke – emphysema and circulatory collapse a devil's dowry for the guaranteed livelihood of mass-market ceramics.

After a squeeze goodbye from Lily at her work-table, Cook was shepherded by Tom out of the decorating room through corridors of palettes stacked ceiling-high with glinting china, and into the thud and thunder of the machine shop, where the men hocked and hissed, clattered and muttered.

"There y'go, Dor – The Beast!"

Tom slid away a grubby sheet of canvas and unveiled his printing machine – an intestinal snarl of rods and clamps and pistons, vaguely concealed behind a front-plate control panel. He turned the key and jabbed a button, stirring the contraption into a waking tremor. Tom shrugged off his jacket and shouted over to a group of men browsing tabloids in a small break area.

"Daz!"

Darren Ray – taller and broader, but oddly diminished by an ill-fitting set of dark blue overalls – strolled over.

"This is my lad, Dorian."

Darren squeezed out a synthetic smile. "I know 'im. My brother's in his class at school. Butcher. I had him when I was there. Nasty fucker."

Cook expected a rebuke for the language, but Tom was busy rummaging through a set of tools. "Show him round for me, son. Stay inside, though. Not out to the yards!"

Darren's shoulders dropped slightly, but he kept his composure. Tom was a floor-worker with no formal management clout, but his alpha status was palpable.

"Alright. C'mon, Dorian."

Darren Ray led Cook out of the machine room, down a thin corridor lined with unglazed jugs and teapots, through a pair of heavy double-doors and out into a small courtyard which faced the central bottle oven. They followed the rim of the yard, sticking close to the main building, until they came to a tall brick partition where their only observers would be the workers emerging infrequently from a storage room below the oven. Darren leaned back against a chalky wall, beneath a 'No Smoking' sign, and lit a cigarette.

"You're not thinking of coming here after you finish school, are you?"

Cook had never considered the existence of anything after school, but, feeling the exposure of being alone with Darren, he played it cool. "Nah, don't think so."

Darren combined an exhale of smoke with a dismissive snigger. "What else y'going to do?"

"Dunno. I like telly. And films."

"No telly and film jobs down the dole office."

"I read books, as well."

Darren laughed. "Only place you'll be reading books is on the shitter between your shifts – probably labouring for your dad."

Cook dragged a stone across the wall, scouring through

a layer of smoky slime. As the factory glazed its product, so the process glazed the factory.

"Remember the day with the dogs?" said Darren, with a half-smile, as if wistfully recalling a moment of great joy.

"Yeah. That wasn't very nice."

Darren looked down at Cook, his smile broadening. "Some things aren't nice, Dorian. But they have to be done. Fuckers over there, placing the ware in that boiling-hot kiln room. That's definitely not nice, but they get it done."

They gazed across the courtyard. A tall placer in white apron and elbow-length asbestos gloves was leaning into an overloaded trolley of unfired plates, wrestling it closer to the entrance.

"Your dad isn't nice," said Cook, cautiously.

Darren drew on his cigarette, tilted back his head and, with venom, spat out a geyser of vertical smoke. "No. He's a cunt. Drinks too much. He knocks my mum about, as well."

Surprised – and relieved – at the complicity, Cook pushed a little harder.

"I'm never going to drink."

Darren chuckled at this, but then darkened and turned to look down at Cook directly. "Johnny's alright. I think he likes you. No-one fucking likes him, though!"

"I helped him with some bullies."

Darren nodded. "I know. Plenty more where they came from."

Later, Cook joined Tom, Darren and the other machine workers for pies, Tizer and off-colour banter about 'wenches'. An obese, neckless foreman called Phil led Cook out to the seconds room, where he was allowed to hurl misshapen plates at the wall like frisbees. Tom joined them with cricket bat and safety goggles, and Cook swung at crockery 'bowled' by Phil, pulverising jugs in mid-air and edging the heftier dishes, sending them tailspinning, intact, to shatter across the floor. As they rested, Tom and Phil drank tea from their flasks and Cook ate lemon-curd sandwiches prepared by Esther.

"Can I have a go on the trucks?"

Phil and Tom glanced at each other. Phil, who Tom had cheerfully called his 'boss-man', clarified. "Not until you're a bit older, mate. Fork-lifts aren't like Tonkas. They're hard to drive."

"Can I see the kiln room, then?"

"There was an accident, Dorian," said Tom. "A few weeks ago. We're not allowed."

Cook separated the slices of his sandwich and peeked in at the thickly spread butter and syrupy curd.

"What happened?"

"They fired up when one of the younger placers was still in there," said Phil. "He must have been stuck or fainted or something."

"Might have been hit by a brick," said Tom, staring into his tea. They're falling apart, them things."

Phil shook his head. "It's happened before, son."

Cook thought of the man waking up to his own cremation. He hoped the heat had killed him before he knew anything or felt any pain.

Darren Ray and a couple of other younger workers from the machine shop wandered in. Darren, annoyed at the lack of fresh seconds to smash, had overheard the conversation and offered a petulant aside.

"He'd been in there for a while, they're saying."

"Daz…"

"Yeah. It was a morning firing – after the Bank Holiday. Fuck me! Imagine that – stuck in there for days, total darkness, nothing to eat. Then you get baked alive."

At the weekend, Cook was picked up at Esther's by his great aunt and uncle, and driven to a local National Trust park in a dark brown Triumph Toledo. In the back seat, he was allowed to have the window open a little while his great grandparents chainsmoked and chattered about the grouse and the heather. As usual, halfway through the journey, he was given tablets for car-sickness, washed down with bottled orange-juice.

To Cook, the 'park' was suspiciously similar to a ragged sweep of fields and trees – no swings or seesaw or roundabout or Witch's Hat. Once the Toledo had been fussily wedged into a muddy verge, Cook was first to escape, stumbling free of his carcinogenic car-arrest to guzzle on the zesty air.

They swished through grass as tall as Cook himself, tottered down into a wooded valley and joined a path by a trout stream which tinkled out of sight. Cook hopped in and out of cow hoof-prints and secretly picked red berries, pocketing them to present to Esther later. An endless hour or so into the walk, Cook's uncle triumphantly raised his hiking stick.

"Look there, Dorian! That's Odin's Cave!"

At the peak of the tallest crag, a symmetrical archway framed the entrance to a natural cavern, large enough to be seen from the valley floor. A log-lined staircase had been etched into the path leading up to the cave, and Cook, craving any kind of thrill, bolted for it.

"There used to be a railway line here, you know – when I was your age."

But Cook was already out of range of his uncle's words and quickly climbing.

"Don't rush off too far ahead, Dorian!"

He scampered up the narrow steps, shoving past elderly ramblers. At the top, the cave entrance – thirty-feet high – swallowed him, and he scaled the angled, rain-glossy rock-base on all fours. He rested by a crack in the seam – a slitted window on the surrounding peaks and farms – before pushing deeper through the darkness and settling into a dank but warm chamber unsoiled by leaking light.

"Dorian?"

His uncle's voice was a whisper from another world. In here, he was sealed and concealed, safe and unreachable – untouchable, unhurtable, invisible. He could remove himself from existence, opt out of the present, freeze the future, deny the past. He tuned in to the surrounding sounds – rattling rainwater, squealing dogs, snarling engines. It was both a thrill and a chill to discover that the world continued to turn without him at its centre.

"Dorian! Come on, son! You can't hide forever."

25

Retreat

"MUMMIES," DECLARED ALFIE, "HAVE got bandages instead of skin and vampires can't come out when it's sunny!"

Gina, whisking something. "They should get some mummy bandages, then!"

Alfie, after a few seconds' thought and a nibble at the edge of his cheese toastie. "They can't, because they are in different worlds!"

Cook clunked a teaspoon into the peak of his boiled egg, marvelling at the complexity of the fracture. Outside, June simmered, in contrast to the domestic frost. Earlier, in bed, at one of their increasingly regular morning summits, Gina had again insisted that they needed 'a break'. Cook, keen to emphasise the temporary aspect, rebranded it a 'trial separation'.

"It's not a trial," snapped Gina. "We're talking about a real separation."

"Yes," sighed Cook, always too eager to tinker with semantics. "For a trial *period*. It's not to see if we want to stay separated, it's to get a sense of how it feels to be separated, to get things into perspective."

Gina nodded, muting her scepticism with a sip of tea. Cook held the moment. He flipped onto his front, head in pillow, then onto his back, covering his face with the duvet – always the comfort and calm of the indifferent dark.

"Do you still love me, Gina?"

Quickly. "Of course, I do. I always will. I just can't *live* with you. Not at the moment."

To her surprise, he absorbed this with relative grace. "I'm hoping I can live with myself."

She spluttered on the tea. "Where's that from?"

"Hmm?"

"It sounds like a line from a film."

They laughed – a tactical solidarity.

"I dunno. Just my head."

Tension unblocked, the plan emerged quickly, lubricated by fifteen years of finely evolved inter-dependency. As with all long-standing couples, they carried an instinct for each other's phoney-tough defences – the tics and tactics, sulks and blusters. At the best of times, this bond was empowering – a hardy symbiosis. But it could also be used as ammunition. Before he met Gina, Cook had fluttered from partner to partner, always alighting at the point where familiarity threatened to mutate into contempt. He suspected that most relationships, if left to endure, simply drifted into a state of mutually assured destruction, where the focus switched from desire and support to the careful cultivation of a status quo, with each partner equally convinced they had the most to lose from a break-up. Now, here, this was confirmed – the shift of imbalance was complete, and Cook could no longer convince his wife of the benefits of his company.

For the sake of Alfie's stability, Cook would move out and live, relatively close, at the recently vacated flat of a university friend who was on an overseas work placement. Cook's usual improvised approach to planning always seemed to improve when his own well-being was at risk. As the marriage had deflated over the last year, he had secured his friend's flat as a housesitting gig, with a vague intention of using it as a bolt-hole ("Shag-shed!" – Will Stone). Now, it was to be his pre-furnished point of exile – for six months. He would be welcome at home, but was expected to give Gina notice of visits, in order to 'manage Alfie's expectations'. Cook had declined the offer of Alfie staying with him at weekends, claiming that he didn't want to confuse things. Secretly, he objected to what was clearly the core of this idea – a rehearsal for permanence.

Alfie finished his toastie, dragged his finger through a swirl of ketchup at the side of the plate and sucked away the sauce.

"Can I take my scooter to school?"

Gina looked over to Cook. He silently signed off the request with a grin.

"Okay, darling. Go and get it from the shed – and brush your teeth!"

As his son scampered past, Cook grabbed him for a squeeze. But Alfie stiffened and strained and wrestled away, dashing out to the garden without looking back.

"He's just a bit excited," said Gina. "I wouldn't get anything, either."

On cue, Cook approached her with arms wide. She abandoned the whisk and edged into an uneasy embrace, nuzzling in close and speaking into his shoulder – as ever, displacing emotional discomfort with practicality.

"Alfie's got a sleepover tonight. Maybe you shouldn't go

until the weekend. I have to work. It means you won't have to pick him up, drop him off and then leave."

Cook was startled at her acceleration of thought, how she already seemed comfortable with the new emphasis on logistics over emotion. He gave her a parting squeeze and looked down into her eyes, ornate with sadness. She turned her head to the side, avoiding his gaze, but he mirrored the movement and lightly cupped her chin with both hands, tilting it up to make eye contact unavoidable.

"It's not forever. Don't worry."

Cook's phone bleeped, puncturing the moment.

Gina offered a broad, forced smile and shook her head – to confirm or deny? She ducked away from the deathly cuddle and followed Alfie outside.

Cook took out his phone and navigated to the *PastLives.com* inbox. There was one message, with no subject header. He tapped it.

what goes around, comes around
D

26
Now Approaching Midnight

December, 1975

Every Christmas Eve, Cook was routinely woken at 11.30pm by Lily and Esther for a bleary force-march to the Catholic Church near Bethesda School. He trailed along, numb-limbed and heavy-lidded, behind his mother and grandmother as they pitched and listed, slurred and cackled, laden with port and lemon. Today, they were joined by Tom and Uncle Russell, both generously refreshed with the brackish bitter they had once insisted Cook sample – to his disgust and their delight. As they approached the steep incline at the top of the oil-works road, there was a synchronised stumble-and-stop, as all four adults seemed to simultaneously doubt their ability to tackle the challenge. They milled and fretted like refusing horses until Cook, laughing, shouldered into the back of Russell, who lurched forward, delivering a shove to Tom which sent him wheeling into front-runners Esther and Lily – and momentum was restored.

The church was deep and tall and splendid: kaleidoscopic stained-glass windows; looming walls lined with solemn effigies clutching emblem shields; a colossal, vaulted apse with rim of hand-woven tapestry. Despite his sleepless delirium, Cook was always jolted by the supernatural contrast as he slipped away from the scruffy streets, inhaled by the sighing organ. He could faintly remember the subject of the tapestry from a school trip to the church (Mary being crowned Queen of Heaven?) and knew a little of communion and confession, but he had no real understanding of the human context. It was all just a soothing escape – a temporary drift.

"Dor-Dor!"

As Cook shuffled into a pew, he felt sticky hands tug at his jumper. In the row behind, Rebecca Goldstraw squirmed on her mother's lap, arms outstretched and flailing, reaching for Cook, trying to hurdle the wooden seat-back and fling herself into his care. Lisa sat beside her mother, hair parted and woven into two shoulder-length pigtails. Her light-brown eyes were cloudy with fatigue, but she offered Cook a wide, sincere smile and, as usual, his stomach flipped.

"C'mere then, young lady!"

Uncle Russell hooked his hands into Rebecca's armpits and raised her up and over into the small space at the end of Cook's bench. She immediately set about scaling Russell's knees in a renewed effort to get to Cook, but Lisa diverted her with a chocolate bar, posted through a carved slot in the back of the seat. Cook watched as Rebecca investigated the lurid pink chocolate, nibbling suspiciously at the edge. He saw that the scar on her chin had now become a feature – an embossed blemish which underlined the base of her face.

The congregation rose and, prompted by the organist's impatient stabbing at a pair of opening chords, mumbled its way into song. Cook normally mouthed and mimed his way through, eyes on the floor. But this time he knew the words, having practiced the hymn at school assembly for the past few weeks.

> *In the bleak midwinter, frosty wind made moan*
> *Earth stood hard as iron, water like a stone*
> *Snow had fallen, snow on snow, snow on snow*
> *In the bleak midwinter, long ago*

As the song ended, and the organ reverb receded to deferential silence, Cook heard a familiar sniffing and snuffling. He looked across the aisle and saw John Ray, with father Frank, brother Darren and – half out of Cook's eyeline – a small, pale woman in a thick fur hat. Frank and Darren stared ahead, stern and savage, while John flicked and dabbed at his nose with the blue-and-white handkerchief. Cook was suddenly light-headed with a loathing that seemed to have no source or anchor but which enclosed the whole family – sickly classmate, hateful brother, brutal father, mousey mother. John pocketed the handkerchief and turned his head, catching Cook's eye. He offered a dutiful smile of recognition, his bleached features an eerie beacon in the unsteady candlelight. Cook pretended not to notice and shifted his gaze to the altar and the priest's halting eulogy.

After the service, the tipsy worshippers hobbled away to reconvene outside, on a raised porch by the front doors. Tom was the first to light up, dragging deeply on an unfiltered cigarette and respectfully expelling the smoke away from the church, high into the frosty air. (Lily flapped at it, coughing theatrically.) There were hair-ruffles and cheek-pinches, overlong bear-hugs and hardly necessary Merry Christmases. As he searched for Lisa, Cook was startled by an eruption of bellowing, libidinous laughter from Tom and Phil – the man who, it seemed, had signed off on the reject-smashing session at the pot-bank. The shock rattled Cook's bones and made him crave his bed and his hot water bottle. He wandered away from the group, around the side of the building.

Rebecca Goldstraw was crouched over a small puddle near the church's side entrance. She had removed her shoe – a pink, buckled sandal – and was repeatedly filling it with water, emptying it back into the puddle, and refilling it again. Cook walked towards her, away from the huddle and hustle of the porch. He was surprised and calmed by how quickly the adult world faded – how it slid backward as he moved forward, through the untended scrubland at the fringes of the church grounds, into the early-morning dark.

As he approached Rebecca, she looked up and, overcome by excitement, raised the shoe above her head and slammed it into the surface of the puddle, splattering her grinning face with muddy water.

Cook chuckled. "Oh no! What a mess!"

"Dory!" squealed Rebecca.

Cook flinched, but was grateful at least for the progression from 'Dor-Dor'.

"Look!"

Rebecca lunged for Cook's hand and yanked him away from the puddle. She pointed at a tangle of bramble near the entrance to a small graveyard.

"Comic!"

Cook knelt down, in the gloom, on the frosted grass,

and reached into the weed-patch carefully, wary of thorns. He pulled out a flash of colour – a torn-away section of a magazine. It was faded and dew-matted, with creases worn into perforated edges. There was a front cover – mostly legible – with a few relatively unsoiled front-section pages. The cover image featured a young woman, shot from the side, wearing white underwear, stockings and suspender belt. She was topless, with her right breast exposed, nipple strategically obscured by the elbow of her right arm. Her head was turned – painted eyes glaring into camera, shoulder-length brown hair blow-dried and centre-parted. In her right-hand, she balanced a hand-held microphone, grille close to her open mouth. A cover-flash announced:

FREE LOVE POSITIONS! LP RECORD INSIDE!

As Cook's eyes adjusted, he could make out a calligraphic logo, top-right *('The Journal Of Love')* and a rack of wordy cover-lines which traced the 'S' shape of the woman's shoulders and back.

SEE YOUR RANDY COVERSTAR IN INTIMATE ACTION WITH HER BLOKE! In mouth-watering close-up full colour!
    YES, HEAR HER TELL YOU ALL ABOUT HER FAVOURITE LOVE POSITIONS & INTIMATE KICKS! While she's hard at it on record!

Cook ruffled through the pages, browsing the tableaux of bodies – scrawny, dumpy, sweaty, always hairy. He gaped at their shaggy plumage – the furry chests and frizzy chins, the flourishing pubic afros. Faces leered and grimaced, as if in alarm or pain. Tongues extended, probing at overlit flesh. Unclipped nails clawed into cellulite.

"Becky?" Lisa's voice, calling her sister.

"*Rebecca!*" Mrs Goldstraw, more urgent.

Cook buried the magazine deep inside the bramble, but the density of the weeds made it difficult to obscure.

"Dory!" said Rebecca. "Funny lady!"

Adults were arriving – Tom, Phil, Mrs Goldstraw. Even Esther had made the effort, accompanied by Uncle Russell. Rebecca was scooped into her mother's arms.

"How many times have I told you? Stay close to me!"

Mrs Goldstraw was half-sobbing with fury and relief. She turned to Cook. "What do you think you're doing? Bringing her down here? She's only three!"

"*He's* only nine!" bellowed Uncle Russell, loud enough to make Mrs Goldstraw cringe.

"Russell!" (Esther).

"I didn't bring her here!" said Cook. "I found her!"

Lily appeared. "Dorian? What's going on?"

"*Comic!*"

Rebecca writhed in her mother's arms, pointing down at the weeds. Russell stamped at the brittle stems, beating out an opening. As he reached in and retrieved the magazine, Rebecca reached out – to *The Journal Of Love* – with both arms. Russell lifted it out of her range, and Mrs Goldstraw snatched it up. She briefly noted the content and jerked away her hands, as if the magazine had suddenly burst into flames. It sploshed into the puddle next to Rebecca's shoe.

"Dorian, where did you get that from?" Mrs Goldstraw's tone remained indignant, but with a softer, enquiring edge.

More adults gathered – murmuring, clucking, tutting, their alcoholic breath swirling.

"I found it!"

"Where?" (Lily).

"In there! Well – Rebecca found it and showed me."

Mrs Goldstraw scoffed loudly at this.

"He's nine years old!" (Lily again).

Cook looked up and searched the spectators' faces, looking for Tom – but he was disappointed to see his dad leaning in to Phil's ear, whispering something that sparked a snigger.

"Well then, he should certainly know better than this!"

"Than what?"

"Than showing dirty books to a young child!"

Barely suppressed laughter from Tom and Phil.

"It's just as well," announced Mrs Goldstraw to the crowd, "that we're moving away from here!"

Cook stumbled forward and snatched the magazine out of her hand.

"Dorian!" Uncle Russell made a grab for the pages, but Cook was too quick.

"Alright, then. Look!"

Cook kicked at the grass by the bramble. He dug in the heel of his shoe, scraped a small pit in the soil and drove the magazine into the hole, mashing it down as deep as it would go. Uncle Russell reached down to pull it back out, but recoiled as Cook frantically smothered the paper with a scattering of large stones.

"See! Look! It's not mine! It's gone, it's gone! I got rid of it!!!"

27

Old Acquaintance

IN HIS LAST WEEK at *Widescreen*, Cook had expected his impending absence to be conspicuous. But, apart from the odd email expressing – with questionable sincerity – how much of a privilege it had been to work with him, there seemed to be little pre-emptive melancholy from either direct colleagues or wider work associates. He was presented with a *Modern Toss* leaving card – a scrawled homunculus shouting into a telephone mouthpiece, with a speech-bubble exclaiming, 'I can't come in to work today, so fuck off!' It had been signed by all the staff, apart from publisher Laura who, perhaps strategically, was away 'on a course'. Most signatures were accompanied with sly little tessellations – doodles, emoticons, kisses, slashed dividers. It was a florid but duty-bound display and Cook looked forward to abandoning the card to a litter-bin once he'd anointed his exit at the bar opposite the office.

It was hardly a conscientious demob. He dawdled through a nominal to-do list and tinkered with an over-detailed handover document, to be passed on to freelancer Nigel Smith, who would cover while the magazine found a permanent replacement. Smith, ever the predator, had scented Cook's lameness well before his *Talking Pictures* appearance, and had been openly circling since the tetchy editorial meeting. Now, on a salary hike after dropping his retainer to *Movie*, he swooped.

Writing came – small reviews, a think piece on the futility of certification in the digital age, a pithy side-bar on Bergman. But the words oozed out, overbaked and redundant, to be shuffled into boilerplate sentences. He was fading – from view, from thought, from connection. Even the technology was tired of him. When his security pass began to insist on multiple swipes, the IT guy questioned the need for anything more than a temporary replacement, and Cook concurred with minimal protest. (Meekness, he felt, was an attitude he would be wise to embrace.) He sensed a collective holding of breath – an impatience for his influence to drift into history. He had become the guest who would have to leave before the party could relax.

At the pub, his backpack bulging with sentimental stationery and gifted hardbacks, Cook chaired a stilted conference with a modest pack of colleagues and industry allies. *Widescreen* art director Warren Plant demolished several bottles of artisan ale and, to Cook's relief, hijacked the farewell banter with a frank assessment of his current girlfriend's sexual appetite.

"She says she's 'OCD'," slurred Plant, his fermented rasp barely an inch from Cook's ear. "And I tell you, Dorian, she is fucking *thorough!*"

Cook pushed out a guffaw, but sex was now lost on him and he was lost to it. The penis-enlargement email had recently ended, in a near overnight shutdown. He had found solace in its absurdity – the offers of swollen girth and surging volume had become more than just commentary on his insecurities. But as the backbeat of his dread quickened from pulse to patter, the sudden silence carried a ghastly implication – his untouchability was now so comprehensive, he was being spurned by spam-bots.

Most of the attendees drifted away, leaving only back-slaps and cliches. ("You'll be able to enjoy films more now you don't have to write about them!")

Last to leave – oddly – was Henry Gray.

"Anyone would think you're the one who's moving on, Henry," said Cook, as his Ed-in-Chief lolled over an empty glass, childishly twanging his bottom-lip against the rim.

"You're not 'moving on', Dorian," said Gray, lifting his head. "You're escaping. Ends as new beginnings – that's all bollocks."

Cook winced away the dregs of his pint. "Are you still excited about film, Henry? Or is it just a job?"

"I *love* films," said Gray, a little defensive. "Good guy kills the bad guy, saves the girl. But I can't stand 'film'. Too much fucking reality."

"And perspective?" said Cook, grinning at the *Spinal Tap* reference, which was lost on Gray who, keen to underline the profundity of his sign-off words, was already rising to leave.

Then, a handshake – too firm and lingering – and, echoing the rehearsed consolation of Cook's GP, that shoulder double-tap.

Cook stayed for another, wallowing in the solitude of a dark and unpopular corner near the toilet door. He pulled a freesheet from a wall-rack and flattened the front page across his table. Towards the end of the front section, slotted into a page-deep side-column, he found what he feared.

ELLIE: POLICE PRESSED ON ENQUIRY

Detectives investigating the disappearance of Eleanor Finch, 38, have been questioned on when the case might be reclassified from one of Missing Persons to Murder.

"Eleanor's last contact with her family was three months ago," explained Detective Chief Inspector John Barrett at an emotional press conference on Tuesday. "But we are continuing to piece together her movements in the hope of information which may help us understand why a woman with two young children would suddenly choose to not return to her home."

With Ms. Finch's ex-husband Gareth, 43, at his side, DCI Barrett fielded strong questioning on his force's progress.

"To date, we are obviously concerned that Eleanor may have been the victim of crime, but we have no direct evidence to confirm this and we will continue to pursue significant enquiries with friends and associates in a bid to shed some light on what might have happened to her.

"Sometimes, adults who go missing may wish for their location to remain anonymous, and they do have that right which we must respect. I have no reason to believe this is the case here. Regardless of what has caused Eleanor's disappearance, we need to find her urgently and give her family some answers. It's vital that people call us if they know anything, no matter how insignificant it might seem."

Cook gulped at his drink. There was nothing insignificant about this for him. He stared at the police-issue picture of a young-looking, near-forty woman leaning self-consciously against a door-frame, smiling but sad-eyed, long brown hair stacked over one shoulder. Their correspondence had never evolved into a meeting, but there was something familiar about her expression – a hint of accusation, a knowing glow of sympathy. For a second, he was carried away and gently settled alongside her, in fragile limbo, hovering out of reach, neither dead nor alive. Like Cook, Eleanor had slowly degraded – from earthly constant to apparition of thought. He hoped there was still life inside him – and her, despite Detective Chief Inspector John Barrett and his unsuccessful enquiries.

Cook's phone convulsed against the wooden table-top. A placeholder image of a silhouetted head-and-shoulders appeared on the screen, below the words 'Dennis Mountford'. Anxiety stampeded over him. As the phone ground out its silent alarm, Cook gathered his coat and backpack and squirmed through a cluster of baying broker types. Outside, he tapped the answer icon and cautiously lifted the phone to his ear. There was a voice – Dennis Mountford's voice, spluttering, half-sobbing against the background drone of traffic.

"Dorian! Dor! Is that you? Someone's been to Jake's school! They were talking to Jake and his friends and one of the older kids said something and he left."

"A man?"

"What? Yes! A man!"

"Did the kids say what he looked like?"

"No! I don't know. I'm rushing back home. I was at a job with no signal. I'll find out."

"What did he want?"

"He was asking Jake about me. Said he knows me."

"It's probably nothing."

"*It is not fucking 'nothing', Dorian!*"

28

Grounded

May, 1976

It was a Raleigh – three-speed, *derailleur* gears, drop handlebars, dark orange frame, and the word 'Chopper' in lemon-yellow, pasted along the lower tube. Cook's annual pester for the bike kicked in sometime around late autumn, as regular as the clocks going back. The hints to Esther and Lily had grown heavier by the year – pointing out other children who had recently evolved from scooters, pushing the kitchen-table chairs into a line to form a 'play-bike' and, most recently, leaving torn-out pages from the Kays catalogue slotted inside Esther's *TV Times*. On Christmas Day 1975, the "We'll see…" refrain had finally delivered his own private fiery chariot.

Cook rode it in the morning before school – a menace to milk-floats. He rode it to school, at speed, whooshing by the pushchairs, grazing the shuffling cliques. He came 'home for dinner', so he could ride it more casually, trundling around the play-park path, gliding down empty streets. He rode it home after school and, on this day, he kept riding – to Dennis Mountford's house, where the two boys drank grapefruit squash, listened to 'heavy rock' records and plotted a robbery.

"You could stick it under your coat," said Mountford. "Easy. My mate gets loads like that."

"I'm not putting your stuff under my coat!"

"Okay, then. You get the lamp and I'll get a pump."

"Lamp will be harder to hide."

Mountford laughed. "We won't get caught, Dor. It's a massive place and we'll be too quick."

They cycled, side by side, parallel, fanning out then drifting back in close. They cycled up steep Lowther Street, to test their gears. They cycled to the gravel wasteground at the edge of the play-park path and – heads down, highest gear – raced each other, completing three full circuits before laying the bikes flat and collapsing by the main gate. Mountford's bike was a metallic blue Grifter – better suited to his older, rangier frame. The fit of Cook's Chopper was a little generous, but he was still too smitten to covet – he wanted to grow into his own bike, not be big and old enough for someone else's.

"Hi, Dorian!"

Lisa Goldstraw skipped off the roundabout and swayed over to the gate, gripping the bars, poking her face through. Cook, mortified at being caught in a moment of recuperation, leapt to his feet.

"Guess what? No more school for me now!"

"How come?"

"We're going to Canada in a few days. Emigrating."

Cook had known and prepared for this, but had kept it safely shut away and suspended – an abstract unpleasantness, far away in the foggy future.

"Wow. Brilliant! When are you coming back? Are you going on a plane?"

Lisa laughed. "Of course we're going on a plane! It would take ages by boat. And we're not coming back. We're going to live there. My mum's family are there."

Cook crouched and sifted through a stack of pebbles by the gate foundations. "So, you're not coming back – ever?"

"Don't think so."

"Are you still at your house?"

"No. We're living with my auntie."

This was a major setback for Cook's long-term plan – to marry Lisa and live in her enormous house when her mum died.

"Is it because of me?"

"What?"

"Rebecca. The magazine."

"Of course it isn't!"

Cook rolled the pebbles, one by one, into the hole that held one of the gate's support posts.

"It's not that far. I could come and visit you."

"Yeah."

"Kissy-kissy!"

A group of boys who Cook recognised from Lisa's class ambled from the roundabout to a perilous-looking rocking-horse in the park's far corner. As they passed by the gate, they giggled and aimed lip-smacking noises at Cook and Lisa.

Cook jumped up. "Got to go for my tea."

Lisa nodded. "Is that your new bike? It's really nice."

"Yeah," said Cook. "The orange one."

A gaping pause. The scene was suddenly drained of flavour. Cook wandered back to his bike and mounted it, hoping he looked vaguely cowboyish – aloof and unhurtable. He pushed away without looking back, reclaiming the betrayal. Mountford had to hurry to catch him and keep pace.

"Dor! You're not going home yet, are you?"

"No! But I couldn't say we're going nicking, could I?"

At the far end of Lowther Street, Cook and Mountford slowed at the sight of a small figure, cautiously wheeling his bike along by the kerb, in the gutter, despite the absence of cars. The weather was mild, but John Ray's top half was smothered in heavy winter clothes – duffel-coat, padded jumper, scarf – while his lower body had to make do with an ill-fitting pair of flimsy polyester flares. He looked like he'd been dressed remotely, by two separate people in different climates. Mountford called to him.

"John! Come with us to the new Tesco!"

Ray glanced over as he dragged his junior racer onto the pavement. He pivoted the handlebars a couple of times, flinching at the squeak. Cook pulled up alongside him.

"Y'need some oil, John."

John Ray stayed silent, keeping his gaze fixed on the far side of the street. He squeezed and unsqueezed his brake handles.

"Do you want us to get you some?" said Mountford, hanging back, circling.

"No, thank you."

Ray looked up and, at last, submitted to eye contact. His pupils had lost a little of their redness, but Cook was startled by how bright and white his forehead dazzled beneath that waxy hair. The heat around his nose and cheeks caused a subtle blood-flush below eye-level, but the upper half of his head was so parched and colourless it seemed to have been dusted in flour. He glanced from Cook to Mountford and back again, accusing eyes staring from the centre of tear-streaked sockets.

"You alright?" Cook posed the question carefully, but it made Ray startle and he pulled out his handkerchief, blowing his nose to displace the agitation.

"Yes. I'm fine. I can't come with you."

The voice – immaculate enunciation but so slender and frail and fleeting.

"It'll be a laugh. Go on!"

"I can't."

He was steadying his bike, turning his back, planning his escape.

"Don't be a chicken, John!" offered Mountford. "We'll look after you!"

But John Ray was done. He climbed aboard and squeaked away, even less convincing than Cook as aloof and unhurtable.

At the new Tesco, Cook and Mountford were detained by a tall and terrifying store detective as they stupidly tried to leave by the fire exit. Mountford had slotted a long, thin tyre-pump under his jumper, palpably impeding his movement. Cook had poorly concealed a bulky detachable head-lamp under his jacket. In a windowless side-office, the store detective smoked gravely and made several phone calls. Cook cried, Mountford held off until his mother arrived. Between sobs, Cook kept asking the same question, over and over.

"Can we go yet?"

The store detective smoked and dialed and typed and shook his head.

Two uniformed policemen eventually appeared and took some details. When Cook finally found the strength to wrench his gaze from the carpet, he saw that one of the policemen was Frank Ray.

("I can't.")

With Mountford's mother and Esther present, Frank Ray explained that the boys were expected to attend the station for an interview within a week, and that their case may be referred to a 'juvenile liaison committee'. Outside, Esther kept her furious distance – five body-lengths ahead of Cook, who wheeled his bike slowly and sniffed and snivelled all the way home.

"Am I going to prison, nana?"

"No. Shame! It might teach you a bloody lesson!"

In the house, Cook hurried through the front-room and tried to dash up the stairs, but Uncle Russell was ready for him and barred the way.

"Dorian. You crackpot! What was that for? What a silly, stupid thing to do!"

"The other boy made me do it!" lied Cook, through a fresh downpour of snot and tears.

"Dorian, it's *stealing!* When you go out now, you're not to go past the end of the street. And you're not going out on that bike."

"*What?* How long for?"

"Until I say so, Dorian! If you go past the end of the street or take the bike out, then I'll make sure it gets sold – to someone who can appreciate it!"

"I do appreciate it!"

Esther came in from the kitchen. "Well, you've got a funny way of showing it!"

"It's not fair!"

Cook pushed past Uncle Russell, thudded up the stairs and dived into the corner closet, shutting the door on it all. The darkness absorbed him – cool and calm and dispassionate. It was above ranting and crying and knew nothing of emigration or juvenile liaison committees. It was the only judge he respected.

In the morning, the smell of poached egg on toast lured Cook downstairs. There had been no familiar call from Esther – she had simply laid the food out on the table before leaving for her Saturday job with a sulky door-slam. He ate and watched cartoons, closely observed by Rusty who was eventually rewarded with a few crusts and a dollop of unwanted egg. He slouched out into the back yard and felt a flex of anger at the sight of his hard-won bicycle, propped against the toilet wall, temporarily decommissioned. On top of this private pain, there was also the public shame, the exposure. PC Frank Ray would surely tell his sons and the thwarted shoplifting story would spread and breed around the school, growing more lurid and shameful in the telling.

Cook climbed up onto the metal dustbin and hopped over the wall, down into the cobbled back entry. Since Uncle Russell's inclusion zone extended only to the end of the street, the old butcher's shop was now an outer marker. As ever, Cook approached it with a mix of fear and fascination, but since it was now the edge of his world, the urge to explore had grown more seductive. If he could conquer the fear, it would surely make an incredible den, and, because other people would have been too scared to go in, there might even be abandoned treasures. He crouched down by the 'Trespassers Will Be Prosecuted' sign and wriggled through the gap by the gate's broken hinge.

The builder's equipment was unchanged – wheelless wheelbarrow, scaffold tubes, metal sheeting. It felt almost theatrical – an ossified exhibit, more arranged than abandoned. Emboldened by outrage at his confinement, Cook aimed a kick at the wooden panel blocking the hole in the brickwork and it flapped over, invitingly, to one side. The opening was roomier than the gate-hinge gap and he barely had to stoop to pass through into a small back-room overrun by chalky chunks of masonry. The walls had shed enormous dunes of plaster and formed a central pyramid of powdery grime. Slender shafts of daylight poked in through gaps in the window-boards, casting a sepulchral shimmer over the clusters of bottle-shards and faded beer-cans. He digested the silence and stepped through a battered door-frame into a larger, less cluttered main hall which served as a central chamber to several box-rooms, all now doorless. The fittings had been mostly hacked away and the floor's uneven concrete crunched and crumbled underfoot. It was brighter in here, with light leaking in from an exposed staircase which led to the first-floor window – the one from which Cook had been dared to wave on the day they had retrieved John Ray's school-bag. Stumbling through a patch of greasy polythene, Cook approached the staircase. He would rehearse the dare – climb to the window, admire the view, hopefully call to someone he knew. But at the bottom step, he peeked through a split in a splintered door and spotted another staircase winding down into darkness, out of sight. To a cellar? If there was treasure here, surely it would be down there. He pushed at the door, surprised at its weight. It swung open, lower hinge screeching in protest.

Cook could only see the first five or six steps. The others melted into the gloom, if they were even there at all. He edged forward, hovering a foot just beyond the threshold of the door-frame. From somewhere down below, something groaned – a swelling, extended rumble, somewhere between pain and fury. Cook turned and tripped and leapt away, skidding on the polythene, crashing through the panel, then outside and running, running, running.

29

Suffer the Living

"MR COOK?"

"Yes."

"I'm Inspector Ramshaw, this is Constable Whitcombe. Would you mind if we came inside and asked you a few questions?"

Cook was underdressed for the occasion – grimy REM T-shirt, elasticated tracksuit trousers, no socks. It was 8.30pm on Saturday night and he was about to settle in for a punishing double-bill of Bergman and Preminger. The doorbell had interrupted a ranting hunt for the TV instruction manual. He had been freeloading here for a week, but he had not yet adjusted to his absent friend's taste for minimalist electronics.

The policemen were positioned a respectful couple of steps beyond the doorstep, offering weak smiles and photo ID.

"What's this about? I'm just…"

Ramshaw's smile broadened into something approaching sympathy. "It's just a few quick questions. We won't keep you for too long. It'd be helpful if we could discuss it indoors."

The rhetoric in the request was now clear. Cook stepped

aside and the officers entered, taking turns to shuffle their feet on the doormat. Cook's phone vibrated – silently – in his saggy pocket.

"Have a seat in the…"

"Sitting-room?" smiled Ramshaw, with a calculated brevity that only made Cook more nervous.

"Yes. Can I get you anything? I was just making tea."

"No, thank you. As I say, we won't be too long."

Cook skulked into the kitchen and checked his phone. There was a missed call from Gina, followed up with a text message.

Police were here! They want to talk to you about something. I had to give them the address. Hope there's nothing wrong! x

Cook pocketed the phone and carried his mug of tea into the sitting-room, where Ramshaw – lanky, smooth-bald – and Whitcombe – shorter, squinty – sat side by side, on the sofa. As he sunk carefully into a facing armchair and clanked the drink down a little too hard on the glass coffee table, Cook rewound his memory through vaguely illicit recent events – cut corners, wily misdemeanours, downloaded BitTorrent files. Perhaps it was something to do with the playground fight? Maybe the Mountford/Brereton thing? Since Mountford's panicked call on his leaving day, Cook had deleted the contact, erased past messages, avoided *PastLives.com* and generally gone entirely dark on his… friend? Old schoolmate? Shoplifter comrade? Surely this couldn't be the re-opening of a cold-case – a crackdown on unresolved petty youth crime from the '70s.

Whitcombe flipped open a notebook. Ramshaw did the talking.

"Mr Cook, are you familiar with a young woman by the name of Eleanor Finch?"

"I've seen the news, yes. Has she been found yet?"

Cook thought he saw a sidelong glance pass between the two officers. Whitcombe, finally, found his voice. "No. Are you acquainted? Do you know each other?"

"I recognise the name."

"Dorian…"

Ramshaw resumed control. The switch to first-name terms was clearly intended to unsettle.

"Have you ever *met* Ms Finch?"

"No. Of course not. Why would you think that?"

The tea was too hot to drink but Cook took a nervous slurp, anyway.

"Our enquiry indicates that the two of you may have known each other."

Ramshaw let this hang. Cook stared into his tea for a few silent seconds, and when he looked up he saw that both Ramshaw and Whitcombe had their heads tilted to the left, like curious dogs.

"She used to write to me," said Cook. "But that was a very long time ago."

"How long?"

"Back when I was on my first full-time job. I'm a journalist. She… had some kind of crush on me."

Whitcombe nodded. This wasn't news to him, but he noted something in his book. Ramshaw stayed silent, giving his partner the opportunity to follow up.

"How old were you at the time?"

"Early twenties."

"That would make her fourteen or fifteen."

"She wrote to me, but I never wrote back. I never encouraged anything."

Ramshaw stepped in. "What was in the letters?"

(A slight smirk from Whitcombe on this.)

Cook's mouth was uncomfortably dry. He took another sip of tea. "Just teenage stuff. It was a bit embarrassing, really. The envelopes were always covered in hearts and things – and the other staff always managed to get to them first."

"How often did you receive them?"

"About once a week. They stopped when I left the magazine and started on a weekly paper."

"And you've had nothing since?"

"No."

"Did you know her by any other name?"

"No. She always signed them as 'Eleanor'. Why?"

"We don't believe that was her real name at the time – although she did change it officially later."

Cook sensed the officers were trying to establish whether or not this was a surprise to him. It was.

"I'm not sure how I can help. Have you had any luck in trying to find her?"

Ramshaw smiled. "We try not to work with luck. It's a complex enquiry."

Whitcombe now, shifting up a gear. "Mr Cook, we have discovered a number of letters at Ms Finch's flat – intended for you, but apparently unsent."

"As I said, I haven't heard from her since I changed my job. It must be twenty years ago."

"The letters we found are fairly recent."

"Obviously," said Ramshaw, leaning forward, "we're keen to understand if there's any connection to her disappearance. I have to question why a woman in her late thirties felt the urge to revisit what was – as you say – a teenage crush."

"Wasn't she separated?" Cook on the attack a little, now.

"She was, indeed."

"That must have been stressful – I saw the press conference with her ex-husband. Maybe she was taking comfort in something from simpler times."

Ramshaw raised his eyebrows, nodded. "It's an interesting theory."

Whitcombe, scribbling.

"And the letters are clearly marked for me?"

"Yes. Your name is on all the envelopes. No address."

"What did they say?"

Whitcombe looked up. "I'm afraid we can't disclose any detail."

Ramshaw sensed progress and took a softer line. "There's actually very little. Drawings, abstract things. The writing seems to be mainly concerned with why you haven't replied to earlier letters. Are you sure you've received nothing since the time you changed your job?"

"Absolutely. Nothing."

"Dorian…" Ramshaw leaned back, scrutinising. The gaze was keen and challenging and Cook had to fight the urge to break eye contact. "I'm sure you can appreciate the seriousness of this case. If you have any information at all, if you feel you know anything about what might have happened to Eleanor, then you must come forward. I want to make it clear that we're not accusing you of anything, but it you do fail to disclose information that could serve the enquiry, then that may well be held against you later."

Cook bristled. This sounded suspiciously like a prelude to arrest. "As I said, I recognised the name from the news and, obviously, I was shocked. But it was all such a long time ago. I've never written back, never been in two-way contact, never encouraged anything. I hope that nothing has happened to her, but I honestly can't see how I can help you."

Later, when the police had left him to tea and toast and 1950s courtroom drama, Cook called Gina and calmed her with a soft-focus explanation of why they had connected him to the missing woman. He heard her sigh down the phone-line – a breeze of enervation.

"All this drama, Dorian."

He spoke to Alfie, mostly about football stickers and zombies. ("They can make you one of them but what happens when all the humans run out and there are only zombies. Will they have to eat each other?")

(Cook had to confess his ignorance on this.)

He wished his son goodnight, told him that he loved him (receiving a mumbled 'uhuh' in return), hung up the phone and pulled a small, lockable leather briefcase from one of the still-unpacked removal boxes. Inside, was a stack of letters from Eleanor Finch, retrieved from a safe in his home office. They were packed into clear plastic wallets bearing month/year stickers. The letters had started to arrive at the *Widescreen* office around two years ago. Their frequency was inconsistent, but rarely dropped below two or three a month. Cook had been tempted to reply a few times, but had managed to keep to his (wise? cowardly?) policy of nonengagement. He sifted through the oldest, sliding the pastel-coloured sheets out through cleanly slitted openings. Eleanor's initial awkwardness at rekindling the contact steadily progressed to tender advances and heartbreaking one-way reminiscence. After a few months, she seemed to accept the silence, and the tone became more diary-like – pining for the happier days of her marriage, deep thoughts on elapsing time, occasional flares of unrequited sexuality. And then, after a year of silence, the letters came again, telling of her 'new man', thoughts on restart and redemption, renewed affection for her children and soon-to-be ex-husband.

> *I can be sexual again, Dorian. It's a relief and a thrill. He's more dominant than I'm used to. I didn't think I would enjoy that but I do. I have my own place now, but I stay with him sometimes. He has a nice big house on the end of a street, high on a hill so you can see all around. He kept it when his wife died. It reminds me of the house I had when I was a child. It makes me feel safe. It's actually helped my relationship with Gareth – although I haven't told him about my man.*

The most recent letters were more confused. She seemed cowed and uncertain.

> *He's so jealous. Doesn't like it when I go out, always wants to know where I'm going and who I'm with. I'm worried that I might have made a bad decision, but he says he loves me and wants to protect me. He almost caught me writing this letter but I managed to keep it out of sight. In a way, I don't mind him being*

jealous. It's something I never had with Gareth. He didn't care who I was with towards the end.

Eleanor's final letter was sent a few days before she was reported missing. Cook unfolded the single sheet of lilac paper and re-read it, for the third time that week.

I'm looking out of the window at the primary school – Vaughan Green. The children are playing happily. I miss Amy and Joe so much. I have to send these letters in secret now. Please take care of yourself. I hope you're there.

Cook folded the letter and slotted it back into its envelope. He shuddered – and remembered Esther's saying in response, back at their old, cold house.

"Someone just walked over my grave."

When he was seven years old, he had asked her what she meant by this. ("It's just what they say, Dor – when someone steps on the bit of ground where you're going to be buried.")

Mountford was right. It was far from nothing.

Cook had identified two primary schools called Vaughan Green. He had compared their positions with online street-map software, and only one – around thirty miles away – appeared to be on high ground near the end of a street, facing a large detached house.

Here sat Dorian Cook – jobless, loveless, a force without form, always passing through, never quite arriving. He was a lonely soul who had hovered too long in limbo. But now, gripped with a fresh panic for life, he knew that his time had come around at last.

30

Who Goes There?

June, 1976

Summer swarmed in – a choking, enshrouding heat which baked itself into the Bethesda School classrooms, melting Plasticine, sealing the over-painted ventilation grids, throttling the assembly hall in a miasma of pre-pubescent musk. The pupils staggered from class to class, flushed and drowsy. Cook and Michael Howell started a betting challenge – predicting the number of fainters at morning hymns. (The record was four – a mass topple during a feeble rendering of 'All Things Bright And Beautiful'.) At home, not even Cook's bedroom could retain its mystical chill. Esther replaced the heavy-duty sheets with something lacy and flimsy and suspiciously net-curtainish, but Cook still thrashed and floundered in delirious half-sleep, repeatedly waking to gulp from a bedside mug of tepid water.

His bike had been re-gifted for the half-term break, but Cook could barely pedal past the oil-works without slowing and panting. Instead, he lazed around the back yard, in Y-fronts and vest, playing mini-cricket with Uncle Russell and zapping ants with a magnifying glass.

A pink-and-white *Mr Whippy* ice-cream van took

residence at the street corner near the bridge, in sight of the old butcher's shop. As Cook queued, he found it impossible to ignore the building's ominous allure, and on the Sunday before school restarted, he wheeled the Chopper out of the yard and convinced David Brereton to join him for an 'investigation'.

At the bottom of the entry, the boys propped their bikes along the shadowy wall of the Cash & Carry, and sneaked in through the gate-gap. Cook was surprised to see the wooden panel still in place – hinge fractured, flapped over to the side, more or less as he had left it. Brereton lingered outside as Cook stooped his way into the back-room.

"What's it like?" called Brereton.

Cook assumed this to be some kind of safety check. "Nothing here. It's alright."

Brereton barged his way in. "Ah! It stinks. Smells like toilet!"

"Ssh! Look over here. Unless you're too scared!"

"Fuck off!" snarled Brereton, his voice booming through the gloom.

They scrambled across a bundle of house-bricks which jutted up through the polythene sheeting that, Cook noted, seemed to have shifted and flattened since his last visit. Something else was different – a half-shredded blanket had been knotted onto a rail and draped over the first-floor window. Sunlight flared through the slits, fluttering over the putrid concrete.

Since he was now not so close to an instant escape, Brereton switched to a whisper. "This is brilliant! You could live here, easy."

"Yeah. I think someone does."

"Oi!"

A shout from near the back door. Brereton hustled Cook out of his way and made a dash for the staircase. Cook watched him, smiling. He recognised the voice, but held off on reassurance, keen to see if Brereton was actually planning to dive out of the first-floor window. Brereton scampered halfway up the stairs, stopped and turned, coiled into a crouch and fixed his saucered eyes on the passage from back-door to central chamber.

"It's Den," said Cook, turning, and then, calling – "We're in here!"

There was crunching, clattering, muttering.

Dennis Mountford emerged, with an impish grin. "Did I scare you?"

Brereton cleared the stairs with one bound, sprinted over to Mountford and leapt onto his back. Cook grappled up onto Brereton, and the three boys veered into a stack of crusty planks, laughing and protesting, eventually collapsing into a corner, consumed by a cartoonish dust-cloud. They sat, huddled close, on the powdered floor, hearts drumming. Brereton summoned the strength to give Mountford a final shove.

"I nearly shit meself!"

Mountford sniggered. "I saw the bikes outside."

Cook was the first to stand. "C'mon. Let me show you something."

Cook led Mountford through to the splintered door and descending staircase. Brereton dawdled and complained, trying to disguise his caution with banter. ("I bet all the tramps have it off in here. You sure this isn't your house, Dor?")

Mountford, the eldest, stepped ahead of Cook and shouldered through the door. A spiral of pitted stone steps led down to a narrow passage half-flooded with spilled plaster. As they reached the bottom, Cook wriggled up-front. Mountford hesitated, Brereton hanging at his shoulder.

"Can't see a thing down here!" said Mountford, hushed. "Have you got a torch at your house, Dor?"

But Cook was away, wading through the rubble, plunging to the end of the passage, submerged by the deep, invincible dark.

"Hang on…" Brereton lit a match. The scraping tore through the stillness.

"Where did you get them from?" asked Mountford.

"He's always got 'em," said Cook, pushing on through the leaping shadows.

They emerged into what looked like an old storage area. Rotting crates lined the walls, poised below layers of ceramic shelving, tilted by time. The floor was carpeted by a congealed layer of old newspapers, cigarette packets, cushions and cartons. Brereton lit another match and held it up to a row of coloured bottles on one of the shelves. Mountford read from the labels.

"*Tippers Healing Oil… Black Lacquer… Turpentine Substitute… Loxene…*"

Cook stooped and studied a rakish fireplace, hacked together from mismatched stone. The raised hearth was coated in a mound of fresh-looking mulch which had spilled from the firebox. Mountford took a match from Brereton and dangled it over the opening.

"Is that *shit?*" said Brereton.

"Soil," said Mountford, giving it a kick.

Still crouching, Cook ran his fingers over a rough metal ring set into a square baseplate, bolted to the floor. It was riddled with rust but, as he clawed at the edges, it lifted away, twisting on its hinge. He gripped it with both hands and pulled upwards, grinding ring against base. The motion disturbed the edges of what looked like a thick trapdoor, but it was far too heavy to open.

"Let's have a go," said Mountford. "Give me some light, Dor."

Cook took a freshly lit match from Brereton and cast its glow over the ring. Mountford tugged and grunted, but the door's edges held firm.

"There's a load of pipes and bars by them crates," said Brereton. "Let's stick 'em down the ends and get it open."

Mountford and Brereton gathered up a few sections of tapered steel tubing. They took a pipe each and stabbed the flattened points into the grooves around the door-edges, prising and rocking until the wood loosened enough for Cook to grip the ring and yank the door open. Brereton wafted a new match over the opening.

A wooden ladder had been fastened to the trapdoor's frame, descending to a tiny, dungeon-like cellar.

"I'm not going down there!" confirmed Brereton.

But Cook was already backing into the hole, finding footing. He climbed down, slowly and deliberately, testing his weight on each rung. As he stepped off at the bottom, Mountford and Brereton lit new matches and poked them in through the trapdoor opening. Under a low, curved ceiling, the cellar was a ten-foot square cavern of nothing – bare stone floor and walls, no clutter, no shelves, no crates, no light, no anything. But, in the current heat, it felt refreshingly brisk.

"We could use this!" Cook's voice was cut short by a squealing creak as the trapdoor swung shut, sealing the frame, casting the cellar into profound blackness.

Muffled shouts – Brereton laughing and protesting, Mountford stern and urgent.

Cook's legs buckled. He kneeled, fingertips groping for the dirty floor. This was a new flavour of void – solid, entombing. Above, Mountford and Brereton scraped their pipes at the trapdoor edges, but Cook was shocked to discover that he felt no fear. He was calm, cool, out of sight, safe from harm, away from the stare of the sun. Down here, there was no closet door for the Sea Devils to fall upon. He waved his hand before his eyes, but only felt a slight air disturbance – he could see nothing.

Mr Pink-Whistle is not like ordinary people. He's half a brownie and half a person, and he can make himself invisible whenever he wants.

Esther had said that it wasn't possible. But here he was, without body. And he still believed it – that if you could make yourself invisible, then no-one could see you or hurt you.

Mountford and Brereton levered open the trapdoor. They had been too busy with the pipes to burn matches and so there was hardly any extra light.

"Dor! Are you okay? Sorry! Sorry!"

"Yeah, it was an accident!"

Cook fumbled around, found the ladder, and began to climb.

"It's okay," he said. "I've got an idea."

31
The Hole in the Noise

COOK LIFTED THE LETTERBOX flap and let it drop – three times seemed reasonable. He waited, noting the flaking paint around the door-frame and the recycle bin propped open with takeaway pizza boxes. William Stone peered through a small window above the letterbox, his features deformed by frosted glass. He studied his visitor for a little too long, before (it seemed to Cook) reluctantly admitting him, door barely ajar. Inside, Cook reeled at the reek of neglect – a microclimate of stale carpets, unwashed dishes, ageing meat, infrequent bathing. He recognised it from his own holding-pattern lifestyle. It was universal, bottleable – Calvin Klein's *Separation*.

Cook searched for somewhere to set down his car-keys, but all the horizontal surfaces had been colonised by mugs and bowls and plates of varying vintage.

"Sorry about the mess," said Stone, unapologetically. He swept a few newspapers off the sofa. "What's up? Do you want a drink, mate?"

Cook detected a faint slur in his friend's speech. It was earlyish – 10am – and he charitably dismissed it as morning grogginess.

"No, thanks. I won't be long."

Stone flopped into an armchair.

"How are things?" said Cook, lowering himself onto the unyielding sofa.

"Could be worse. They've done a 'conduct investigation' review and now I've got to agree an 'improvement plan'. My brief has got the complaint reduced. It's all bullshit, though. I'll be back soon. Main thing is that I'm still fucked for any promotions. Unless I can find Lord fucking Lucan."

Cook greeted all of this with a few well-practiced grunts of sympathy, marking time until he felt it appropriate to attempt a subject-change. He had mentally rehearsed a subtle transition, but in the event, realised that he simply didn't have the skill or inclination for diplomacy.

"I'm in trouble, Will. I need your help."

To Cook's surprise and irritation, Stone unleashed a belly-laugh which triggered a convulsion of breathless rasping. He burrowed through the detritus on a side-table, plucked out a cigarette and sparked it up, puffing and coughing. "Mate. I'm a man whose 'standards of professional behaviour' are probably being discussed right now by a bunch of cunts in suits. What help can I be to you?"

"It's nothing major," said Cook. "I need your advice – and maybe a bit of, uh, insurance."

Stone spluttered, spouting a flurry of smoke. "Dor, I know you're a movie man, but this isn't the fucking *Godfather*. It's reality. I can't just call in a fucking SWAT team. I'm serving this out, staying good as gold."

"It's nothing that elaborate."

Cook rescued a soft-porn magazine which had almost slipped out of sight beneath the sofa. He turned a few pages, squinting at the prurience. He was both acting and feeling casual. "Gina and I are on a break. It's been coming for a while. You know that. It's just... There's something else."

"Oh my God!" said Stone, smiling. "You're going to kill your family and top yourself. I had one of them a couple of years ago. Fuck me! One of the kids *survived.*"

Cook looked up from the magazine but didn't indulge the banter.

"No. Nothing like that. Gina and I – we might be okay. This goes a lot further back."

That evening, at 'home', Cook poured himself a glass of red wine and scrutinised the letters from Eleanor, cross-referencing her descriptive asides with the detail in his own research. When he was satisfied, he made a few brief notes in his old screening pad and headed into the kitchen, where the radio babbled, tuned to a news and sport station.

He took a knife from a drawer, butter from the fridge, cheese slices, ham slices, relish.

He listened to the news.

"Police have launched a murder investigation after the bodies of a man and a child were found at a house in Edgware."

He laid out two rounds of bread. He opened the butter.

"Dennis Mountford, 47, was found along with his seven-year-old son Jake at their home on Tuesday."

He did not release the knife in horror. It did not tumble to the floor in slow-motion.

"Detectives have issued an appeal for witnesses and are studying CCTV footage of the area."

He layered the cheese and ham onto the bread.

"This is a particularly brutal and callous crime, with an added element of outrage due to the involvement of a young

child. We would ask if anyone has any information – no matter how small it might seem – to please come forward, in confidence. It's crucial that we apprehend whoever is responsible for this appalling act as soon as possible."

He squashed the ingredients between the buttered bread slices, turned and walked out of the kitchen into the living-room.

He took his car-keys and notepad.

He left the house and got into his car.

He drove to the town-house flat-block and pressed the button marked 'D. Brereton' over and over again.

He got back into the car, drove out of the town centre, onto the motorway.

He left the motorway and stopped the car by the side of the road.

He consulted his notes and drove to a low-lit suburban street.

He parked at the corner, near a sign – 'Vaughan Green Primary School'. Opposite, stood the house where he was sure that Eleanor Finch was being held prisoner.

32
Destroyer of Worlds

Cook lay starfished, on his stomach, in swimming trunks, too close to the black-and-white TV. Esther's needles ticked and tapped as she – absurdly – worked through a pattern for a winter sweater. Rusty sprawled, panting, in a puddle of shadow near the kitchen step, as the midday sun blared in through the sitting-room sash window. Earlier, as he propped open the loose frame with two slender sterilised-milk bottles, Cook had suggested closing the curtain to keep the room cool.

"Shutting the curtains on a day like this?" said Esther. "People will think we're tapped!"

"But no-one can see in, nana! It's the back yard!"

"Makes no difference! You don't sit in the dark in the middle of July!"

The television spoke of ladybird plagues, heatstroke, failing crops. The temperature had been locked at around 32C since the end of June. Today – at 35C – was emerging as the annual high. A hirsute man in a heavily patterned jacket insisted there were "questions to be asked" over why the Met Office warning of a possible drought had been ignored. Water was rationed, communal bathing encouraged (in no more than five inches of bathwater). Grimy cars became a badge of upstanding citizenship, as detector vans with coathanger-like 'pipe monitors' stalked the streets. Neighbourhood standpipes were installed, drawing clucking queues of pail-bearers. Toilets were to be flushed with dishwater, lawns left thirsty.

"It's like the bloody war, this!" said Esther, fanning herself with the knitting pattern.

For Cook, the heat was just a backdrop to the invasion of insects – eddying and fluttering through the dead air, crunching underfoot. Out on his bike, he had to be careful to keep his mouth closed, or risk an involuntary gulp of aphid or ladybird.

"Turn it over, Dor!"

Cook thumbed in the channel-change button.

"...known as 'The Black Panther' has been continuing at Oxford Crown Court. Neilson faces four murder charges, as well as attempted murder, GBH, robbery, kidnap and firearms possession. He was apprehended after the kidnap and murder of heiress Lesley Whittle, who was held in a deep storage drain at Bathpool Park in Kidsgrove, before being..."

"Bloody hell. Get the telly off!"

"...maintains that Ms. Whittle's death was an accident and that she was not pushed off a ledge but died after..."

Esther dived forward and twisted the on/off dial. She set down her knitting and trudged off into the kitchen, tutting.

Cook unpeeled himself from the carpet. "Nana? What's 'GBH'?"

The front-door letterbox clattered. Rusty, too hot to fuss, stayed in the shade, ears pricked, clunking his tail against the table-leg. At the door, Mountford (polo shirt, long trousers, sandals) sat on the step, lapping at an ice-lolly. He looked up over his shoulder as Cook appeared.

"Hey, Dor. Get your bike!"

Brereton (T-shirt, testicle-crushing shorts, socks, sandals) hovered by the kerb, astride his bicycle. "Yeah. Come on! Let's go! Unless your mum says you've got to stay in again!"

"Shut up, David," said Mountford.

"It wasn't my mum!" said Cook, pulling on a T-shirt.

Esther appeared with a pair of suitably inappropriate trousers. "And don't forget your shoes, Dor!"

Brereton sniggered and took a swig from a bottle of strawberry-flavoured fizzy pop.

"It's okay, Mrs. Cook," said Mountford. "We're just going to call for someone."

Esther was already halfway back into the sitting-room. "Alright. Keep away from you-know-where!"

"We will!" called Brereton, smiling.

'You-Know-Where', as they all knew, was a concept open to interpretation. Given recent events, Esther was most likely referring to Tesco, but she could have had several other places in mind: the school playground, accessible through a widely known but unrepaired split in the wire mesh at the corner of the car-park; the Lyons Maid factory, where Cook and friends were regularly gifted 'reject' tubs of buttery ice-cream by an ex-Bethesda pupil; and – their first planned stop-off today – the clay-extraction zone known as the marl-hole.

The three boys cycled side by side, in ragged formation. Brereton and Mountford dawdled, oppressed by the heat, while Cook took point, forging forward, tipsy with excitement. They freewheeled down an undulating tarmac slope, onto the upscale estate, down the side of the tightly shorn lawn, and into the back-garden of the blue-painted house, where they laid their bikes flat on the decking. John Ray opened the door before they'd had a chance to knock. He was, as ever, overdressed – in long-sleeve burgundy cardigan and heavy corduroy trousers.

"C'mon, John," said Brereton. "We're going to the marl-hole! You can join our gang!"

"It's too hot." Ray ran a palm across his matted white hair, sweeping it away from a flushed forehead. "I need my cream."

"Put some on, then!" said Cook, leaking more irritation than he'd intended.

"And it's way too bright. It's dangerous for me when it's bright."

"Have you got any sunglasses?" said Mountford, a little bored.

"My mum has. They're in the drawing-room."

Drawing-room!

"Put them on, then!" (Cook again – calmer, brighter.)

"I'm not supposed to go out. Darren is at work and my mum and dad…"

"Come on, John!" said Brereton. "You've got to come with us if you want to be in our gang. Find the sunglasses. Get your bike out!"

Ray turned, stalled a little, and disappeared into the kitchen, leaving the back door open.

"It's hot out here!" called Brereton. "Have you got any Jungle Juice?"

Cook and Brereton screeched with laughter. Mountford smiled and tinkered with his bike-chain, before wiping oily fingers on Cook's sleeve.

"Oi!!" Cook was on him – wrestling, grunting, reaching for his own chain-ring, planning to smear oil into Mountford's hair.

John Ray's reappearance stopped and stunned them all. His hair and cheeks were covered by a silk head-scarf knotted under the chin; his skin was shiny with liberally basted sun-cream, eyes concealed behind a pair of vast, circle-framed sunglasses. He looked like a scaled-down parody of his mother – the woman Cook had glimpsed at the church on Christmas Eve. Ray dawdled in the doorway, suspended in multi-state reality – on the threshold, between in and out, light and dark; neither young nor old, male nor female, dead nor alive. He was crepuscular – creature of shade, enemy of light. He needed to be concealed and protected. He shouldn't be out at this hour, not at any hour. He wasn't built to be out at all. He was an outsider, caught in the unblinking glare of the outside world – easy prey for the blinders and brutalisers. His flesh wasn't willing and his spirit was weak. The bullies called him 'The Ghost' – because of his skin, his hair, his spectral pallor. But it was also because they were scared of him – more scared of him than he was of them. And that was his tragedy – he didn't know it. He didn't yet know that fear was more powerful than love.

"Excuse me, Mrs Ray," said Brereton, laughing. "Can John come out to play?"

To the marl-hole, and its petrified mud-flats, cracked barrels of chemical waste, patches of fibreglass insulation ('itching powder'), powered-down (but not off) industrial vehicles, jutting nails and lurking hooks. In this heat, it was a lunar wasteland – the earth blistering beneath wilting weeds. Cook, Brereton and John Ray tore wooden sticks from a splintered selection of planks near the central work-hut, while Mountford uprooted a metre-long iron pole from a prehistoric gateway which led through to the oil-works. They prised the lid from a small barrel near the hut and disovered scrapings of tar, liquefied by the weather. The three with wooden sticks dunked them into the barrel, with a vague plan of constructing flaming torches. Brereton took out his matches and tried to ignite the gloopy tips, but they wouldn't catch. So they swished and whipped the sticks through the air, flicking the tar at each other – into hair, onto cheeks, over ears, somehow avoiding eyes. Ray took a splash across his sunglasses and Mountford called a halt.

They ate meat pasties, drank cans of Tizer and cycled to the old butcher's shop, propping their bikes in the side-entry. Mountford held the gate open as they wriggled through to the yard.

"Is this the den?" said Ray, as they filed in through the door-flap.

"Yeah!" said Cook. "We've got a game you have to do before you can be in the gang."

They scrambled through to the main room. Sunlight seeped through the tainted walls and windows, tinting the squalor in honeyed yellow. Cook pointed to the staircase leading up to the first-floor window.

"We'll all go outside and wait by the window. You have to go up the stairs and wave to us. Then we know you're brave enough to be in the gang."

"But you can't start until we're all outside or it doesn't count!" warned Brereton.

John Ray took off his head-scarf and sunglasses. He studied the room, looking back to the entrance, forward to the staircase, up and around at the first-floor window. He cringed at the drifts of plaster and rotting rafters.

"Okay!" he said.

Brereton, Cook and Mountford back-tracked, out into the yard – still with its undisturbed wheelbarrow, cement bags and scaffold tubes.

"Go and stand outside," said Brereton. "I'll scare him when he comes out!"

Cook and Mountford squirmed through the gate, back out into the street, sniggering. They stood on the corner, directly beneath the first-floor window.

"Ready!" shouted Mountford.

No answer.

They listened, expecting the sounds of scurrying, running, swearing. Then, Cook heard Ray's footsteps, heavy on the brittle stairs, thunking their way to the top.

"Hello there!"

Cook and Mountford spluttered with laughter at the formality. They looked up and saw Ray, pale face at the window, hands waving.

"Okay, John!" shouted Mountford. "Now you have to come back out."

Again, the thunking – this time coming down. Then more nothing.

Then Brereton.

"*Wooooooaaaargh!*"

Then John Ray, wailing and squealing.

Brereton emerged through the gate-gap first, holding it open for Ray, who stumbled forward onto the scalding pavement, sobbing and re-concealing himself behind scarf and sunglasses.

Brereton and Cook were breathless with laughter, but Mountford stooped down in consolation. "Are you okay?"

Ray squatted against the yard wall, sniffing and whimpering. He shook his head, pulled out his blue-and-white handkerchief, mopped his eyes, blew his nose. He quivered and snuffled, chin firmly on chest, hands on head, fingers ruffling the head-scarf.

"Sorry, John," said Cook. "We didn't think it would frighten you like that."

John Ray slowly raised his head. "Am I in the gang now?"

Later, they all sat flat against the entry wall, in the cooling afternoon shade, eating '99' ice-cream cones. Ray had recovered, even brightened.

"My dad told me about Tesco."

Cook glanced at Mountford. "Yeah?"

"Yes. He says your details were taken and their new computer system will remember you if you do it again."

"He's not supposed to talk about it," said Mountford.

"I know," said Ray. "But he always does."

"Talk about what?" demanded Brereton.

"We got caught nicking." Cook expected mockery, but Brereton kept silent, extracting the chocolate Flake from his ice-cream and gnawing at the edges.

"Why didn't you tell me about it?"

Mountford laughed. "Why? Are you sorry you didn't get caught with us?"

Brereton shrugged, screwing the Flake back into its hole. "Wouldn't have got caught if I'd been there."

"That's impossible!" insisted Ray. "They have people dressed like shoppers who watch everyone – and there's cameras, too. They film the whole shop so they can check up on every minute."

"Let's go back inside," said Cook. "Now you're in the gang, you can see the den."

"Yeah," said Brereton. "We were only messing about. Promise we won't scare you again."

The boys finished their ice-creams and squeezed in through the gate. As they opened the flap at the back-door, Ray had to crouch to avoid a strip of sunlight. Cook saw him squint and cower, noting his keenness to follow Brereton and Mountford back into the dark. At the staircase leading to the cellar, Mountford flicked on a small pocket torch. He shuffled down the steps, casting an anaemic glimmer, stalked by shadows. Cook followed, then John Ray, then Brereton. They stooped, in single file, through the lower passage and out into the trapdoor room where the blackness leered – loud and untameable, beyond the reach of any residual light.

"SHHH!" hissed Brereton.

They all froze.

"Listen…"

Brereton held the tension for a few seconds, before launching a long and fulsome fart.

No-one laughed – apart from Brereton. "Fuck off, David!" said Mountford. "Tell John about the rules."

They squatted down in conference – a circle of four.

"This is where the gang hangs out, John," whispered

Brereton. "We keep all our stuff down here and have secret meetings."

"The things you steal?"

Cook caught a look from Mountford.

"Yeah," said Cook. "Stuff we bring from home, too."

"You are in the gang now," said Brereton. "But we still have to do a swearing-in ceremony."

"Yeah," said Mountford. "And then you'll be in our gang forever and nothing will happen to you. We all have to protect you. And you have to protect us."

Ray laughed at this – a cynical tremor from an older, wiser soul. The sound sent Cook's mind tumbling forward, through the years ahead, extrapolating the adult from the child. He saw the future John Ray as a man-sized boy – scaled but not grown. Internally, he would mutate, but on the outside remain, without blemish or blossom – a freeze-framed caricature, suspended in agony. He was more specimen than human – something to be preserved, kept safe, turned to stone. But he was not a display piece. His strangeness would be forever undimmed – there was no need for it to be illuminated.

"The den is down here," said Mountford, motioning for Cook and Brereton to help. Ray aimed Mountford's torch at the iron handle as the other three grunted and prised and gouged the trapdoor from its frame. Cook was first to the ladder, descending with stuttering stealth as the frail beam flitted from rung to trapdoor to darkness below, steered by Ray's curiosity. Brereton and Mountford followed and, after some cajoling, Ray probed and groped his way down to the cool stone floor. He trained the faltering torch up at the curved ceiling, guiding its glow slowly down and around – a soft-focus searchlight inspecting the featureless walls.

Behind him, Mountford was climbing back up the ladder. "I'll get the matches, just in case."

Cook followed him up, unnoticed by Ray.

Brereton took the torch from Ray, slipped his arm around his shoulders. "Now, you have to close your eyes."

"Okay. But don't scare me too much!"

Brereton turned and quietly climbed the first few rungs. He passed the torch up to Cook, who shone it down into the cellar, lighting the way as Brereton crawled out through the open trapdoor.

"Now you have to count to three," said Brereton.

"Okay! One…"

John Ray's voice – wavering and diluted – wafted up from the cellar. To Brereton, he seemed absent, a thousand miles away. Mountford heard something exquisite – anticipation, not fear. For Cook, it was a sign-off – a last transmission, soon to be tuned out and wiped over with silence.

"Two…"

Cook screwed the lit torch into a gap in the wall, spotlighting the scene. Brereton and Mountford lifted the trapdoor away from the floor. Cook grasped the iron handle as they heaved it upright.

"Throw down the torch," whispered Mountford. "Dave's got matches."

Brereton, straining against the trapdoor's bulk, nodded impatiently. Cook poked his arm down through the frame, shoulder-deep, reducing the falling distance.

"Three!"

He let the torch drop. It clinked against the stone floor, flickered, stayed alight. John Ray opened his eyes at the noise.

Cook, Brereton and Mountford pushed the trapdoor.

Thunk.

It slotted into place with a gust of dust – sealing the hole, stealing the light.

Silence.

Brereton lit a match.

Screaming.

Watch! He hates this!

Cook had first heard this screaming in the passage by Lisa's house, when the boys had tied Ray's hair up with his handkerchief. It was more like a howl of outrage – primal and jarring, but tainted by impotence. Back then, it shuddered out in bursts, between breaths. Now, it emerged as a single, sustained note of immaculate terror.

And so they left him there – to scream in peace. They bolted – scampering back through the passage, up the stairs, through the central chamber, out into the yard. They huddled by the back door, panting.

Brereton – delirious, cackling.

Mountford – startled, cry-laughing.

Cook – listening, listening for Something.

Instead, there was Nothing.

No screaming.

"I can't hear 'im," said Brereton.

"It's too deep," said Mountford. "I thought we'd be able to hear everything outside."

They cycled back to the marl-hole. Mountford stayed with the bikes while Brereton squeezed onto Cook's long saddle and hitched a ride back to the butcher's shop. Brereton dismounted and hopped onto Ray's junior racer. They paused, listened. Still nothing.

"We should leave him his bike," said Cook.

"Someone might nick it!"

"Just stick it round the corner, by the gate."

They wedged the bike in next to the Cash & Carry side-entrance, not obvious to anyone passing at either end of the entry, but hardly well hidden.

They went back to the marl-hole.

They talked for a while, worried about whether they would 'get done' or not.

They didn't go back. They didn't go back to John Ray and they didn't open the trapdoor.

Later, in the airless night, Cook was inside the old butcher's shop, looking out of the first-floor window. The scene shifted to the view from his own bedroom window – the Sea Devils rising from a lake of hot tar, swarming across the road, dripping black, herding towards his front-door.

He heard them bustle together at the foot of the stairs and begin their ascent.

He waited for the bedroom door to open.

He cowered in the closet, straining hard to wake up.

He heard them crowd into his room.

John Ray screaming.

But it was Cook screaming and he woke, with Esther there, asking what was wrong, saying the heat must be giving him bad dreams.

Saying, "Don't worry, Dor. It's not real. If it's not real, it can't hurt you."

33
The Fourth Wall

THE IMAGE WAS SURPRISINGLY clear, with a wide field of view which monitored the front and side of the house. The camera was intentionally unremarkable – off-white and about the size of a cigarette packet. It ran for forty-eight hours off specialist batteries which could be replaced in seconds, with one hand. (Thumb-flick and slide open the panel, release the old, slot in the new.) It had an automatic, light-sensitive infra-red mode and could be switched on and off remotely, via a unique website. Live footage was viewable by web or dedicated app. Cook had used adhesive strips to fix it – high enough to deter accidental curiosity – on a street-corner lamp-post. To the unsuspicious eye, it looked like some sort of micro alarm system. Suspicious eyes were an unavoidable risk, but he'd been viewing the pictures and changing the batteries for two weeks now with no threat of interference – apart from one tense afternoon when the lens had been partially blocked by a maintenance worker on a hydraulic platform.

Cook had sourced the camera by reviewing the notes for the section in his social media article on live-blogging and lifestyle-tracking. His world was now so condensed and constricted, the observations sounded like mutterings from a mind adrift in some parallel reality.

The 'new solipsism'... Free and open platform for opinion regardless of insight makes more noise... Difference between panel debate and room full of shouting people (number of followers equates to loudest shouters)... Blogs more like scrapbooks than diaries... Experience-driven analysis given way to indiscriminate leakage... Quantified self and Orwellian impulse to monitor others...

The piece was spiked due to 'space issues', but even as he filed, Cook knew the copy was too hostile and soap-boxy for the flippant brief ('Diary Of A Social Media Naysayer'). There was comfort in the irony of his kill-fee covering the camera purchase.

He reviewed the images twice-daily – cutting and pasting significant sections, noting timings and repetitions, cross-referencing irregularities. He drew up a colour-coded chart of occupancy and activity. A pattern was forming, but not as quickly as he'd hoped, and he would not act until he was confident that the risk of discovery was virtually zero.

Cook drove to the house on two consecutive Saturday afternoons, parking round the corner, but still in sight of the gate. He rehearsed his approach vicariously, through several cold-callers and once, a parcel courier who rang the doorbell after receiving no answer from a neighbour. Each time, Cook was satisfied to see that the outcome tallied with his chart.

Today – a Sunday – he arrived home, feeling almost optimistic after a day at the cinema with Alfie, and made the mistake of turning on the radio in time for the half-hourly news bulletin.

"Police are still hunting the killer of a 47-year-old man and his seven-year-old son. Dennis and Jake Mountford were brutally murdered at their home in Edgware last month."

Mountford's death had slipped down the news agenda, behind a crisis in Estonia and a scandal involving a married politician housing his lover at public expense. Cook had tried to keep the implications corralled in a corner of his aching mind, but this was denial most foul. After the initial panic, he had cooled on trying to contact Brereton and was starting to convince himself that the crime was just an appalling fluke.

"After conducting house-to-house enquiries and several forensic investigations, we are appealing to the public to come forward if they saw anyone acting suspiciously in the area from late afternoon on Saturday 28th September to around 10am on Monday 30th September. Please contact us, in absolute confidence, if you know anything at all, as it could be important to the investigation."

Cook had taken a call from the police, who explained that they were conducting a 'routine elimination' of every number in Mountford's mobile address book. He confirmed that they were old school friends who had recently caught up after a chance meeting. He heard the junior-sounding officer sigh and type something. There was a possibility of a follow-up interview, she said – probably within a day or two. He had heard nothing more.

"The case is to be featured on BBC's Crimewatch this Thursday at 9pm."

Cook brewed some strong coffee and opened his laptop. He logged in to the camera website, accessed the clipping section, activated the live feed and resumed work on his private directorial debut. (He was, of course, also producer, editor and cameraman.) The evening ahead was clear – a couple of hours' work on the latest footage, reheated lasagne, half-bottle of Rioja, a new Herzog documentary. Then, he would open the small package he had received yesterday from William Stone.

34

The Life of the Mind

September, 1976

The heatwave faded, doused by ferocious thunderstorms which rolled in with supreme comic timing – soon after the government had appointed a 'Minister for Drought'. Back at school, Cook, Mountford and Brereton gathered in the upper playground, by the utility shed.

"What did Mrs Mellor say?" asked Cook.

"She said she didn't know," said Brereton, already a little bored by the fuss.

"It's been in the paper," said Mountford. "My dad was reading it. He told me to make sure I always come straight home from school."

Brereton unwrapped a blob of bubble-gum, rolled the wrapper into a stiff tube and scratched out a lump of crumbled mortar from the shelter wall. He mumbled into the stone. "It was an accident."

"No, it wasn't," said Cook.

That afternoon – the third day of the new term – Cook waited for the rest of his class to leave for lessons before summoning the nerve to approach his fearsome new form teacher as he cleaned the blackboard.

"Sir?"

"Dorian Cook…" said Mr Corlett in sinister reply, not bothering to turn.

"Was John Ray meant to be in our class?"

Corlett faced him. He was improbably tall, with a lumpy, reddened nose, hair waxed flat.

"I think he's off sick at the moment, lad."

The storms were triggered by a dense humidity which seemed to intensify Cook's nightmares. Sleep became an oppression, ripening his guilt with a clarity which could not be dampened by rationalisation or denial. His resting mind had settled deep inside a narrative furrow through which the creatures travelled – across the road, through the door, up the stairs and into his hiding-place, desecrating the darkness. Before, although they carried panic and pain, he knew he would eventually open his eyes and escape. Now, they threatened irreversible shutdown – the totality of death.

And in the waking light – at the park, by the ice-cream factory, on the school-walk, along the over-groomed avenue where his imagined girlfriend once lived – John Ray remained, banished from sight but not from mind. The three boys did not dare return to the scene of the crime, but they did sometimes pull themselves up to peek over the wall, where the building materials sat undisturbed, in shrine-like repose.

That year, Cook's birthday – his eleventh – fell on a Saturday and he was allowed a small party in the parlour. Michael Howell came, as did Brereton, Mountford and a few others. For the first time, in the presence of Tom, Lily, Esther, and Uncle Russell and girlfriend, Cook toiled beneath the weight of his secret. It was there in the glances between the three who shared it, and he realised that the story they had used to lure Ray – the imaginary 'gang' – was now a reality. They were a complicit collective, bound by mutual self-preservation.

There was lemon squash and jelly and ice-cream. They played a rigged version of Musical Chairs, with Tom strategically lifting the stylus from one of Cook's records whenever he approached an empty chair. After all non-family had been ushered away with birthday cake wrapped in tissue paper, Cook squeezed onto the sofa with Tom and Russell. His uncle had threaded a copy of the *Daily Mirror* through the elastic slats under the seat-cushion. He slid it free and flattened the front-page across his knee. A bruised, black-eyed face stared out, contrasting with an older, more composed police mug-shot. Beneath the battered version, the caption ran:

THE KILLER: Neilson after his arrest. He was attacked by members of the public as police struggled with him.

And then, the bellowing headine and main story.

CAGED FOREVER
– PANTHER JAILED FOR LIFE

Donald Neilson, the Black Panther, was caged yesterday… for the rest of his life. He was convicted of three more murders to add to his shocking tally of crimes. Neilson had already been found guilty of murdering 17-year-old Lesley Whittle, the heiress he kidnapped and imprisoned underground. He was, the judge said, a killer without mercy.

Under this, a portentous sub-splash.

FOUR-PAGE DOSSIER STARTS ON PAGE 13

Cook turned the pages, eager to study the contents of the 'dossier', but a few flicks in, his eye was drawn to a text-only story compressed into a side-column.

HUNT FOR MISSING BOY

Tom laughing with Esther.

    Russell shovelling up a bowl of trifle.

    Lily suddenly there, stroking his hair. ("Have you had a nice birthday, darling?")

Police are 'extremly concerned' for the welfare of thirteen-year-old Robert Gillham…

The missing boy was thirteen-year-old Robert Gillham, not ten-year-old John Ray.

    The Black Panther had been caged.

    Yes, he told his mother. It had been a nice birthday.

Something was coming up the stairs. But Cook was already half-awake. Was this residue from his dream or a new twist of reality? He could smell smoke, wisping in through his bedroom window. Outside in the street, someone was shouting, banging on front-doors.

    Esther barged in. "C'mon, Dor. Get yerself out of bed! There's a fire!"

    Cook jumped upright. "Here?"

"No! In that old house down the end of the street. Fire brigade are there. We've got to get out."

Cook dived into shorts and T-shirt.

"I've got your shoes. Come on!"

Esther grabbed and squeezed his hand, too hard. She yanked him down the stairs, out of the house and over the road, falling in with a group of bleary neighbours – fluffy slippers, 'house-coats', pre-breakfast cigarettes. The old butcher's shop was almost completely obscured behind rippling swirls of dark black smoke. Flames surged through the half-boarded windows, tamed – but not extinguished – by columns of water from two hoses directed by yelling firefighters. Their actions were futile – the sun-baked timber was easy prey for the inferno and, as the building was apparently uninhabited, the fire had already savaged most of it before anyone had raised an alarm. Cook watched through droopy eyes as the structure buckled and shrivelled. He gazed, bewitched by the orange-and-black fury. He watched the embers take flight and twist skyward, tracking their escape up into the morning haze.

Further down the street, he saw David Brereton, skulking under the iron bridge.

And down came another shower of summer rain – too late to snuff out the fire or wash away any sins.

35

Something

COOK WASTED TWO DAYS trying to contact Brereton. No answer from his flat, no joy from a trawl of likely hotel kitchens. (He had doubted his claim, anyway – sous-chef seemed too close to the frontline for someone so slippery.) This urge to connect was driven by impulse over reason. Brereton may have been the only other person alive who knew the back-story, but Cook had no need of advice or solidarity. He already had clear sight of his final act – the spy-camera footage was writing the script. He sat here now, on someone else's sofa, watching their television, drinking wine from their glass. Maybe soon, he would pine for the stolid certainties of the world he had been forced to abandon. But he had been still for too long. After years of deferral, he was a man with momentum.

"Welcome to Crimewatch. On tonight's programme..."

The Mountford murder was trailed as part of an opening preview, by the show's male anchor, striding through the live incident room, booming significantly into a roving camera.

"A man and his young son brutally murdered in their own home. Can you help lead police to the killer?"

After the opening item – a typically am-dram reconstruction of a robbery on an industrial estate – the focus switched to a more sympathetic female presenter, standing in front of a transparent bulletin board decorated with hand-written case comments and photographs of Dennis and Jake Mountford. As she spoke, the camera drifted back to reveal incident-room workers hunched over computer monitors, shouldering telephones. A startled-looking man in a short-sleeved shirt stood beside her.

"Now, a case which contains detail which some viewers might find upsetting. At the end of September, a 47-year-old man, Dennis Mountford, and his seven-year-old son Jake were murdered at their home in Edgware, north-west London. With me is Inspector Adam Claymont, one of the officers leading the enquiry. Inspector Claymont – this is a particularly appalling crime and one which you're obviously keen to get to the bottom of."

Inspector Claymont shuffled in position. Cook thought he seemed a little junior for a national spotlight.

"Indeed. It's a savage and heartless crime and the attacker is obviously still a huge danger to the public."

The director – clearly sensitive to the gulf of composure – was quick to cut back to the presenter. Cook, ever the critic, was so distracted by the random pace and artless shot-framing, he found it difficult to absorb what was being said.

"The thing that's so unusual about this case is that there doesn't seem to be any obvious reason for the crime."

"Yes. There's no evidence of robbery or sexual motive. There's also no sign of a break-in – which raises the possibility that the killer was known to Mr Mountford. But he may also have tricked his way onto the property under false pretense. As far as we can tell, the deceased lived a relatively simple life. He owned a small signwriting business and lived in a usually

safe suburban area. So we're keen to understand whether anyone might have cause to hold a grievance against him – perhaps as a result of business dealings. If there was friction in this area, someone knows about it – and I would ask them to please come forward, in absolute confidence."

Cook sipped his wine. Could these two people really be there together, in that studio, at this time, because of his actions, another life ago?

"I believe that Mr Mountford's family have given you some interesting information…"

"Yes. We understand that Dennis had been concerned about a man who was seen talking to Jake outside his school on the 18th September. We don't have an accurate description of this man, but we're obviously keen to trace him. I would urge anyone who was witness to the conversation or who might have an idea as to the identity of this man to please call the Crimestoppers line immediately."

"He might, of course, be unconnected to the case."

"Indeed. But we do need to speak to him urgently."

"As I said, the details of this crime are extremely upsetting. Both Mr Mountford and his son suffered a great deal of violence."

"That's correct, yes. Although it may seem like an isolated, spontaneous incident, this has the hallmarks of a carefully planned attack and we have to assume that the killer is capable of doing it again. We need to find the individual who did this very urgently indeed."

"What sort of help are you looking for? Do you have anything that might lead you to understand more about the killer's motivations?"

"We do have an item found at the scene which isn't

familiar to Mr Mountford's family. I would urge anyone who
recognises this to please get in touch."

The camera cut to a close-up shot of Inspector Claymont's hands. He was holding a plastic evidence bag containing a blue-and-white handkerchief.

PART TWO

THE MAN WAS ALWAYS alone. He left the house alone and he entered it alone. Every Friday evening between 7 and 8pm, he arrived with two grocery bags, one in each hand, switching them both to one hand as he unlocked the door and shouldered his way in. From Friday to Monday, he only ever left the house once – for two hours on Saturday afternoon. From Tuesday to Thursday, he emerged at 8.30am and returned at 4pm, always double-locking the front door and always checking the back door and side window, tugging and testing. He was tall and large, but moved at quickstep pace. His hand-speed – reaching, lifting, key-twisting – was brisk and dextrous. Dorian Cook had monitored the man for six weeks now and he had seen no sign of anyone else entering or leaving the house, and no evidence of internal activity when the man was out.

Early on Saturday morning, Cook drove to Vaughan Green Primary School and parked on a corner of Peakvale Avenue, a few streets away from the man's house. He walked the short distance to a local cafe, and slid into a booth seat, trembling with dread. Worries over arousing curiosity were unfounded – his absence of charisma was natural camouflage, and it took the over-tattooed waiter ten minutes to approach and take his order, despite the cafe being half-empty. He nursed a butterless scone and large mug of tea through the rest of the morning, grazing on a newspaper and keeping the camera app in view on his phone – a full-screen window featuring a live feed of the house. At 12.30pm, the man appeared, as usual. He ran through his door and window checks, and, after pausing slightly to look back over his shoulder at the front door (listening for something?), he crossed the street and walked, hands in pockets, up the inclining main road before taking a left turn, as usual, down a side-street. After a judicious fifteen-minute delay, Cook requested his bill from the passing waiter, who jumped slightly at the noise, as if he had not only forgotten about Cook being there, but had detected an adversarial edge to his voice. (He was evidently doing a poor job of remaining – and appearing – calm.)

At his car, Cook opened the boot and took out the small package from William Stone. It contained two items, one of which he slipped into his jacket's inside pocket, not expecting to need it but feeling better with it to hand. The other was a small set of standard cylinder-lock keys with the cuts planed down to maximum depth. There were versions for tumbler locks and dimple locks, and all of them had small strips of shock-absorbing material glued to their top edges, to prevent detectable damage. Stone had shown Cook how to partially insert one of the keys and, while twisting it in the desired direction, whack it with a screwdriver handle. As long as the key's teeth aligned with the top pins of the lock cylinder, the impact would 'bump' the pins upward, enabling the key to turn and open the lock. Cook had practiced the technique on his kitchen door and had been surprised at how quickly he developed a process – insert key, wriggle it forward and back into position, bash it with screwdriver head while applying turning force. He pockcted the keys, took a small screwdriver from the glove-box and approached the house.

Cook did not indulge in a portentous pause at the back-garden gate. He strolled straight in and walked, with authority, up the short path to the back door, which the man always checked last. The lock was a simple tumbler and he found the right key after only two attempts. Cook felt that gaining short, sharp entry would be less risky than taking a shifty look around, and so he jiggled the key, rapped the head with his screwdriver, unlocked the door, and immediately stepped inside.

He was standing in a long, slim side-return, extended onto the main building. It was a neat and clean-smelling space, with glossy, chestnut-brown floorboards. The walls were lined with precisely stacked storage boxes – all white. A wheeled office-chair and expensive-looking glass-topped desk gleamed beneath a deep-set skylight. There were few open surfaces and no loose or discarded items. He removed a pair of light leather gloves from his pocket and pulled them over twitchy fingers. He stood motionless, breathing slowly and deeply. This was either the man's home office, kept minimalist and uncluttered to ease concentration and emphasise separateness from his living space, or the sterile decompression zone of an unstable and divided mind – an airlock between the outside world and the horrors within.

Cook twisted the handle of a locked wall-cupboard. The violation was now complete. He had identified and seized an opportunity, gained illicit access, crossed the threshold and connected with the environment. There was relief in the commitment. His threadbare heart, thunking with the terror and the thrill of it all, was most definitely *in it*. At last, he could – in the words of his old Film Studies teacher – 'interrogate the plot'. In movies, Cook knew that it was all about the edit – the director's meticulously gathered ingredients were sliced and spliced and rechannelled for pace, logic and dramatic intensity. Here, though, was the unrewinding world – one take, no reshoots, no post-production failsafe. The final act was live and loud and upon him – a man who had spent most of the second half of his life in self-imposed captivity, under cover of darkness.

All this drama.

Cook turned the squeaky handle on a heavy adjoining door and crept across the hall into a gigantic fitted kitchen so obsessively antiseptic it could have passed as a laboratory. He moved slowly and silently across the stone-tiled floor, casting a fractured reflection in the polished chrome of the integrated oven. Who was that, he wondered, and what was he doing here?

He reached a gloved hand out to a bright yellow waste-bin, slotted out of sight around the back of a curving breakfast bar. The motorised lid flipped open unexpectedly, startling Cook into a whispered, 'Fuck!' He studied the bin's contents – mostly cellophane, cereal wrappers and fruit-peel. There was a second sensor-bin, in complimentary turquoise, next to the first. He opened the lid and rummaged around inside – cardboard, plastic milk cartons, tin cans. He sifted a little deeper and spotted the colour and typography of a familiar brand – a crushed blue-and-white box – Tampax.

Footsteps outside, approaching the front door.

He inhaled.

Then the letterbox.

Then something flopping onto the doormat.

Then the footsteps again, receding.

He exhaled, closed the lids of both bins, and opened the door to a shallow utility room, which housed little more

than a few propped long-handle brushes, an ironing-board
and an upright Dyson. The smell – sweet polish clashing
with sour paint – reminded him of Esther's 'scullery' – a
poky box-room opposite the outside toilet, home to an old
vertical-drum washing-machine and mangle. It was one of
the first places Cook had adopted as a hideaway, tucking
himself into a shady corner by the broken rubber wash-
basket and Rusty's dog-bath. Drawn to the sense-memory,
he edged into the room, groping for a ceiling-cord.

Inside, under an energy-saving half-light, Cook could see
that the room was longer and slimmer than it appeared from
the kitchen, with a ceiling that sloped down towards the far
end. The walls were bright and scrubbed – recently
whitewashed – with shelves holding regimented racks of
uncrusted paint-pots and fluffy rollers. A small door, secured
by a heavy latch and padlock, was set into the wall at the mid-
point of the ceiling slope. Cook drooped his head and shuffled
forward. He used the in-built light on his phone to examine
the lock closely, being careful not to touch it. None of the bump
keys would work on the mechanism.

"Hello?" Cook was startled by the authority in his voice.
He waited, listening.

Again.

"Hello?"

There was a shuffling from behind the locked door.
Then a voice – female, adult. *"Hello?"*

"It's okay," said Cook. "Please don't shout."

"Who is that? *Help me!*"

The door clattered from the inside, rattling the lock. The
woman's voice – ragged and hoarse – was now just inches
away. "Who is it? Get me out! *Open the door!*"

Cook pressed his cheek up against the door and kept his voice at a low level, hoping the woman would do likewise.

"Please. Listen. I can't open the door. But – I will help you. Really."

"Who are you? Where is he?"

"You'll be okay – I promise. But I can't help now. You have to wait a bit longer – and you *can't say anything*. He can't know that someone has been here."

"Please..." The woman was sobbing – her flash of hope short-lived. "Please help me! How did you know I was here?"

In his internal rehearsal, she had been more yielding and compliant. But there was impurity in Cook's urge for dramatic redemption. Eleanor's survival was a by-product, and he had to stay true to her bit-part role.

"I will help you. But not now. I know you're here, and that's enough. You can't tell him. I can never help you if you say anything."

"Don't fucking leave me here!"

"I won't."

And he left her there.

He back-stepped out of the utility room, closed the door, and hurried out through the kitchen, checking he'd left no footprint smudges on the stone floor.

Across the hall. Fresh junk-mail on the doormat.

Into the side-return and back outside, re-closing the door, which clicked back into its locked position.

Giddy with adrenaline, he walked back to Peakvale Avenue, got into his car and drove away.

37

The Abyss

DAVID BRERETON WAS MURDERED three days later, sometime between 2am and 3am. He was found the following Saturday, after an anonymous phone-call to police advised them to investigate the locked storage cellar of an abandoned spinning-mill a few miles from Brereton's flat. There, they found a body – sitting, propped upright in a corner, head drooped, arms and legs tightly bound with thick rope, eyelids crudely sewn shut. The wall to the left of the body was splash-scarred in dirty-red, the floor slick with blood and urine. When the coroner lifted the body's chin from its chest, he noted probable cause of death as 'haemmorhage from the left common carotid artery'.

"Nasty…" said the Senior Investigating Officer to the coroner, as they watched the forensic team go to work. "Why the eyes?"

The coroner shrugged and dragged a palm across his unshaven chin. "Cheaper than a blindfold?"

Dorian Cook did not know any of this, as he sank into the sofa and opened his laptop. He did not know that the boy who used to be so shrewd and elusive had been stalked and cornered and starved and beaten. He did not see the face – so moulded by that signature sly smile – defaced by panic, bruised and bulbous. He did not hear the punching and crunching or the yelps for mercy or the scream, through splintered teeth.

"It was Dorian! Dorian fucking Cook! It was his idea!"

Cook sipped his tea and navigated to the home-page of *PastLives.com*. The site's user interface had been recently overhauled and he had little difficulty setting up a fake profile under the name of 'Michael Howell'. He carefully confirmed Bethesda in the profile's Primary School field and wired up a few token one-way connections to other pupils. He logged in as himself and found the message he was after, originally sent over three months ago.

what goes around, comes around
D

'*D*'...

He thought of Darren – Darren Ray – and 'not-nice' Frank. All those fatherly sins, trickling down through the ages, blotting and blossoming. But, although time had rendered a gauze of naivety over his actions as a child, the adult Cook took no comfort in piety. He had watched as the puppies were drowned, he had restrained the bullies as Darren had beaten them, he had pissed into the bottle and conceived the 'gang'. He had grown tired of his protector fantasy and turned away, stifling the symptoms instead of addressing the cause. A chill had stolen over him and, adapted as he was to the cold – of his bed, his home – he had welcomed it as a pain he was used to.

'*D*'...

Before the handkerchief, there was hope that this was all

just a David Brereton tease. It was not beyond a man who, as a boy, had chosen to conceal his involvement in a prank by potentially burning the victim alive. Perhaps, in the face of Mountford's paranoia, he had decided to cover his tracks completely – using the handkerchief to implicate Darren, if only to Cook. It was comforting to believe that Brereton would have murdered Mountford's son reluctantly – to eliminate a witness. As he had started the fire to ensure their victim's silence, Brereton would simply be repeating himself, using a different method. Implicating voices had to be silenced, regardless of age.

Cook did not know that Brereton had followed John Ray into the darkness, head steadied between his killer's knees, eyelids stretched and pinched and knitted together with needle and fishing-line. He did not know that his friend had ended his life in abysmal isolation, sealed in a vacuum of hurt, his rage and pain left to incubate for two days, before he was fed and watered and informed – in a whisper – that there was no use in hoping for rescue or respite. He did not know that Brereton had cried at this, or that the tears – unable to escape through unopenable lids – had scorched his eyeballs, or that his keeper had left him alone for another two days before returning to release him with a serrated kitchen knife. If he had known all of this, then Cook would have no need to ponder the identity of 'D'. He would have recognised the fury in the violence.

He noted the 'D' profile name, logged back in as 'Michael Howell' and typed out a message containing the address of the house where Eleanor Finch was being held. He tapped 'return' twice and wrote:

DC is here.

38

Hour of Defeat

WILLIAM STONE WALKED INTO the *Seven Stars* and sat at the usual corner bench, opposite his friend and occasional banker. The pub had only been open for ten minutes, and, as the barmaid upturned the chairs, she regarded her sole customers with more pity than irritation.

"What's going on, Dor? Bit early for you!"

Stone took off his jacket and leaned back, opening his body, offering himself to whatever was coming. It was about time for Cook to ask for some kind of repayment. The items he had sourced were specialist and tricky to obtain, but the summoning suggested there was still debt to negotiate. Stone had calculated he could spare a £1000 severance fee without too much pain.

"Hello, Will," said Cook, looking up from a cup of black coffee, casting his eyes across the table, around the room – anywhere but Stone's gaze. "I'm a bit off-kilter with timing at the moment. Not really sure if it's day or night – or what difference it makes, anyway."

Stone reached over and stole a slurp of coffee. "Fuck me, mate. I know it's hard, but – y'know – crisis/opportunity, all that. Get out there! Fill your boots. Empty your bollocks!"

Cook smiled and looked up. "Did you read about the murder last week?"

"Which one? Front cover of *Murder Monthly?*"

"The bloke who had his throat cut. He'd been kept at some factory, tied up."

Stone brightened at this. He was already starting to assign the £1000 to other debtors. "Yeah. Why?"

"I was at school with him."

The barmaid – drawing blinds, scraping chairs under tables – called over.

"Can I get you anything, love?"

"Coffee, please," said Stone. "White, no sugar."

Cook was hardly deflected by the interruption. "Will – how would you feel if..."

Stone cut him off, surprised at his own irritation. "Happens all the time! He was a name, mate."

"What?"

"You're talking about Dave Brereton, right? Drugs. Small-time, big in his head. Cocky bastard. We've had him on possession a couple of times but he was definitely dealing. I remember he came in a few years ago – speed freak. Maybe even injecting. It's a big drug with chefs and kitchen staff. They work silly hours. Keeps 'em flying. Most of 'em are on shit money so they can't afford coke. We think he probably had a steady supply network, then as he got higher up, more funds, more time, started dishing it out himself, thought he was untouchable, pissed off somebody he shouldn't be pissing off – probably one of his dealers went freelance without telling him. That's how it goes. You mess with someone who's fucked-up enough to think he can do it without competition and who has a couple of nasty connections, and you might find yourself dead."

"Will…"

"They were probably told to scare him but one of them went too far and they finished him off because it was less risky. Seen it loads of times, mate. Yardies or fucking Armenians – they fly in, spend a weekend whoring, do the business and then fuck off on the next flight out. Always helps when the victim is someone who no-one gives enough of a fuck about to follow up on. Either that, or they're too scared."

The coffee arrived. Stone snatched up the mug, sipped at the milk-foam.

"Will… It said he was blinded or something."

Stone took out a sweetener capsule and clicked a couple of pellets into his drink. "So? What do you want me to do?"

"Help me!" said Cook, loud enough to divert the barmaid back to the near edge of the bar, within earshot. He softened his voice. "Help me. Well – it's not me. It's Alfie and Gina."

"And what's going to happen to them? Dor, you're sounding mental, mate."

"I am not *mental*. You don't know what I know."

Stone took this partly as an insult. "No. I don't! I'm not as clever as you – well done for spotting that. I'm just telling you what I think, based on my experience. I don't know what this has got to do with your family, but it sounds like you're in a mess. Get away for a bit. Clear your head."

"Will. There *is* no 'away'."

In the evening, Cook dined alone at an obscure Italian restaurant near his temporary home. He sat away from the windows, swivelling spaghetti with one hand, prodding at his laptop with the other. The feed from the Eleanor house was comforting – static and predictable. He pondered the psychology of a captive given hope of rescue, but then abandoned. Would she think of her encounter with him as psychosis? Fantasy? A twisted ruse from her keeper?

And still, the nightmare loop, round and round on his inner widescreen – Gina jumping, screaming. Alfie sobbing. Panic and trembling. A calm voice asking for information. Confusion and fear. Then a louder, more volatile voice – demanding, threatening. Then, Gina dead. Alfie dead. He had sifted through the detail too many times, refining it beyond recognition, scrutinising the connections for evidence of delusion. But he knew that true insanity was a work in constant progress – it could not be soothed by reason or cured by reflection. Cook was still a man in deep sleep, desperate to wake and welcome the world outside the veil. But, however hard he flexed, he could not give clear and tangible form to his torment. It was a terror that coiled tighter the more he struggled.

Will had provided a contact – Avi Ackner, a friend who ran a private security firm. The phone-call had been cordial – Ackner sounded wise and well aged, clearly accustomed to troubled clients. Cook was heartened at how his requirements were absorbed without suspicion.

For two weeks, his family home would be watched, round the clock, by two guards in unmarked cars – one at the front, one round the back.

"Other methods of access?" asked Ackner.

"Not that I know of," said Cook.

"And this *is* your house, yes?"

Cook resented the implication – of sloppy security awareness, or worse. "Of course. There's a front door and a back door, that's it."

"Any side entrance? Alley? Cut-through?"

"No. Can I ask – what do they do all day?"

"The operatives? They'll vary their routine, swap positions, plan patrol routes. They won't just sit there – that would obviously attract interest. Don't worry. They're all ex-army. They're used to it."

"Do they just watch? How do they see detail at night? Binoculars, or infra-red…"

Ackner chuckled. "Some of them use pinhole cameras. Hook them up to the cars. Blends in very well. A lot of employers use them – embedded into ceilings, walls. They can monitor live, images can be reviewed, memory flushed every few days."

"Yes," said Cook with a half-smile. "I think I've heard of that."

They agreed on 'alert criteria' and exchanged a couple of emails – a disclaimer, photographs of Gina and Alfie. Cook transferred £8500 to *Frontline Protection* and, shortly after, received a text message informing him that the payment had been processed and the 'operation' would begin the next day. Cook now had a fourteen-day window of opportunity. As ever, his reaction to a solid deadline was a mixture of reassurance and panic.

The restaurant was approaching closing time, and Cook realised he was the only patron remaining, apart from an elderly couple chatting to the owner in tipsy Italian. His waiter approached and offered a scripted endorsement of the chef's 'special' tiramisu. Cook declined and ordered

coffee. He logged into *PastLives.com* on his laptop. The
Michael Howell account showed one new message – from
the 'D' profile (status 'Online').

how do I know your MH

With a flush of smugness, Cook logged out – and back
in, via his own account. He swept the messages and profile
detail for anything that seemed out of place or indiscreet,
reset the password to 'bethesda' and logged back in to the
Howell account. The site offered a live-chat window which
could be accessed with a profile-to-profile request. Cook
sent:

chat in 2 mins?

Almost immediately, a window popped up.

*You have received a request for private live messaging from
user >D<. Do you accept?*

Cook, light-headed now, accessed the chat window,
exclusively shared between 'Michael Howell' and '>D<'.
There was a conversation thread already open – a repeat of
the inbox message.

how do I know your MH

Cook typed:

Jungle Juice

Instantly, a reply.

?

Cook's stomach lurched. He had mentally rehearsed this
encounter, but only after seeing the words on-screen did he
realise that Darren Ray (if that was who he was talking to)
had arrived after the bottle-pissing and so wouldn't get the
reference. He typed:

I saw the dogs but ran away

"Would you like anything else?"

The waiter reappeared with coffee. Cook flinched and almost snapped the laptop shut. "Uh, no. Just the bill, please."

In the corner of the chat window, a looping animation showed fingers fluttering above a section of computer keyboard and, redundantly, the word 'Typing'. Cook stared at it, nauseous.

how did you get my profile

Back on-script now, Cook typed:

Hacked DC account. 'doriancook'. Password too obvious!

Typing fingers.

?

Cook replied:

School name

No typing fingers.

Cook drank the tepid coffee in a couple of gulps. Darren Ray was big enough and scary enough back then. What would he look like now – hunting through Cook's profile, walking over his grave?

Typing fingers.

ok

With a couple of authentic errors, Cook typed:

I didnt knwo about anything else honest

The '>D<' profile status changed to 'Offline'.

39

Final Cut

"ZOMBIES EAT YOUR BRAINS," said Alfie. "But it doesn't make them clever."

"I can't imagine it would do you much good, though!" said Cook.

Alfie pondered, draining his milkshake. "It might – if they ate the stupid part of your brain."

"Let's not talk about eating brains, any more."

Cook and son were gnawing their way through functional cheese-rolls at a cafe near the cinema entrance. Cook was still faintly traumatised by the film – *The Dancing Dead* – about a troupe of stage-school kids fighting off a zombie invasion. (After being bitten, the group's alpha-teen realises that the only way to defeat the infection is to keep his blood pumping – by dancing. The kids rally around him, working to spread the positive message of dance-based counter-attack quicker than the zombies can overcome the population.)

"What about ghosts, Alfie? How do they work?"

"They don't eat. They are floating souls. If you see one and it knows you've seen it, then it haunts you forever."

"How does it haunt you?"

"They haunt you," said Alfie, with exaggerated

impatience, "by making monsters scratch on the door and doing red eyes in the dark."

Cook smiled. "Can you kill them?"

"Dad!" He sighed – a glimpse of the teenager to come. "They're already dead!"

Cook had collected his son just after breakfast, releasing Gina to an early work meeting. As he approached the house, he had expected to see a burly brute in an armoured van, skulking behind tinted sunglasses. Instead, he passed a slight-looking character in a scruffy suit, pacing – with little urgency – around a dark blue Ford Focus, speaking quietly into his mobile. Five minutes later, as he left the house with Alfie, the man was sitting in his car, still on the phone. This was either an illustration of *Frontline Protection's* mastery of blended surveillance, or Cook had spent close to £10,000 on glorified babysitters. It was now the second week of the 'operation', and Ackner's daily updates had offered nothing to raise concern. Cook had spent the first three nights parked at Peakvale Avenue, monitoring his live feed, seeing little outside the usual routine.

As he dropped Alfie back with Gina in the early evening, Cook saw that the Ford Focus had re-parked further up the road, and that the man inside had been replaced by a reassuringly broad colleague, shaven head bowed to his lap where he seemed to be jotting notes. To the curious eye, this activity would raise slight interest, but the variation made it difficult to pin down as unusual and, Cook supposed, that was the point – not too visible, not too invisible.

For another two nights, Cook hovered around in a state of calculated insanity, monitoring the house on the corner from the discomfort of his proxy home. He walked

from room to room with his phone held up at head height
– a sterile spirit guide. He propped his laptop on top of
the television, balanced it on the toilet-seat lid as he
bathed. With tablet PC and live feed on his bedside table,
he slept late and woke early, gambling that 'D' would not
approach the house between 3am and 6am. Cook had
estimated that he would be able to make the drive in
around twenty minutes, as long as he reacted quickly to
any movement.

On Monday morning, for the first time since leaving the
magazine, Cook sneaked a look at his bank balance. He
could afford to live without income for another couple of
months, as long as he didn't need to extend the surveillance.
The tracks were rumbling. A kind of closure, he felt, was
inbound. It would either rattle on in regardless or, ideally,
arrive as a result of his own action. He couldn't allow himself
to stumble now – to succumb to a craving for an ending. He
had set his scene. Now he had to ensure that his players
found their marks.

In the evening, an hour after the lights had gone out –
at 11.30pm, as usual – Cook's lips paused at the rim of his
tea-mug, as he watched the fence at the back of the house
dapple with torchlight. He was up and out and on the road
in minutes, laptop on the passenger seat – feed window
showing more of nothing and then flickers of torch-beam
and then, as he left the motorway and slowed into the
deserted slip-road, a tall and unfamiliar figure lingering near
the back door. By the time he had parked – a little further
down Peakvale Avenue than usual – the figure had gone. He
killed the engine and sat there – in the darkness, in
withering silence – leering at the screen. He was disturbed

by his arousal, but also irritated by the sense of masturbatory seclusion. He pined for an observer.

A low light flicked on upstairs. A ground-floor light – almost as dim – followed soon after, and was instantly extinguished. Cook launched the camera app on his phone and connected to the feed. He closed his laptop and slid the bump-keys out of the dashboard. The other item received from William Stone had been with him constantly since the day he had discovered Eleanor. Outside, he kept it in his inside jacket pocket. At home, it moved around with him – beside his phone on the coffee table, within reach on a glass shelf when he was in the shower, next to his digital radio in the kitchen. Depending on the rhythm and volume of the house's night-creaks, he occasionally stuffed it under the pillow.

He slotted his laptop under the passenger seat, pulled on the leather gloves and stepped out of the car. His heart was neither hammering in his chest nor did it leap into his mouth. If this *was* the end – if he was striding into his final escape – then there was always Alfie, and the love he would leave behind. At least he would succeed where his own father had failed.

It was almost late enough to be early. Cook walked slowly and quietly to the house, glancing at his phone. The feed was now a reflection of his reality – it showed the upstairs light still on and a shadowed figure at the back door, examining a phone. He was quite the auteur – writer, producer, camera-man, director and, now, star.

The door had been clumsily forced – there was no need for the bump-keys. Cook listened – to nothing – for a few seconds, and entered the dark side-return, guided by the glow from his phone screen. He advanced a few feet into the room, casting the light over oblivious furniture. All was clean and correct and undisturbed. He moved on steadily, step by silent step, towards the hall and kitchen. The adjoining door was closed and, as he reached for it, there was no longer nothing. Something stirred – a shuffling sound, beyond the door – not directly in the hallway but close by. Then, more than a shuffle – a thud. Something small but heavy dropping to the floor. Cook touched his ear to the door. Something was alive, in a room across the hall. He reached for the door-handle and, remembering the squeak, turned it carefully and gradually, just enough to release the latch. He opened up an inch-wide gap and squinted through. The weak light from upstairs revealed a scattering of glass fragments from a mirror which lay face-down across the lower legs of a body – also face-down, its upper half slumped across the doormat. Cook pointed his phone-light through the gap in the door. A small table lay on its side, sprinkled with mirror-shards, beside a lamp with a flattened shade and smashed bulb. He opened the door a little wider and stepped through.

The glass crackled beneath his feet. He scanned the body with his light, tracing up from leg to torso to where the head used to be – now a detonation of meat and bone. The arms were posed mid-swim, squelched into a glinting puddle of gore. A metallic smell wrinkled Cook's nose and he quickly shifted his light back down to the body's feet, noting the leather slippers and pyjama trousers. This, it seemed, was the owner of the house – Eleanor's captor and keeper no more. It was his second dead body and despite the violent contrast with Mr Smith's melancholy exit, Cook was troubled by the absence of shock or empathy. He stepped over the legs, crossed the bottom of the stairs and made for the open door to the sitting-room.

As he approached, there was more thudding and shuffling from further inside the room. Hand on his inside pocket, Cook stepped through the door. As his eyes adjusted to the deeper dark, he saw the outline of someone – not Something – sitting on the floor, back propped against an armchair, shoe-heels kicking and scratching at the wooden floor. He lifted his phone and pointed light at the someone, which flinched and lifted a forearm over its eyes.

Watch! He hates this!

Cook dipped the beam and the figure's red eyes rose up behind its arm. He saw the white hair, the glassy gaze, the sallow skin. He saw the figure's trembling hands, clamped over a wound on the right side of its chest. He saw a heavy-handled kitchen knife, a lump-hammer, more blood – smear-tracks from the hall, fresh on the figure's hands, matted around his shirt.

"Hello, John," said Cook, remaining in the doorway. "What happened? I was expecting your brother."

John Ray coughed out a chuckle. "I learned to fight my own battles. You might have noticed."

The voice had roughened with age but still retained its stilted eloquence – the flaring vowels, the stinging consonants. Cook moved further into the room, caution yielding to fascination.

"Well," said Ray, squinting through the pain. "You haven't changed."

Cook stared, in horror and admiration. Was he smiling?

"What's wrong, Dor? You look like you've seen…"

"How did you get out?" said Cook.

"A gentleman of the road," said Ray. "After you all left, I screamed myself to sleep. The next day, the trapdoor opened and he let me out. I think he was angry that I was squatting in his toilet or something."

"I heard him," said Cook. "We saw his stuff."

"I did think you would have come back for me. Obviously. Until the place burned down. That *cunt*, Dorian... I wanted him to suffer a lot more, but the last time I saw him, he was so abusive. And he was a coward, you know. He admitted the fire was him, but he blamed you for everything else."

"Where did you go? You didn't come back to school."

"Yes. I'm sure you all missed me. It threw a switch in my mind. I couldn't speak. My parents wanted to know where I'd been, but I couldn't tell them. They were separating, anyway – about ten years too late for my mum and her bruises. At least you sped all of that up. She thought it was the bullying, wouldn't let me go back to Bethesda. She already had her own place so I moved in with her, transferred schools. I'm sorry about your housemate out there, by the way. I got him as he came down the stairs. Didn't see the fucking knife, though... It wasn't Brereton who told me you were here, by the way. That was someone else."

Cook saw little point in giving him the true picture.

"John. I am sorry, you know."

"Of course you are. Sorry it came to all this. It all ended for me last year. Both parents gone, Darren moved to Spain about ten years ago with a woman he met on holiday. He never knew, Dorian. I thought the 'D' thing would get you

– before I realised how there are 'D's everywhere! Dennis…
David… Dorian… I apologise for the melodrama. I honestly
didn't mean to be so cryptic."

"Where's Darren now?"

Ray paused to push a hand down on his wound. He took
a few cautious deep breaths. "Died. Jet-skiing. Dad went ages
ago – lung cancer. My mum killed herself after Darren. You
know how tragedy just follows some people around? I
suppose all they can do is hope they're not the last one
standing. That didn't work out for me. The only thing left
was to… settle up."

Grunting and grimacing, Ray dragged himself up off the
floor and flopped into the armchair, clutching his bleeding
side. Feeling bolder, Cook moved closer and slowly lowered
himself into the sofa opposite, keeping his eyes on Ray. He
upturned his phone and set it on the cushion beside him.
The sharp light was unhelpfully eerie, but just enough to see
by.

"Your message was wrong, you know," said Cook. "No-
one is keeping score."

Ray raised his eyes. "What?"

"What goes around doesn't necessarily come around.
It's all a continuum. Bad behaviour goes unpunished, good
behaviour isn't always rewarded. It defies all we know about
human nature – to impose any logic or order on all of this."

Ray lifted his head and coughed into the air – atomised
crimson. "I know that. And who really wants to be a part of
that chaos? Mountford, Brereton, Darren, your friend out
there… They're the lucky ones. I'm getting luckier by the
second. You're stuck with this. You've got to find a way to
cope – maybe for a long time, yet. The worst thing is that

you have to cope in the knowledge that you're basically nothing – that you don't matter. We all have such a fine opinion of ourselves and our position in the world. But it's just delusion – the pathetic twinge of human self-esteem. We all think we have a 'part' to play – that we're something. But really we're just a collection of self-conscious nothings."

"But we can choose," said Cook. "And given the choice, it's better to be alive. 'The dead know only one thing – it is better to be alive'."

Ray smiled. *"Full Metal Jacket!* I would have thought you'd be more of a *Paths Of Glory* man. Go on, Dorian. Confess! You might as well. I won't tell anyone. Do you really think your future holds anything but suffering?"

"Yes, I do!" snapped Cook. "Why the fuck do you think I went through all of this? Yes – I'm miserable. But I'm learning to reject pessimism. Imagine something truly terrible – like being blind. How do you keep *going* through that? Perpetual darkness. Nothing but nothing. But where are all the blind suicides? Obviously, it's better to be alive in the dark than alone in the light."

"You're not alive in the dark. You're a *hider*, Dorian. You always were. You chose the dark because it felt safe. I had no choice. Yes – I suppose it is 'good' to be alive and aware and full of possibility. But it's even better to have not been born in the first place."

On cue, he coughed up something primal – a belly-deep rasp. There was an impatience to the sound which startled Cook.

"Why did you do it? Why didn't you come to get me out? Remember what that girl said – what had I done to hurt you?"

"You were different. As different as it was possible to be. And we were kids, and kids are cruel. They have to be. It's how they deflect and free themselves from all that control and belittlement – all that spite and *structure*. Remember the world back then? Teachers who could hit us with bits of wood – fucking mark us for life. It was too dangerous to speak up or stand up or stand out when the adults had such a license to keep us quiet, keep us down, keep us in the dark. *Teachers* – who taught us that physical abuse was just the way of the world. All of that – all the violence it spawned. We weren't trying to hurt you. We were trying to stop everyone else hurting you."

John Ray smiled, exposing bloodied teeth. "It's almost endearing, how much control you think you had then – and still think you have, now. It's always been my comfort, accepting how little control we have over anything. Because of how I am – how I was – I gave up on conventional happiness before I could walk. You're not a plotter or a director, Dorian. You're a walk-on. Like I said – I don't matter, you don't matter, this doesn't matter. The world will just shrug and keep on turning – long after we've gone. Once you abandon the silly selfishness of 'personal fulfilment', you can zoom right out and embrace insignificance. If you squeeze tight enough, it's almost spiritual. I didn't scheme a way towards achieving justice – revenge as a way of restoring some kind of karmic balance. It was animalistic – I had no control, no free will. It's what I've always been used to, and you should start to get used to it, too. However you got me here, I don't see why you should see any success in it – your grand whitewash. Redemption by disavowal."

His eyes were frosting over. Cook flinched at the scraping breaths. "What's it like, John?"

"What?"

"Dying."

"It's okay. You'll like it."

With a ruinous extended wheeze, Ray rose up from the armchair. He tried to lunge for Cook, but fell forward, emptied of energy. Cook scrambled over the back of the sofa and pulled the yellow-and-black M26 Taser from his inside pocket. He aimed with both hands, pointing the weapon at his near-helpless assailant.

Ray dropped to his knees and raised his head. "What are you trying to do? Finish me off or shock me back to life?"

He crawled back onto the armchair, sighed, and closed his unseeing eyes.

The world turned.

John Ray died.

The world turned.

Cook kept the Taser raised. He stood there, stiff and solemn, scanning for signs of life. After a few minutes, the reverie broke and he dared to divert his gaze to an ugly clock on the wall above the television. It was just past 3am. He slid the Taser back into his pocket and stepped forward, avoiding the puddle of blood coiling across the carpet from Ray's legs. He picked up the lump-hammer from the floor, retrieved his phone from the sofa, tore away one of the curtains and backed out of the room, aiming light at his shoes to check he wasn't trailing anything. At the hall, he covered the body with the curtain. He turned right into the kitchen, opened the door of the utility room and pulled the light-cord. The door beneath the ceiling-slope was still padlocked. He lifted the lock and twisted it round, so it jutted out horizontally. Cook had anticipated a protracted session of swatting and swearing, but the lump-hammer crushed the clasp after two strikes and the lock fell to the floor with a clatter. Behind the door, Eleanor shrieked.

"Who's there? Who's that?"

Cook held the latch. A simple lift and shift and the door would open – outwards.

"You can't look at me!" he shouted.

"I can't see! I've got a blindfold on! He ties me up for the night. Please! Don't leave me again! Help me! I don't care who you are."

Cook leaned his shoulder into the door and unhooked the latch. He opened a gap of around an inch and peeked through, recoiling at the sulphurous stench. Eleanor Finch lay naked and foetal on a rotting mattress, ankles bound with tape, wrists rope-tied in front, black blindfold tightly knotted. She was trembling – convulsing with cold and terror. As the utility room light passed over her, she spoke – shrill but steady. It was the voice of someone with an urge to make themselves understood quickly.

"I can't. I can't take the blindfold off. I managed it once. He didn't feed me for two days. Don't hurt me!"

It sounded more like a command than a plea.

"I won't."

Cook crouched and began to unravel the rope. Eleanor clamped her palms together, reducing the tension in the knots. He realised that he was now God-like – in complete control. He could stop, stand, walk out, close the door and drive away, and she would die – here in the dark.

"I'm going to untie your hands," said Cook. "Then,

you'll stay here for fifteen more minutes. Count to one-thousand. Then you should leave, by the back door. Don't take the blindfold off until I've gone. Did you hear me? Do you understand?"

She nodded, whispered yes.

"Don't leave until you've counted to one-thousand. Don't go down the hall or look in the sitting-room."

"Why?"

"Just leave. Go. Don't look back. Don't even think of looking back. It won't be good."

The ropes fell away, revealing livid red grooves, scored in spirals down both forearms. Eleanor massaged her wrists together, groaning with pain and relief.

"Why are you wearing gloves?"

Cook ignored this and turned his back. He stooped and headed for the door.

"Thank you," said Eleanor, turning her face in his direction, tilting her head up to see him, sightlessly.

And he looked back and saw the scar – the scar at the base of her chin.

A really nasty cut.

His mind scurried back to the day with Inspector Ramshaw and Constable Whitcombe. Ramshaw saying something about her officially changing her name.

She had some kind of crush on me.

Cook squatted down and leaned in for a closer look at the scar. It was absolutely the one – carved in like an emphasis, tracing the curve of her chin. He wanted to say it ("Rebecca?") but of course he could not. Instead, he removed one of the gloves and, for once, he was the one reaching out. He groped for Rebecca Goldstraw's hand, squeezed once, skin on skin, saw her smile, and left her there, counting out loud. He eased through the back door, into the muggy morning, unstrapped the spy-camera and walked to his car. He was not the good guy, but the bad guys were gone, the girl was safe and he had not been turned into a pillar of salt.

Acknowledgements

This story has been a long time in the making, and I'm grateful to the friends and family who supported me through its telling.

From the decades, my love and applause to Keith Groom, whose classroom beard-shaving taught me the pleasures of creative expression.

And to my immense, unimpeachable grandmother – so long, and thanks for all the chips and beans.

Andrew Lowe
London, 2015